USA TODAY BESTSELLING AUTHORS

THE VOW

USA TODAY BESTSELLING AUTHORS

J.L. BECK &
C. HALLMAN

1

SEBASTIAN

*S*itting at the large desk in my brand-new office, I sign the last stack of papers for the day. It's still weird to write my name on the line above *Dean of North Woods University*, but I'm slowly getting used to it. It's not like I never thought I would make it here. I just didn't think it would happen so fast.

Thanks to the old dean's sudden early retirement, my career got fast-tracked exponentially. Not that I'm complaining at all. This is a great job, my dream job, to be honest.

My stomach growls just as I sign the last dotted line, reminding me that lunch was a long time ago and that I stayed late yet another day to get shit done. Shoving the papers in an envelope, I move to get up, grabbing my jacket from the chair behind me when a soft knock on the door fills the room.

"Come in," I call as I slip into my coat. It's probably just a student needing assistance with something. The door opens, and I look up to see a woman hovering in the doorway.

My heart stops beating in my chest. All the air leaves my lungs, and every thought evades my mind. All I can do is stare at the small woman standing in my office.

Shoulder-length blonde hair, a heart-shaped face with a small button nose in the middle, two large blue eyes the color of the summer sky, and pink pillowy full lips just begging to be kissed. Her skin is the same pale shade of ivory I remember, everything about her is just like I remember... *my Amy.*

"I wasn't sure if you would even remember me, but the look on your face tells me you do." Her voice fills the room, and like a needle popping a balloon, I deflate. It's the voice that does it because it's not Amy's voice, it's not her soft sing-song voice I hear and how could it be... Amy is dead.

"I'm sorry, I..." I trail off, still staring at the woman like an idiot. I know it's not Amy, deep down I do, but the woman before me looks so much like her, and then it hits me like a pile of bricks falling from a tall building.

She just said that she wasn't sure I'd remember her. Which means I do know her, and if I know her, and she looks like Amy...

"Lily?" Her name slowly falls from my lips.

A smile spreads across her beautiful face, and again I'm rendered speechless. The similarities are too much. My heart aches just looking at her, and it's a stark reminder of everything I've lost. Of everything that I'll never be able to get back. Still, I can't stop myself from looking at her. My eyes are glued to her face, taking in every breathtaking inch of her.

"I just wanted to come, say hi," she explains sadness seeping into her eyes. "I'm a new student here. I just moved into the dorms." She takes a step forward, closer to me, and I can't handle it. Glancing away from her face, I drink in her body.

The last time I saw her, she was only a child. Amy's little sister, with pigtails in her hair and barbie dolls in her small hands. She was mourning the loss of her big sister, of her parents, while I was mourning the loss of my world.

She's not a child anymore. She is all woman now, her hips swaying from side to side as she steps closer. I swallow hard as she gets close enough for me to catch a whiff of her. Coconuts and jasmine; exotic and forbidden. I force myself to look back up and into her eyes. She might be all grown up now, but in my eyes, she'll always be Amy's little sister.

"You're a student here?" I ask, trying to keep my voice even.

"Yes, starting classes next week," she beams at me.

"Wow, that's crazy... I mean... You're all grown up, going to college... *here*. That's great," I say, stumbling over my own words trying to catch my footing before I stick my foot in my mouth and say something stupid.

"Yeah, I can't really believe it myself. But I'm glad it's happening, I'm glad to finally be out on my own. I didn't think it would happen, but I ended up getting a scholarship. The dorms are really nice, by the way, and I like my roommate."

"That's amazing. I'm glad you like it here. North Woods is a great school... and the new dean is amazing, so I've heard." At my joke, she starts giggling softly, the sound vibrating through me, and I don't understand what it does to me. It stirs something inside me, something I haven't felt in so long that I don't remember what it is. Shoving that feeling down, I try to compose myself, standing up a little straighter.

"I've heard the same." She smiles. "Congrats, by the way, on your promotion."

"Thank you, and congrats on your scholarship." For a moment we just stare at each other, neither of us saying a word. This odd feeling overcomes me that she is taking me in, the same way, I'm taking her in, with a sense of reminiscence.

"Well, I better get going. Got to prepare for classes and stuff," Lily says, breaking the awkward silence.

"Yes, good luck, and let me know if you need anything," I offer, but some part of me regrets doing so. I already know that I need to stay away from Lily. I should try to avoid her at all costs. Too many feelings are stirred looking at her. Feelings I swore to bury and never dig up again. She's trouble waiting to happen, and I'm not about to find myself in that kind of situation, least of all, with my dead girl-friend's baby sister.

"Thanks, Sebastian... I mean, *Dean Miller*," she smirks. "See you around."

"Take care, Lily," I call after her as she disappears from my office.

The door closes behind her, and I slump back down into my leather chair. Why does it feel like I just got hit by a bus? *Mother-*

fucker. My jaw aches with the tension inside of it. I wasn't even aware I was clenching it.

All the walls I've so carefully built around me for the past ten years are suddenly cracking, leaving huge empty spaces to let light, sand, water, and most of all, feelings in.

That damn woman. Why does she have to look so much like my soulmate, the one I was supposed to be with for the rest of my life? Is this God's way of saying fuck you? I've tried my hardest to be a good man. No, I haven't been perfect, but I've been damn near close to it. Did he send Lily to me just to torment me?

Thrusting my fingers into my hair, I hold my head in my hands. This is crazy talk, and I need to shut the fuck up. Lily isn't Amy. She's not. End of story.

It takes me about thirty minutes to compose myself enough to get up and finally exit the room. The hunger I felt earlier is long forgotten. The emptiness in my stomach is now replaced with an assortment of feeling, none of them good.

I'm worried about what Lily is going to stir up inside me, how my heart is going to handle seeing my soulmate's lookalike walking around campus. I only saw her for a few minutes, and it took me half an hour to recover from it.

Is this going to be a recurring thing? How it's going to be every time I see her on campus? I decide that the answer is no. I can't let her distract me like this.

Once again, I tell myself that she is not Amy.

Not Amy. She's not Amy. I need to remember it, burn it into my fucking skull.

On the drive home, I let the words run rampant in my mind over and over again.

She is not Amy. It's not her. Amy is gone.

The same chant replays, like a bad pop song, caught on repeat inside my head.

By the time I walk into my place, I must have said the words in my head over a hundred times, but the ache in my heart still remains. In my head, I know it's not her, it's Lily, her baby sister... but my body responds to her, just as it did to Amy.

To my body, there is no difference. My heart yearns for me to be near her, and it's earth-shattering to my brain. In the ten years since Amy's death, I've been with a handful of women, but none to which my body reacted like it did when I saw Lily today.

Stop this. Make the ache in your chest disappear.

Heading straight for the kitchen, I get out a bottle of whiskey and a tumbler from the cabinet. Generally, I don't make it a habit to drink on school nights, but I don't give a fuck right now. I have to stop this before it gets out of control.

My hands shake as I pour myself a glassful before taking it and the bottle to the living room. Settling down onto the couch, I start to sip on the amber liquid, welcoming the burn in my throat and the warmth in my stomach that it brings.

I can't remember the last time I got drunk. I prefer to keep a clear mind, but it doesn't matter today. Everything inside my head is fucked now, her presence ruining everything. I down the glass in two gulps and pour myself a second one right away. I can still feel her eyes on me, and my skin burns. *Wrong. It's wrong.* I take another gulp.

Briefly, I consider calling Rem over to talk but decide against it. He doesn't need to see me like this. No one needs to see me like this. I'm a mess, a fucking complete and utter mess. So instead of doing what I preach most and reach out for help, I sit by myself like a loser in my living room and get drunk. The world around me is spinning, maintaining the same speed but everything inside of me has stopped, the air, my heartbeat, it's all unmoving.

Don't break. Do. Not. Break. I grip the glass in my hands tighter. Tight enough to shatter it. Tight enough to break me. It's been years since I wanted to use anger as an outlet to my pain. Years since... the memory pulls me under, the memory rushes in before I can stop it and just like that I'm back there, being the old me.

I slam my bare fists into the walls of my room over and over again. The anger inside me so great, I don't know any other way to let it out. It's like a volcano of rage, erupting, spewing from deep inside me.

The rest of my room is already destroyed. I tore it apart when I got home from the hospital. The same hospital where she took her last breath. The doctors said they did all they could... but it wasn't enough. They did all they could? A cruel smile appears on my lips. If they did all they could, she would be here, right in front of me.

The skin over my knuckles is gone, blood drips from my hands and paints the walls. My hands should hurt, but I don't feel the pain... not there at least. My body is too overwhelmed with a different kind of pain, a pain a thousand times worse than any physical pain.

She is gone... dead... she left a hole inside me so deep that I know there is nothing to fix it. No one will ever be able to fill that space again.

She left a void that will forever leave me empty and alone.

Drink, after drink, I try to drown the memories I've been trying to forget for so many years. Amy, my sweet, Amy. God, how I miss you. I look around this room, and all I can think about every day is how empty it is. How pathetically alone I am because I refuse to move on with my life.

I should be married and starting a family right now, not drowning myself in a bottle of fucking whiskey, all alone.

Loser. You're a loser, Sebastian Miller.

Raising my glass, I drink like it's a celebratory event. My thoughts shift and swirl like shit being flushed down a toilet.

"Lily..." I say her name out loud just to see if it burns as badly on the outside as it does on the inside. *Nothing.* Slamming the glass down on the table, I force my shaking hands away from the whiskey bottle and into my hair. Even as angry, and hurt, and burning with sadness as I am over Lily reappearing in my life, I'm concerned for her. Riddled with worry.

Is she alone? Why is she here? How is she doing? What's her life been like the last ten years? The questions stack up, higher and higher, threatening to topple over.

Is she suffering like me? Does she hate herself for not being in the car that night, like I hate myself? When she moved away with her grandparents, I never once stopped to check on her, to consider what she might be going through. I'm not really sure why. Maybe I figured she still had someone to hold onto, to make sure she pieced herself back together again. I had no one, at least, not anyone that would really understand.

She didn't just lose her sister, but her entire family all in one swoop. Where I had lost the love of my life, she lost it all.

Ha. Pathetic. Here I was whining over something as superficial as lost love when the person who should really be hurting was smiling as if the world hadn't done her wrong. Hadn't taken everything from her.

Selfish asshole. I was going through my own shit, yes, but she was just a kid. This is dumb, ridiculous. Why the fuck do I even care? The past is the past. It's not like I can go back and change what I did, or what happened.

Nothing can, because if I could, I would find a way for Amy to be here with me.

Fuck, I need to get out of my head. Stop thinking about her. About all of it. It was easier when I pretended that part of my life never happened. I thought I was over this, over Amy but one look at Lily and the flood gates opened.

Lily was a reminder of everything I had lost, and everything I would never have.

There was no moving on from someone you loved, someone you never got the chance to say goodbye to. All there was, was learning to deal with the absence that they left in your heart.

Nothing will bring Amy back. It's now a reminder I'll have to repeat again to myself often.

But Lily... she is still here and as badly as her presence made me feel it also brought me a sliver of excitement, a zing of pleasure so foreign I nearly forgot what it felt like to be even a little joyful. I feel like an even bigger ass thinking about it. I shouldn't feel this way about anyone, especially not about Amy's sister.

Betrayal. I know the feeling all too well. It burns through me like a hot knife slicing through butter. Every time I would fuck another woman, look at another woman, it would sneak up on me and sink its razor teeth into my back. It was always there, in the back of my mind, eating away at my subconscious. Gnawing on me.

I was good, but I wasn't good enough to get Amy back.

I wasn't good enough to let go of her memory, and now I was thinking about her sister and how much they looked alike. Making a fist, I slammed it against the side of my head over and over again. The fucking thing inside my head had better start working or else...

Finally, the whiskey I all but guzzled down starts to work and my brain slows, a fog settling over my thoughts, and lifting the elephant sitting on my chest just enough for me to suck in a full breath. Everything inside of me screams for me to leave Lily alone to forget about her. To forget about Amy.

Forget, forget, forget.

She's happy, going to college, finding her way. She has her whole life in front of her, a promising, happy life. If she hasn't already, she'll find love and a life worth living for.

Falling back against the couch, I tilt my head back and stare up at the ceiling. I don't know where the thought comes from, but something inside my head says...

Do what Amy would want you to do. Be there, but only if you need to be.

The voice inside my head calms me enough for me to rationalize with myself. Yes, I'll only be there if I need to be. Only help if I'm needed.

A little of the guilt in my gut fades away, but I still feel it deeply, like a crater of an asteroid impact it remains, the gaping hole refusing to ever heal. Lily already left her mark on me, and it's going to take an epic amount of effort to forget that she fucking exists again.

2

LILY

*S*ebastian was different. Yes, I expected him to be different given the last time I saw him I was only nine, but I just didn't expect him to stir all these feelings inside me.

It left me breathless, and dare I say, flustered. Age looked good on him. Tall, toned, and tanned. Sebastian was gorgeous, and he knew it. Guys like him always knew how good looking they were. At first glance, I thought maybe he was a student and not the Dean of the school, he looked young, and very much like the rest of the men that I had seen roaming around campus.

I tried to stop myself from thinking about him, his face that looked like it had been carved from stone, his lips, full, and his eyes dark and brooding.

He's the same guy I remembered him to be, but without the sparkle, the life in his eyes had dimmed. I knew all too well about that. Every day, I thought about how I was still here, and they weren't.

Every day, for the last decade, I've beaten myself up for being alive; breathing air, and doing all the things Amy never would, because she's dead. *Dead.* All of them are dead, and a part of me wishes I was too.

Stop. I mentally tell myself. I need to stop thinking like that. I need to live up to my family's wishes because, in the end, that's all I have left of them. This is where Amy and my parents would've wanted me to be... in college, living my life to the fullest.

Sipping on the piping hot cup of hot cocoa that I'd ordered, I make my way to a corner seat near the window. My roommate, Delilah, is still upfront trying to decide what she wants. I can see her from where I'm sitting, her long brown hair bobbing in a high pony-tail, while she has her hands on her hips and stares up at the menu board like it's her enemy.

When she demanded we come to this place, I wasn't so sure about it. I didn't intend to make more friends than I needed to while at school. All my focus needs to be on my art and my homework, not on expanding my social circles. I don't have the same luxuries that many of the other students do here.

I'm riding high on a scholarship; one I've worked exceptionally hard for.

Finally, having made up her mind, Delilah walks over to me, her own steaming cup of mystery goodness in her hands.

"What did you get?"

"Tea," she answers before bringing the mug to her lips to take a tiny sip.

Wrinkling my nose at her, I reply, "Ewww, tea is gross. What's it got in it? Flowers?"

Delilah's blue eyes narrow. "Maybe? What's it matter? You drink your disgusting chocolate stuff, and I'll drink my flowers steeped in water."

Shaking my head, I smile. Back home, or at my grandparents' house, I had only a handful of friends, and none of them were anything like Delilah. She's goodness, with a touch of light. She makes me smile when I don't feel like smiling, but above all, she's the friend I wish I'd had in high school.

Bringing my mug to my lips, I'm seconds away from taking another sip when the bell above the door sounds, and I glance up, seeing *him* walk in. Sebastian, and he's not alone. It only takes me a second to recognize who it is standing beside him. *Remington Miller.* He looks so grown up now, mature, his body having filled out from the little boy that I remembered him to be.

My gaze flickers back to Sebastian. Is it wrong that my stomach starts to flutter in his presence, and my heart hammers against my ribcage, threatening to break free? If so, then I don't want to be right, at least not until the guilt trickles in a second later. He hasn't noticed me yet, so I use the moment to my advantage and drink him in.

His suit is tailored to his body, showing off all his sharp edges. My teeth sink into my bottom lip as I wonder what he looks like beneath that expensive suit.

Does he have an eight pack? Does he work out?

I can tell just from his frame that he does, the bulging of his shoulders, and biceps. The way he carries himself and how the fabric clings to him. He's hiding a whole lot of deliciousness under that suit, and I'll be damned if I don't want to peel back all that fabric and take a peek. Just a peek. A tiny little one.

Those hazel eyes of his swing around the room as if he knows I'm staring at him. At the last second, right before his eyes land on mine, I look down into my mug, watching as the little marshmallows dissolve. *Stop thinking about him, Lily.* I scold myself.

"Earth to, Lily. I've been calling your name for like ten minutes now," Delilah huffs, dipping her tea bag in and out of the hot water, as if that could possibly make it taste any better.

"Don't be so dramatic, you were not."

"I was, and you were off in space, gazing at..." Delilah's voice trails off, and she twists around in her seat to look at what I was staring at. Leave it to D to draw more attention to a subject than it needs.

"Stop, you're going to embarrass me," I growl, slapping her arm like a small child, after a second.

"Please," she twists around, but not before locking eyes with Sebastian who is still standing in place, off to the side, just inside the door. He looks like I feel—uncomfortable. Why is this so weird? It didn't feel this weird the other day in his office, did it? Maybe I'm just making it out to be weird. It must be all in my head.

"You aren't the first to drool over the newly appointed Dean, and you won't be the last. He looks young enough to be a senior attending the university, never mind, running the place. Don't be embarrassed."

She's right, but that doesn't mean I should be staring at him, basically drooling over him. Other students don't have a connection to him like I do. *He's your dead sister's boyfriend.* The thought appears like a bright blinking warning sign in my mind. As if I need a damn reminder of how wrong it is for me to want his attention or affection. He might as well be fucking forbidden at this point. Not only is he the Dean of the university, but he's also everything I shouldn't want or need.

Pretending not to exist, I wait for the floor to swallow me whole as he goes up to the cash register with his brother and orders. This is normal, right? Us being in the same place at the same time? It's not weird besides the fact that I kinda-sorta-want him?

My stomach twists and knots, so badly I'm certain I won't be able to unknot myself later. I feel sick like I might actually vomit on the floor.

"You're staring at him. Like staring deeply. Like maybe you *know* him?"

Know him would be an understatement.

My lips press into a hard line, and I avert my gaze back to Delilah, brushing a few strands of blonde hair from my face. I try my hardest not to take notice of him as he and Rem take a spot a few tables away from us.

"Oh, that's it. You know him. Otherwise, you wouldn't be turning pink in the cheeks, and look like someone's taken your panties, and hung them up next to the school flag in the quad." Del announces in a whisper.

If I could will knives from my eyes right now, I would. Luck must not be on my side because as if they can hear what she's said both of the Miller brothers look up, and in my direction. Sebastian, of course, looks away first, but Remmy holds my gaze, his eyes narrowing but not in a way that is worrisome, but more of an I-think-I-Might-Know-This-Chick.

The brothers lean in and start talking amongst each other, and I let out a heavy breath, thanking God that I wasn't forced to face them right this second. I don't know why, but Sebastian makes me nervous, antsy, like a crack addict on the search for her next fix.

Taking a sip of my drink, I nearly spit the now somewhat cool liquid on Delilah when she leans in and whispers, "Shit, they're getting up and walking over here."

Dear Lord in heaven...

"Lily Kline, is that you?" Remington stops at the edge of the small round table. His presence is one you couldn't ignore even if you tried. Peering up through my lashes, I give him a smile. Remington Miller is as beautiful as he was the day I left. All the Miller boys are, taking after their mother. Toned, tanned, and a smile that owns every room.

"That's me," I chirp, trying not to sound nervous, or excited, or anything at all.

Sebastian grunts beside him, and I let my gaze slowly drift to him. He's holding the paper coffee cup in his hand so tightly it looks like he's going to crush it at any given second. Does my presence annoy him that much? He seemed fine in his office the other day.

"What's it been, ten years?" Rem strikes up a conversation like time never passed between us. Like we're the same two kids that lived a few houses down from each other.

"Yup." I pop the P.

"Are you studying here?" Rem asks.

"Yeah, I'm starting classes on Monday. I just moved back here," I explain.

Glancing over at Del, I wish I hadn't. Her blue eyes look like they're about to burst out of her heart-shaped face. An awkward silence settles over the four of us, and Del nibbles on her bottom lip nervously.

"Cool, do you remember, Jules?" Remington asks, breaking the silence.

"Yes," I smile. How could I forget such a kind person? She was one of my first friends in elementary school, even though she was a year ahead of me, we used to ride the bus together, and play on the playground after school.

"She is a student here too, you know," Remington smiles, and elbows Sebastian in the side not so subtly.

What the hell is that about?

"Jules' birthday is this weekend, and we're having a little gathering at my dad's place. Think maybe you would want to come and hang out?"

I chew the inside of my cheek. *Say no, Lily, say no.* The last thing I should do is hang out with Sebastian, considering that I've basically just lusted after him for the past ten minutes. Against my better judgment, I still agree.

"Of course, that would be awesome. It's been forever since I've seen her."

Rem's smile widens, and his eyes glitter with happiness. "Cool, Seb, can bring you over to the house if that's okay, or Jules and I could swing by whatever works."

"It doesn't matter." It sure as hell does, but I don't say that. Thinking about being inside a car with Sebastian has my heart racing.

"Perfect, let me give you my number, and then I can let you know the exact time on Friday." I pull out my phone and type the numbers he rattles off into it. Then I save his number and send him a text message with a smiling emoji, so he knows it's me.

When I look up from my phone, I see Sebastian staring at me, his gaze pierces through my skin, and into the deep layers that hold all my secrets.

I wonder if when he looks at me, he sees her?

The thought vanishes into the air when Rem clears his throat and says, "Okay, well I'll see you this weekend, can't wait to catch up. I know Jules is going to flip when she finds out you're back in town."

I try and smile, but my lips don't move. Rem doesn't wait for me to say anything and instead starts for the door. Sebastian remains standing there like a statue with his feet sinking into the concrete. One look at his face and I see the anguish flickering in his eyes, and even though I didn't ask the question out loud, I know what the answer is.

Yes, he sees Amy when he looks at me.

THE DAY of the shindig arrives, and I get up, straighten my hair, and search through my closet for something to wear. Delilah crawls out of her bed after I've tossed the third pair of shoes from our shared closet toward her. Each pair landing harder than the next.

"Okay, okay, I'm up. Quit throwing things at me!"

"I don't know what to wear," I huff, blowing a piece of hair from my face. "I need your help picking something out."

"It's just a birthday party with old friends. Who are you trying to impress?" Delilah questions with one eye open and the other half-closed.

"No one," I say defensively. "I just want to look nice, that's all."

"Nice for whom? Mr. Miller?" By now she's fully awake, her eyes twinkling with amusement.

"Don't be ridiculous. I told you how I know him. He dated my sister. Not to mention that he is ten years older than me, and the Dean of the university that I'm attending as a student."

"First of all, that was a long time ago, Lily. You are not a child anymore, and even though you might be a student here, you are still an adult. If you're willing and he is willing…"

I can't with her. I literally can't.

"It doesn't matter how long ago it was. They would still be together now if… if she was still alive." I look down at my hands. "I saw it in his eyes the other day at the coffee shop. I'm just a reminder to him, a reminder of my sister, of what could have been. He'll never see me as anything else, and I'm not sure if I want him to anyway. Every time I look at him, it feels like I'm betraying her."

Delilah rolls her eyes at me. "You don't know that. You've only seen him twice, and both of those times were brief. It's obvious there's chemistry there. Anyone with a pair of eyeballs can see that. I didn't know your sister, and I don't know you all that well yet, but I'm sure your sister would've wanted you to be happy."

She is wrong. I just know. He doesn't want me.

"It's just a dinner party with old friends. Nothing more, nothing less."

Delilah doesn't look like she believes me, but she doesn't say anything. An hour later, I end up picking some leggings and pairing them with boots, and an oversized sweater that falls off one of my shoulders. It's not overly sexy, but it's cute.

"I'd bang you." Delilah giggles as she shoves a spoon full of cereal into her mouth.

"Does that mean I'm decent enough to be seen in public with you?"

"It means," *crunch*, she pauses as she shoves another bite into her mouth, "that you're gorgeous, and that if I were Mr. Miller, I would snatch you right up, and make you mine."

"Stop calling him Mr. Miller and stop talking with your mouth full of food."

"Okay, Mom." Del taunts, and I twist around, pinning her with a grin, that she returns.

Five minutes later, I'm standing outside, waiting for Sebastian to pull up. Rem and Jules were originally going to pick me up, but Rem messaged me last minute asking if his brother could instead. Everything inside me screamed *no,* but my fingers typed the word yes instead, and I hit the send key before I could think any longer on it. Fiddling with my phone, I try and do something with my hands to curb the anxiety I'm feeling. It's going to be okay. Everything is going to be okay. It's just dinner with his family. It's not a funeral, not a date. Just dinner.

Tires crunch against the road and I look up from my hands, my gaze colliding with his through the window of his blacked-out jeep. I don't know why, but every time I'm in his presence, I'm pulled toward him. Even through the window, I have that weird feeling, like he's a black hole and I'm the galaxy just waiting to be sucked into his darkness.

God, please don't let me screw this up.

3

SEBASTIAN

Time. It's supposed to heal you, make things easier, but I think that's a lie. Time doesn't heal shit. It isn't time that makes things easier. It's you. You either learn to cope with it, or you let whatever's eating you fester. I thought I was coping well, but the moment Lily walked into my office, I knew that was a heaping pile of shit.

One look at Lily and I knew I still wasn't over *her,* or anything that had to do with her for that matter. Maybe this whole thing would be easier if Lily didn't look like the spitting image of her sister. Maybe I could look at her without feeling like my heart is bleeding, shattering into a million pieces all over again.

When I pull up to the dorm, she's already waiting for me, standing at the curb like she's waiting at a bus stop. As soon as I see her all the feelings in my gut swirl together.

Guilt, anger, loss, and... lust, the worst feeling of all. They all blend together like a wet painting, the colors bleeding, seeping into one another, making it harder to decipher one from the other. She climbs into the Jeep, sliding slowly on to the leather seat.

She isn't wearing anything sexy, thank fuck for that. Still, I can't help but look at her legs as she buckles up, and I have to fight the urge to not reach over and run my hand over her thigh.

Not, Amy. Not fucking, Amy.

"Thanks for picking me up," she says softly, as I pull out of the dorm's parking lot. I try my best not to white knuckle the steering wheel. The last thing I need is for her to realize she has any type of effect on me. That would make all of this worse.

"No problem," I respond tight-lipped.

A second, then two, then three passes, and I exhale a breath, but as I'm sucking in another, I'm assaulted by her sweet but exotic scent. She smells like what I would consider a tropical island; coconut and vanilla.

Fucking Christ. I choke on the air in my lungs and start to cough. Out of the corner of my eye, I can see Lily watching me cautiously like I'm a hungry lion who hasn't eaten in days. Truthfully, I haven't *eaten* in about a year, but that's none of her business.

"Are you okay?" Again, her voice penetrates my skull, and while her voice is a pleasant sound, it still finds a way to annoy me.

"Fine." The word comes out more like a hiss, the message behind it is clear... back off and leave me alone. Even in the low light of the car, I catch her shocked expression. Her beautiful features twist into confusion before she turns away from me.

I know I'm an asshole for brushing her off, it's not like it's her fault that she looks like her sister, but I don't know what else to do other than to push her away. I just can't bear to be around her and if that makes me a selfish prick, so what. I won't stop. If she's uncomfortable around me, she'll stay away, which is the entire purpose.

The rest of the drive she stares out the window, and I stare out onto the road. Neither of us speak, making the tension in the car so thick it's hard to breathe.

I'm anxious as fuck by the time we arrive at my father's house and all but bolt from the car. Sucking a sharp breath into my lungs, I exhale her stupidly good scent. It clings to my nostrils, refusing to let go, just like her presence.

By the time I walk around the car, Lily has already gotten out and is walking toward the front door without me. *Very well.* I follow her to the porch where she stops, waiting on the doorstep. Holding my breath, I brush by her and open the door without knocking. It's not like I'm an unwelcome guest.

We step inside, and I can already hear Rem's loud voice carrying through the house. I follow the sounds of laughter through the hallway and into the living room, while Lily follows close behind. I don't have to look back to know she is, it's like I can feel her haunting presence.

"There you are!" Rem calls, a beer already in his hand. I tip my chin toward him, Dad, and Lex.

Jules who is sitting beside him lights up, her eyes landing on Lily as she gets up from the sofa and walks over to greet us.

"Happy birthday," I tell her as I give her a quick hug and a peck on the cheek.

"Thank you," she says before letting me go and looking at Lily next to me. "Lily, I'm so glad you made it. It's been so long."

"It has, but I'm so happy to be here, to celebrate with you. I just hope I'm not intruding."

"God, no. We're practically family." Jules smiles infectiously.

I try not to stare as they hug, and instead walk straight into the kitchen to grab a beer from the fridge. I don't want to see their reunion or any shred of happiness. Twisting the cap off my beer, I toss it into the trash. If I didn't have to drive, I'd grab something stronger, something that would make me forget *her* completely, at least, for a little while.

"You okay, son?" Startled, I turn around at my father's voice, he's standing right behind me.

Jesus. When did he get up?

"I'm fine," I lie, before taking a sip of my beer.

"She looks a lot like her," he points out the obvious. "That can't be easy for you."

"Yeah, not so much, but it is what it is." Shit, I sound like an asshole.

"So, you're not fine?"

"No, but I will be. Don't worry about me, pops." I try to smile, but my lips won't work.

"Hard not to worry about you when you're the kindest of your brothers, and your behavior right now isn't something I've ever seen before."

I shrug, "I don't really know what's going on. Ever since Lily walked into my office, things have changed. I'm moody and angry... so angry." I squeeze the glass bottle in my hands.

"If you want to talk about it, you know I'm here. I'm not going to make ya but remember what happened with your brother and Jules. Feelings build, pain turns into anger which is where you are right now. Don't be that guy. Don't let it build up." I nod, acknowledging what he says, but saying nothing in return. He's warning me like I'm the problem in all of this. I didn't come trapezing into her life looking like her long-lost love.

Lily's soft voice carries into my ears as she takes a seat in the living room besides Jules. They talk while I drink, trying my best to drown myself in the bottom of this bottle. Dad walks back out into the living room, while I remain in the kitchen watching from a distance as *my* family welcomes her with open arms.

Now I know how Rem felt when I brought Jules here without asking him first. I guess payback is a bitch, huh?

Rem and Dad drill her with questions; like what she's been up to, how her grandparents are, what she's studying. Things of that nature. It's nauseating to hear her spew all these wonderful things about her life.

Stop, Sebastian. Stop being a douchebag.

It's wrong, deep down, I know it's wrong to be angry with her, but I can't help it. It's like something inside of me has snapped, and all the ugly, dark pieces I've swallowed down over the years are leaking out. I can feel Rem watching me, and I do my best to ignore his cynical gaze.

Tipping my beer back, I let out a grunt of disapproval when nothing comes out. Guess I've drunk it all. My body itches for more alcohol, but I don't grab another beer. Instead, I lean against the counter and stare off into space. A moment later, Rem gets up from the couch and enters the kitchen plucking a chip from a bowl on the counter.

"Why the depressed face?"

"Not depressed."

Rem smirks, "No, you're just in a sour as fuck mood. Any particular reason why?"

My eyes turn to slits, it's not often I want to slug my brother, but right now, I would love to. "No reason at all. I mean it couldn't have anything to do with the fact that you made me pick her up, then there's the little tidbit of inviting her without even talking to me first."

He shrugs, "How was I supposed to know you would be so butthurt about it. I figured you would like having her around." *Idiot.*

"Like having the spitting image of my dead girlfriend sitting in the same room as me." I mock, and give him a fake smile, "Totally excited, just bursting at the seams with joy over it."

Rem taps his chin, his lips curling into a smug grin, "This kind of reminds me of a similar situation. Remember when you didn't ask me when you invited Jules?"

"Don't act like that," I hiss, my fist clenching without thought, "this isn't even remotely the same circumstance, and if this is some sick twisted way of you getting back at me..." My voice trails off. I don't finish because I'm not sure what I would do. Nothing. There is nothing that I can do. If it wasn't for her being here, I wouldn't be in such a shitty mood. She's a permanent reminder of what I lost, and I hate it.

"It's not. I'm not an asshole." Rem smirks, adding, "Most of the time."

"Then why invite her?" Feeling like a cunt for even asking.

He shoves another chip into his mouth, "Her and Jules were friends, plus her whole family used to be close to ours. Not to mention that Lily lost her family the same way Jules lost her father and brother. I mean they've both lost everything. Have you ever thought about that? About how much she lost that day? I know you lost too, but Lily lost a sister, her father, and her mother." There's a brief pause, and I know what he's trying to do, trying to break through my senses, but what he doesn't know is that I know all these things already. I feel them. I feel Lily's pain. It surrounds me.

"I don't understand why you are so pissed about her being here.

Did something happen between you two?" Rem interrupts my thoughts.

I don't even understand why I'm so pissed. What the hell am I going to tell him? That I'm secretly drowning in my own misery because a girl I loved died, but her sister didn't, and she's a walking reminder of her.

Ha, no. I'm not ready to talk about this yet. I'm barely ready to recognize it for what it is. So instead of giving him an answer, I ignore his words and stare at the wall blankly.

Rem's gaze narrows conspicuously, "You aren't acting like yourself, so whatever it is that's bothering you so much, it's not my fault. I wasn't going to go home and tell Jules that I saw Lily, but I didn't invite her when I had the chance. That would've been a shit thing to do, and we both know it."

"Whatever," I shake my head, and shoulder past him. As I enter the living room, all conversation stops. Lily's gaze drops to her hands, and Jules stares daggers at me like I've done something to piss her off.

Great. Less than twenty minutes in their presence, and Lily already has them all hating me.

Shoving down into the other recliner, I look to the TV where Dad has a football game on, I stare at the screen pretending to be immersed in the game.

Pretending like she isn't even here.

The doorbell rings a moment later, and Dad shoves from his recliner with a groan.

"Don't get old girls, it's all downhill from here."

"Already there," Jules laughs.

When he reappears, he's holding four pizza boxes. Everyone gets up all at once, and piles into the kitchen to eat while I remain glued to my seat. My appetite is gone, and even though I know I'm being a party pooper, I can't seem to let go of the feelings I'm having.

It's annoying. Infuriating. I should probably just go home, but I can't do that to Jules. Call me a sadist, but I'd rather suffer through the pain. I spend the rest of the night trying to ignore everybody.

Jules seems to have a great time even with me dragging down the party.

Lily sips on her root beer, pretending, just like I am. I can see it, the tension in her face, the way her body is angled away from me. She's uncomfortable. *Good.* At least I'm not alone.

Fuck there is something wrong with me.

Lex and Rem continue drinking, guzzling beer down like they're frat boys, and as much as I would like to join them, I choose not to, I already got drunk the other day. Once a month is plenty for the newly appointed Dean.

"What's the matter with you, Seb? Why such a sour puss today?" Lex yells from across the room like we aren't all sitting a few feet from each other. Rem, of course, laughs in his drunken state. I don't know why but I've always been closer to Rem than Lex. Maybe because Lex was gone.

"Maybe he just needs his ass kicked," Rem chuckles loudly. "A few punches to that noggin will set him right." My dad shakes his head from where he is sitting but doesn't say anything. He knows how we get. Us Miller boys are a rowdy bunch, always have been, always will be.

"Okay, you, time to go home," Jules takes Rem's hand and pulls him to his feet. She's tipsy herself but has nothing on Rem and Lex.

"Come on, boys. I'll drive you home," Dad announces, getting up from his own seat.

Lex follows suit, and we all get up and walk toward the door. Shit, I've done well all night, now all I have to do is drop her off at the dorms, and I'll be free of her, at least till she shows up somewhere else in my world.

"You guys going to be good?" Jules asks, her eyes slicing through me.

"I only had one beer, and that was two hours ago. I'm fine," I attest, knowing damn well that's not what she is talking about.

"You and I are going to have a nice talk next week," Jules whispers as she leans in to give me a hug. Wrapping my arms around her, I give her a tight squeeze.

"Night, and be good, Rem," I warn him over Jules' shoulder before releasing her.

"I'm always good," he slurs and presses a sloppy kiss to Jules' forehead as he pulls her into his side. The rest of my family walk out through the kitchen and into the garage, while I head for the front door.

Walking outside, I hear Lily's soft pitter-patter behind me. I don't even bother to turn around and look at her. I simply get into the driver's seat and watch her slide into the passenger's seat out of the corner of my eye, refusing to look at her straight on.

Once she's buckled up, and I pull out onto the road. I can't stand the heavy silence that's settling between us. I know what I need to do, what I need to say.

I'll make sure that this was the last time she invades my private life.

Strangling the steering wheel, I reason for control over my emotions.

"You shouldn't have come... this was a family gathering, and you didn't belong there." My tone's clipped, and my gut twists just hearing the words I spoke out loud. I'm such an asshole, but I have to be if I want to protect myself, my emotions, my heart.

"Look, I'm not stupid, I already gathered that you didn't want me there, but you don't have to act like I invited myself or intruded on some secret gathering. Rem invited me and I said yes, because Jules and I are friends."

I almost snort. "You knew each other as kids, that hardly accounts to being real friends." I know that's a low blow, but since I'm already going to hell, why not go all the way.

"You're a real prick, Sebastian." Her words are emotionally charged. Good, she's pissed off, now she knows how I feel.

"I know that. Always have been..."

"We both know that's not true. The way you've been acting today, that's not how I remember you," she interrupts, "you didn't treat Amy like this or anyone for that matter. You've always been a kind person, the one who would give the skin off his back to help someone else."

Her name. That's all I really hear. It's like nails on a chalkboard to my senses, and I damn near swerve into the other lane trying to rein myself in.

Clenching my teeth, I grit out, "Do not say her name. Don't talk about her, don't even mention her in my presence. The person you *remember* me being isn't the person I am right now."

Lily crosses her arms over her chest, and I swear, I see fire flicker in her blue eyes.

"Pfft, that much is obvious. The Sebastian I knew never would've talked to me like this or made open-ended threats to me." There's a pregnant pause, and it looks as if she is gathering her thoughts, getting ready to attack me with another set of verbal rage. "You have a lot of balls telling me that I can't speak my sister's name in your presence, and even more acting like an asshole to me. I lost so much more than my sister that day, but yet you want me to pretend..." She looks away, and strands of blonde hair fall into her face. When she looks back at me, it feels like I've died and gone to hell.

"Maybe you can pretend that she didn't exist, but I can't."

Pretend? Didn't exist. She's lost her fucking mind.

I bite my tongue, wanting to scream, wanting to tell her that I could never forget her sister, much less now with her sitting beside me as a never-ending reminder but I don't because I'm afraid of hurting her, of the words coming out wrong.

The air inside the Jeep grows hotter and hotter, and I'm so close to snapping it's taking every shred of patience I have not to lash out at her, to say something that will most definitely cut her down the middle. I'm not a mean guy, but I want to hurt Lily, simply because she exists, and her sister doesn't and that's not me.

This angry, vicious, cruel bastard isn't me.

Reaching the dorm, I pull the Jeep to the curb and watch as Lily's hand hovers over the door handle. She turns in the seat, and our gazes collide.

The vibrant blue of her eyes darkens, and I wonder if she's going to cry. *Fuck.* I hate myself for being like this, but I can't explain it. I can't fix it, not without removing her from the equation. Opening my mouth, I will words to come, but they don't. With the way she's looking at me right now, I'm not sure if there is anything that I could say to make this better.

I've already hurt her enough, it's probably best if I keep my mouth shut.

"Do you think I don't see her every time I look in the mirror? That I don't wish it was me that was in the car that day instead of her?" Her voice breaks at the end, tears brim her eyes, and all I can do is sit there, clutching onto the steering wheel. She's just sucker punched me in the gut with nothing more than her words.

How do I respond to that? Can I even?

Before I can tell her that I'm sorry, that I don't know what's wrong with me, she climbs out of the car, slamming the door shut behind her.

Goddamnit. This isn't how I wanted any of this to go. I don't want to hurt Lily but being near her feels like I'm losing Amy all over again, and I just can't bear it...I just can't.

4

LILY

I thought coming to North Woods was the right thing, coming back to where I grew up, where I was born, but I'm starting to second guess that. Not when I can't stop thinking about him. I know it's wrong, especially after the way he acted, and the things he said to me.

I should hate him. I should never want to see him again, and forget he even exists but, stupidly, I don't. All of this is wrong. Sebastian and me. The feelings I have.

As a student, I shouldn't be wondering what he is doing, hoping that I might run into him every time I walk across campus. It's sick and twisted, and I can't put it into words. The hate but need that I feel. He's the last piece I have of my sister and, as wrong as it is, I don't want to let him go. I can't.

Two weeks have passed since I last saw him. Classes have started and are in full swing now. College is definitely harder than I expected. For some reason, I thought studying art would be more fun and include less math and English classes. Welp, I thought wrong. I've already flunked a surprise math test that I had on Monday.

Which is shit for me being that I'm here on a scholarship and can't afford to let my grades drop below a certain GPA. Of course, not having the textbook for said class doesn't help. The scholarship only covers housing and tuition, not textbooks or anything else you might need to live. So, when I saw the price tag on the books, I had to make a choice between food for the next two weeks or printed paper. In case you were wondering, I chose food.

I try to throw myself into homework, hanging out with Delilah, and finding a job but every spare moment or thought leads me back to him. I'm so caught in my own head as I head to class that I almost run over Professor Berg, my beloved math teacher in the hallway. Luckily, I stop a few feet short of colliding with him.

"Ahhh, Miss Kline, I'm actually glad to have run into you. I was going to talk to you Monday before class but since I've got you now, would you mind stopping by the Dean's office to talk to your academic advisor."

"Uh, sure," I say, but it almost comes out as a question. Why the hell is he sending me to talk to my advisor? Have I done something wrong? Broke some sacred rule? I should probably ask him. My mouth pops open, a question on my lips when he starts to walk away.

"Great, see you Monday then."

What the hell?

Taking out my generic phone, I check the time. It's late, and they'll be closing soon, but if I hurry, I might make it. Slinging my backpack over my shoulder, I speed walk down the hall and toward the administration building which thankfully isn't that far from where I am right now. Students rush past me, all of us clearly in a hurry.

By the time I reach the building, I'm a tiny bit out of breath, but I still don't slow down. Pushing open the large door, I step inside, my sneakers squeaking against the linoleum. Pausing briefly, I stare at the front desk. No one. There's just a sign that says be back tomorrow.

Well then... Deciding that tomorrow is just too late to wait, I walk down the long hall toward the offices. When I find my advisor's office, I lift a hand and knock on her door.

"She's already gone," Sebastian's voice rings in my ears, and I swear my whole body reacts to the deep gravelly sound.

Goosebumps spread out across my arms, and my heart starts beating just a little faster.

I ready myself, before I turn around, puffing my chest out to show him that I'm not scared or affected by him.

I turn expecting to find him scowling at me, maybe even preparing to yell at me to get out, but instead, he just stares at me, his eyes softer than I've ever seen them. I'm so shocked by the way he is looking at me that I forget to respond.

"Is there something I can help you with?" He breaks the silence, and a shiver runs down my spine.

"I... I don't know," I admit. "Professor Berg sent me here, he didn't say why."

He doesn't look angry or irritated, and I'm not sure what to make of him at this point.

"Come here. I can check your file on the school database." He motions toward his office, and I follow him like a lost puppy.

He sits down behind his desk and starts typing something into the computer, while I sit nervously in front of him, wringing my hands in my lap. I try my best not to stare at him because every time our eyes meet this stupid warmth fills my abdomen.

"Professor Berg made a note that you failed your first test, you didn't submit your homework, and you didn't bring your textbook to class." Sebastian looks up from the screen and finds my eyes. An unspoken question hangs between us.

"I don't have my textbooks yet, but I will get them soon and make up all the work I've missed," I sigh. I was really hoping this wasn't that big of an issue, but obviously, it is.

"Why don't you have your textbooks yet? You should have gotten a supply list a long time ago."

A flush works its way up my throat and onto my cheeks. Embarrassed, I look away, finding some spot on the wall behind him to concentrate on.

"I just... I don't have the money to pay for them right now." I try my best to make my voice strong and even, anything but what I'm truly feeling, but instead, it all comes out in a rush like the air deflating from a balloon. He shakes his head and leans back in his chair. For some strange reason, I feel the need to explain.

"I'm looking for a job right now, so it shouldn't be much longer."

"Why didn't you come to me and ask for help?" I swing my gaze back to him just to make sure he isn't joking. His expression confirms that he's serious, which confuses me even more.

"Are you serious, right now? You really expect me to ask *you* for help? When should I have asked... before or after you told me that I'm nothing to your family?"

Regret fills his eyes, and his face twists as if he's in pain.

"I'm sorry about what I said and how I acted that night." His apology takes me by surprise, the insults I had lined up for him are now suddenly stuck in my throat.

"You... you're sorry?" I can't pull my gaze from his, and not just because he's gorgeous, no it's because of the way he's looking at me. Like I matter. Like I'm important to him. There's a stark difference between who he was that night and who is he is tonight.

He nods his head, "I am. Let me make it up to you... let me buy your books for you?"

"No!" I yell without thinking. I shove from the chair nearly causing it to crash to the floor. Once on my feet, I move toward the door. I didn't come here for his pity, or his money and the fact he's acting otherwise infuriates me. Twisting around, I stare at him with fire in my eyes.

"You can't just buy me off to make yourself feel better, and I don't need or want your pity." I turn fully, prepared to storm out, but I make it all of one step before he is on his feet quickly, coming around the desk.

Confidently, he walks across the room and over to me. "That's not how I meant it, and you know it. I would never pity you or buy you things as a form of apology. I want to buy you the books to show you that you can count on me for help... if you need anything, just ask."

Exasperated, I growl, "Just ask? Just ask?" I repeat. I cannot believe him. Maybe I'm blowing up over nothing, but I'm exhausted, tired of thinking about him and wondering if he's thinking about me too.

Invading his space, I crane my head back and raise my hand. Sebastian gives me a confused look, but I don't give him a chance to question me. Using my index finger, I poke him right in his perfectly muscled chest.

"I don't need *your* help."

Confusion bleeds into an emotion I can't quite read, and then he does something I would never in a million years expect him to do. He grabs my finger and uses it to pull me closer. The softest of gasps slips past my parted lips. With his other hand, he gently grabs me by the back of my neck, holding me in place while he bends down, bringing his face impossibly close to mine. Too close. Breathing through my nose, I catch a whiff of lemongrass and orange, realizing a moment before it's too late that I'm smelling him.

Before I can think on that embarrassment, his lips crash into mine. There's a hunger to his kiss, it's wild, unhinged passion. He pulls me flush to his body, leaving no space between us. Our chests press together, my hardened nipples rubbing against his skin through both of our shirts.

I want him *bad.*

I need him *bad.*

It's wrong, but it's so damn right.

Fisting his shirt in my hands, I pull him closer, deepening the kiss. The friction against my pebbled nipples causes me to groan, and Sebastian takes my open mouth as an invitation, his tongue sliding past my lips to stroke my own.

His strokes are steady, firm, and they make a slow heat build low in my abdomen.

I've never kissed like this before, with so much passion and heat. It feels like I'm burning up, my skin burning where he touches me. When he starts to move, I don't think twice. I let him guide us back to the couch, and then he pulls me down onto his lap.

Straddling him, I let my hands wander over his broad shoulders, and down his sculpted chest, slowly trailing down to the abs I know he's hiding beneath his shirt. I run my fingers over each hard indentation before coming to rest on the zipper of his dress slacks.

In one small motion, I unzip him. I have no clue what I'm doing, or why I'm doing it, but I want this. No, I need this. As if his brain has finally caught up with my actions, he breaks the kiss and presses his forehead against mine.

We're both panting, gasping for air. Sebastian releases his hold on the back of my neck, and his hand falls to the cushion beside us. It seems like he's giving up. As if he's defeated.

Does he want this as badly as I do? As badly as I need him? Our eyes bleed into one another, my blue into his hazel. I can see the confusion, the anger, and sadness lingering there, and I want to make it go away. I want to heal both of us, to forget just for a minute.

Reaching for the button on his slacks, I flick it, and only then does he make an attempt to stop me, his hand coming to rest against mine. His hold is lax as if he doesn't really want to stop me. There's a firm bulge pressed against my core, and I know for certain he wants this, so why is he stopping? Looking up at him through coal-black lashes, I question him without even speaking.

"We shouldn't." His voice is smoky, it clings to my insides like glue.

"Please," desperation drips from that one single word, but I don't care how desperate I sound or look. I just want him.

After a moment, he releases my hand, letting his fall back to where they were before. He leans back into the cushion, his chest rising and falling quicker, and quicker giving him away.

I take that as an invitation and continue undoing his pants. I might have held onto my virginity, but I'm no saint. I've fooled around and given a blowjob or two before, not enough times to be considered a pro, but enough times that I must've been decent enough because it didn't take long for them to come.

Crawling off his lap, I drop down to my knees in front of him, freeing his massive erection at the same time. I can't help myself. I need to see him. Peeking up at him, I take his heavy cock into my hand. His eyes are hooded, almost closed, but I can still see the lust and need swirling in the depths of them.

Leaning in, I take the velvet mushroom head between my lips. Never breaking eye contact, I press my tongue to the underside and listen as he releases a low rolling groan.

That sound, it zings right through me, making my core pulse with need. His hand comes up to my face, cradling my cheek, his thumb gently skimming over my heated skin.

It's such a simple gesture, there is something so endearing in that touch, it makes my chest swell. My heart feels full, fuller than it's ever been. For once, I feel whole, normal, less broken. With his other hand, he threads his fingers into my hair and strokes my scalp, making tiny rivulets of pleasure cascade down my spine.

I groan around his cock, working more of his length into my mouth.

He's bigger than I'm used to, so it takes me a bit to get a good rhythm going, but once I do, I start to bob my head up and down, my tongue flicking over the slit of his cock, before circling back around the head. He tastes like soap and salt, and I can't get enough of him. He's like a bad habit that I can't kick.

With every pass of my tongue, the muscles in Sebastian's legs and abdomen tighten. His touch becomes rougher, and his fingers dig into my scalp. Intentional or not, he ends up holding my head in place while thrusting his hips upward at the same time. He's chasing his release, asking for it without words.

His cock hits the back of my throat, and I gag around his length.

"Fuck, I'm sorry..." He whispers harshly, skimming his fingers over my cheek. Looking up at him, I can see his dilated eyes, the pleasure of what he just did seeping from every pore on his body. He might be sorry mentally, but physically he wants to do it again, and I'll be damned if that doesn't influence me to do it again.

Breathing through my nose, I swallow as I work him to the back of my throat, but I still gag around his length, saliva dribbling out the side of my mouth and down onto his muscled thigh. Sebastian groans, his head tipping back against the cushions.

"I'm going to come in your mouth if you do that again..." He tells me, the deep sexy tone of his voice makes it feel like I've been struck by lightning, and I'll be fucking damned if I don't make him come.

I've never failed at a blowjob, and I'm not going to start now. Sucking on the head before moving down the rest of his cock, I cup his massive balls in my hand. Then, I sink down, taking him all the way to the back of my throat again. This time, I gag massively, my eyes watering, as I suck in a sharp breath through my nose.

A knocking noise meets my ears, but I ignore it. Pulling back, so I have only the mushroom part of his cock in my mouth, I massage his balls, and smile around him as his hands ball into two tight fists that rest against his thighs.

Yes, yes. It's wrong, so wrong. He's the dean. He's ten years older than me. He's my dead sister's boyfriend. I shouldn't want his cock in my mouth. I shouldn't be wet with need for him, but I'm all those things and more.

His muscles tense beneath my touch, his chest rising and falling in rapid succession. He's close, so close. I'm just about to take him to the back of my throat again when the door to his office flies open. I sit up straight, letting Seb's dick slide out of my mouth. Swinging my gaze toward the now open door, I find two people standing in the office looking at me in shock.

Like a deer caught in the headlights of a car, I freeze.

Shit. Shit. Shit.

For one long, excruciating moment, no one does or says anything. Peeping over my shoulder, I find a girl with long red hair standing in the doorway, a guy beside her. The girl's eyes are squeezed shut as if she could unsee what she just caught us doing.

I'm so embarrassed, beyond embarrassed. I'll never be able to show my face again at this school.

With a mask firmly in place, Sebastian springs into action, pulling up his pants and tucking his quickly deflating dick away. Pushing up from the floor, I move away from him as if that could make the situation better.

They already saw him with his dick in your mouth.

"Seb, we are so sorry," the guy who walked in on us tells him. At the same time, he grabs the girl who still has her eyes squeezed shut and starts walking backward, taking her with him.

"Clark..." Sebastian starts, his voice brimming with shame, but the guy merely shakes his head.

"Dude, we didn't see anything." The guy's hand finds the door handle, and he pulls it closed, leaving us inside the now tension-filled room.

My stomach churns, as bile rises up my throat. *What have I done?* My cheeks flame and I don't know what to do. Do I run, or do I stay? Sebastian has his back to me, but I can still see the agony, the shame rippling through him, and I know without even asking, without even speaking, that he regrets this, regrets what we've done.

"This..." He twists around, his eyes refusing to meet mine and instead fall to the floor at my feet. "This shouldn't have happened. It... it can't happen again. This is wrong for so many reasons."

I nod, not only can't it happen again, it shouldn't. That, however, doesn't stop my emotions from going haywire. It feels like I'm losing a piece of him like whatever I gained from him in this room a couple minutes ago he has taken back.

Finally, he looks at me, but instead of finding the Sebastian I need right now, the one that could make all of this okay, I find the one that dropped me off at my dorm.

Angry, brooding, cold. His features are clear, uncut, and his eyes pierce my skin like a thousand tiny knives.

"This was a mistake, and it cannot happen again," he repeats. "It will not happen again."

Swallowing down the words I want to say, I head for the door. He doesn't reach for me or make an attempt to stop me, and that only drives the knife deeper into my chest. Doesn't he care? Didn't he feel the passion between us? The heat? Didn't his heart beat again for the first time? Gripping the knob, I open the door, walk out, and close it gently behind me. As soon as the click of the door sounds the tears I've been holding back start to fall.

This was a mistake...

That's all I can hear. All I replay in my mind.

I know it can't happen again, that I shouldn't have crossed the line for more than one reason, but I can't help but feel the pain of his words being etched into my soul.

This was a mistake.

We are a mistake.

You are a mistake.

That's what he thinks, that's what everybody else is going to think. I need to make sure that I never get swept away like this again. I need to forget Sebastian Miller as much as I can.

5

SEBASTIAN

*A*nd the asshole of the year award goes to me, for being a dick... a selfish, irresponsible, utterly unprofessional dick. In my defense, Lily has found a way to slither under my skin, every single time I see her. I can't outrun her, she's everywhere, and when she isn't everywhere that I am, she's in my head, her memory etched into my thoughts. I tell myself it's Amy that I see when I look at her, but it's not just her that I see anymore.

Staring at my computer screen, I try and focus on my work, it really shouldn't be that hard for me, but it is. My eyes keep moving back to the couch across the room. Every day I have to remind myself that what happened between us can never happen again.

And every day I'm reminded of what her hot, wet mouth felt like wrapped around my cock. *Jesus.* My cock starts to harden at the memory. I never did get to come that night. All that build-up and for nothing.

Shaking the thought away, I open a new tab on my laptop and type in the school's website, navigating to the university bookstore. Is there a way for me to send these books without me looking like an even bigger jackass?

I don't want her to think I'm buying her off or thanking her for a blowjob—which was spectacular. On the other hand, I'd be a jackass if I didn't get her books, right? Who fucking knows anymore? My moral compass has been off, to say the least. Fuck, right or wrong. I'm ordering the damn books.

Double-checking her class schedule, I order all the books she needs and have them sent to the on-campus bookstore. I pay with my credit card, but list Lily's phone number and her name as the pick-up person.

Closing my laptop, I check the time on my phone. It's past eight o'clock, and I'm the only person left inside the building. It's been like this almost every day this week.

All I've been doing is throwing myself into work. It's the only way I know to take my mind off her, off the image of her on her knees with that perfect pouty mouth wrapped around my cock. *Damnit.* I have to stop thinking about her.

Shoving from the desk, I grab my jacket and slip it on as I'm walking out of the office. I lock up the building behind me and drive home trying to think about anything besides Lily. Spoiler alert... it's not working.

Once home, I strip and take a cold shower, before heating up a frozen meal for dinner, Shortly after, I brush my teeth and crawl into bed. Old. That's what I am. Any man my age would be out having a drink or two on a Friday night, maybe even bring home a woman. Nope, not me. I've been lying in bed staring at the ceiling for the last hour, trying to go to sleep, or merely trying to get myself to stop thinking about her.

I've just rolled over to my side, hoping that a new sleeping position will help, when my phone starts to ring, the sound piercing through the otherwise silent night.

A little startled, and worried by the late-night phone call, I quickly grab my phone. I have to squint at the screen, my eyes not yet adjusted to the bright light. Across the screen, Rem's stupid face grins at me, and I almost roll my eyes.

"Yeah," I grumble. If he's calling this late, that can only mean one thing, he needs me to come be his DD.

"Hey, sorry to wake you," Rem's voice comes through the line, and I immediately start to worry, he doesn't sound drunk at all. I'm worried because if he's not calling about needing a DD, he's calling about something else.

"What's wrong? Are you okay? Is Jules okay?" I question anxiously while shoving the covers back.

"I'm okay. Jules is okay. I'm not... I'm not calling about us. Actually, I'm not... ah, I'm not even sure if you want to hear this..." He's stalling, elongating the inevitable, and I'm starting to get annoyed.

"Out with it, Rem. What the hell is going on?"

"It's Lily," he murmurs, and the breath stills in my lungs. "She's here at the frat house, drunk off her ass, and hanging out with some people she probably shouldn't be."

The air slips past my parted lips, and disappointment and anger overtake the fear I was feeling a few moments ago.

"Where are you?" I don't even ask who she is partying with, if he says they're no good, then I trust his judgment. All that matters now is removing her from the situation, which I intend to do.

"I'll text you the address," Remington says. "It's not far from your place."

"Get her away from whoever she is with and take her outside. I'll be there soon."

Hanging up the phone, I shove from the bed, and pull on a pair of sweatpants, before grabbing my keys and heading for the door.

Checking the address Rem sent me, I find it's only four miles away. *Thank fuck.* She's practically partying in my neighborhood.

Five minutes later, I pull up to a frat house that I've never been to. Cars are parked along the road, and even with my windows up, I can still manage to hear the loud music blasting. People are scattered out in the front yard, stumbling about.

Ignoring them, I scan the area and spot Rem, at the same time that he must spot me. My gaze homes in on Lily. She's swaying on her feet, so unstable a small breeze could knock her over. Rem leans into her ear, and says something, before all but carrying her toward the car.

Getting out, I run around the car and open the passenger door for him, and together we get her inside the car. She smells like an entire bar full of liquor, but beneath that is her normal tropical scent and, of course, I would smell that, of all the smells that she's giving off right now.

She mumbles something incoherently, and I look down at her, wondering what the hell happened that made her act out like this? This is Lily. She's smart, beautiful, she has the world at her feet, and she's doing stupid shit like this? With a barrage of emotions assaulting me, I close the door behind her and turn to my brother.

"Who was she partying with?"

"Just some guys, I know... some who I'm pretty sure are slinging dope."

"Did she take anything?"

"I don't think so. I kept an eye on her. She did outdrink everyone though, so she'll definitely be feeling it tomorrow."

Yeah, she will, among other things, once she's awake and lucid.

"Thanks for calling..."

"I wasn't sure if I should call you, but then she started saying your name and..." Rem eyes bleed into mine, and I swear it looks like he's trying to decode something. "I just wasn't entirely sure since you were acting so fucking weird at Jules' birthday party."

Shit. I fucking forgot about that. I was such a moody asshole that night.

"I'm sorry, I was..."

"Don't worry about that right now," Rem interrupts. "Take her home and then get some sleep. I'm sorry I woke you. We'll talk tomorrow."

I don't tell him he didn't wake me, that I had been sitting up for the last fucking hour thinking about the blonde in my passenger seat, who was apparently trying to make herself forget about something.

"Talk to you tomorrow," I say, walking around the car and getting into the driver's seat. Lily's head shifts back and forth against the headrest, as I lean over the center console to buckle her up.

This close up, I look at her, really look at her. Her heart-shaped face is beautiful. Her bright blue eyes are framed by coal-black lashes that are barely open, and her creamy white cheeks are flushed from all the liquor she's drunk. Her pink pouty lips are parted, and a puff of breath passes through them.

Even in the obliterated state that she's in, she still maintains her natural beauty.

Fucking Christ, I shouldn't be staring at her, much less when she's passed out. Coming to my senses, I finish buckling her in and start the car. Driving off, I head to the dorms, but when I'm about halfway there, doubt starts to slither in, and I wonder if I should take her there.

She's pretty much blacked out. I would have to carry her in and up the stairs. What if other students see me carrying her unconscious body up to her room?

Yeah, that's not going to work. Exhaling a frustrated breath, I take the next turn and drive to my house instead. This might be an even worse idea, but it's the best I've got right now.

At least I won't be seen by any students, and I won't have to worry about anyone messing with her. The mere thought of some young ass frat guy touching her has me seeing red, and I tighten my hold on the steering wheel out of anger.

By the time I pull into the driveway, I'm still not sure how I'm going to make this work. I'm supposed to be trying to forget her, and instead, I end up bringing her back to my home, my domain? I'm the Dean of the university, bringing a student home with me.

This isn't just a bad idea, it's the worst fucking one I've ever come up with. This could cost me my position. *She* could cost me everything. What am I thinking? *You're not.* Stupid, that's what this is. Exiting the car, I come around to the passenger side and open the door. For a second, all I do is stare. How the hell am I going to get her inside without her puking?

She's still pretty much unconscious, so my options are limited to carrying her or leaving her here, and I didn't drive all the way to the house just to leave her in the car. Sighing into the night air, I lean down and unbuckle her. Not a twitch, or growl, or anything escapes her lips.

Yeah, she's gone. Picking her up, I gently set her on my shoulder, praying the movement doesn't spark some insane bout of vomiting.

Walking slowly up to the house, I find she weighs nothing, and that concerns me. Is she getting enough food? Is she eating? I ask myself all these questions as I unlock the front door and carry her inside.

Without even thinking about it, I take her into my bedroom and settle her onto the mattress gently. Then I step away and squeeze at the tightened muscles in my neck.

She looks like a damn angel with her silky blonde hair circling her head like a halo against the black sheets. Right then, all I can picture is her beneath me, those big blues of hers peering up at me as I drive into her, again and again.

Holy hell. I shove the thought to the furthest corner of my mind. That will never happen. It can never happen. I recite to myself as I peel her boots off.

Situating her better against the pillows, I decide against removing any of her clothing.

I don't want to invade her privacy or make her think I'm some creep. The blowjob incident was bad enough, even if I really did fucking enjoy it. Giving her body one last once over, cringing at the leggings and T-shirt she's wearing, I pull the comforter over her and tuck in around her. As I'm doing so, I lean over and press a soft kiss to the crown of her head.

She stirs lightly, her eyes just briefly fluttering open before closing again.

"I hate you..." Her voice is hoarse like she's been screaming all night. For a second, I think I've made up hearing her speak, but I didn't.

She definitely said she hates me.

She hates me.

The words sting and I'm not quite sure why. I deserve that, I guess. I'd hate me too after the way I acted. Staring at her a second longer, I wait for her to say something else, but instead, she starts to snore softly, her chest rising and falling evenly. The urge to crawl into the spot beside her and watch her all night long tugs at me.

No. She shouldn't even be here and crawling into bed and holding her isn't going to make forgetting her any easier. Shoving all the thoughts away, I pull the comforter up to her chin and slip from the room, closing the door softly behind me.

Then, I strip down to my boxers and make myself comfortable on the couch. It takes me forever before my eyes start to drift closed, and even when they do, my thoughts circle around her.

Lily... the one thing I can never have.

6

LILY

*I*t takes me forever to open my eyes, far too many bottles of liquor are stacked on top of them. My hands slide across silky sheets, sheets that are definitely not mine, and as I breathe deeply into the pillow beneath my head, I discover it smells like lemongrass and citrus, two things that, I, myself, do not smell like.

Shit, this isn't my bed. Panic zings through me. Realizing this, I bolt upright in the bed and force my heavy lids open. It makes my head hurt even more, but I push the pain away and scan the room. My vision blurry and my head swimming, as I do so. It feels like I'm on a boat, traveling on rough seas.

My stomach churns, and I press a hand to my mouth. Oh, sweet baby, Jesus.

Don't throw up, don't throw up.

Barely containing the vomit that was just rising up my throat, I decide to give myself a moment to recover and retrace my steps from last night.

Did I go home with someone?

No, I wouldn't do that. My gaze drops down over my body. The clothes I was wearing last night are still in place, the only thing missing are my boots, which I find sitting beside the bed.

Scrubbing a hand down my face, I release a soft groan, racking my brain for memories of last night. I remember being at the party with some guys who invited me, then Rem and Jules showed up. I hung out with them, Rem stepped away to call someone while Jules and I did a line of shots. After that, everything is black. Well, minus the dream with Sebastian, where I told the asshole, I hated him. That I remember.

Breathing through my nose to ease the churning in my gut, I slowly move to the edge of the bed. There's already a constant drumming behind my eyes. I need some Advil and water, stat, but before that, I need to figure out where I am and get the hell out of here.

Reaching the edge of the bed, I lean over and grab my boots. My fingers have just barely grazed the fabric of said boots, when I hear the door to the bedroom creak open, and catch sight of the hulking shadow of a man standing in the doorway.

I fully expect for one of the guys I was partying with to walk in. Instead, Sebastian greets me with a scowl. "I'm surprised to see you up so early after drinking all that liquor last night."

Without answering him, I grab my boots and start to pull them on my feet, ignoring the dizziness I feel as I lower my head.

"You know you couldn't even walk on your own, right? Getting that drunk is reckless and irresponsible. Do you have any idea what could have happened to you if Rem didn't get you away from that party?"

"Are you seriously giving me a lecture, right now?" My throat hurts, and the words come out raspy, but I don't care. I push myself up from the bed, ignoring another dizzy spell. "I don't need you or Remington to babysit me. I was fine where I was... and with who I was."

"Debatable," he says through his teeth, and I'm surprised by the amount of anger contained in that single word. I pretend not to notice and head toward the door with my head held high. I expect him to step away and let me out of the room, but instead, he crosses his arms over his chest. With his wide shoulders filling the door frame, there is no place for me to go past him. He is like a wall in front of me.

"Move," I order.

"No, you're going to listen to a whole lot more *lecturing* before you go anywhere. Plus, how are you going to leave? You gonna walk the ten miles to campus?"

If I wasn't feeling like shit and had more comfortable footwear available, I would probably say yes, but since neither is the case, it's going to be a hard pass. "Can I, at least, take a shower and get something to drink before I have to listen to more of this?"

Sebastian's frown turns into the ghost of a smirk and for some reason that pisses me off even more. "Clean towels are in the bathroom cabinet next to the shower. I'll make you some coffee," he says, before unfolding his arms, turning his back to me and walking away.

I didn't realize the amount of tension in this room, and my body until Seb is gone, and my shoulders slouch down.

How can a simple conversation be so intense?

Shaking my head, I find my way into the bathroom. First thing I do is turn on the water and hold my mouth under the faucet. The cold water hits my parched throat, and it feels so heavenly that I drink until my stomach protests.

After that, I start stripping out of my clothes and turn on the water in the shower. It's not until I step under the hot stream that it hits me. I'm in Sebastian's bathroom... naked, using his shower, shampoo, and soap, after sleeping in *his* bed. I suddenly feel like an intruder, like I invaded his private space, all of this feels terribly intimate. I almost laugh out loud. I had his dick in my mouth the other day, not sure how much more intimate and personal you can get.

When I'm done with my shower, I wrap myself up in one of the fluffy towels and dry my hair with a second one. I already feel a million times better, but then I look at the discarded pile of clothes on the floor, and cringe. I don't want to slip back into the old dirty clothes I slept in. I wonder what the chances are that Sebastian has some clean clothes for me to wear?

Testing my luck, I sneak out of the bathroom and back into the bedroom, wondering if I should go and find him or just try to find something myself. Not wasting too much thought on it, I waltz over to the dresser like I own the place and open the first drawer. *Bingo.*

The drawer is filled with stacks of folded T-shirts. I grab one, drop the towel around my body, and pull on the shirt in one move.

Opening the second drawer, I was hoping for shorts or sweatpants. Instead, I find socks and boxer briefs. Like an idiot, I stare at the black underwear for a moment, imagining them on Sebastian... imagining me pulling them down and freeing his hard cock...

"Looking for something?" Sebastian says behind me.

I'm so startled, I jump back what feels like three feet. My heart slamming against my ribcage in an irregular rhythm as I turn to face him, now only a foot away.

"I-I was just looking for something clean to wear," I explain.

"Looks like you've already found something."

Luckily, his shirt goes to right above my knees, so he can't see that I am not wearing anything underneath, but when his gaze wanders down to where my panties should be, he must realize it anyway. The air between us sizzles. Zings with heat. I can feel it in my core, rippling through me. I have to ignore the connection, the simmering heat.

His eyes snap back up to mine, the hazel in them has turned darker, turning almost dark honey or maybe his pupils are dilated. Either way, he looks like he is about to devour me, and I'm not sure if I'm scared or excited by the sudden turn of events.

"You don't happen to have some clean sweatpants I can wear, do you?" The question hangs in the air between us. Licking my dry lips, I wait for something to happen, and then it does. Sebastian lunges forward, taking me by surprise as he slams his lips against mine.

His hands land on my hips gripping onto me possessively while pulling my body toward him. Even though the kiss is deep and passionate, it only lasts about two seconds. It's then that he must realize what he just did.

Breaking the kiss, he stumbles back. Before I realize it, my hand is flying through the air, my palm connecting with his cheek, the sting of the hit radiating across my hand. The sound of my hand on his face fills the room.

His head snaps to the side, his jaw clenched so tightly I can see the muscles tightening along it. Through it all his eyes stay glued to mine, a mixture of shock, and desire flickers in his hazel depths. Shame paints me from the inside out. How do we keep ending up like this? Inside my head, all I hear is *this was a mistake.*

I don't want to be a mistake.

I don't want to be anything.

Another moment passes between us before those two feelings fade molding into a ball of regret and sadness. *No.* I don't want to be a regret to him. I don't want to see sadness in his eyes. Emotions are a fickle thing, and mine are spiraling out of control like a plane that's been shot down out of the sky.

I want to replace those feelings with something else... need, want. I want to feel anything but the things I've felt since losing my entire family, ten years ago. Crossing the space separating us, I sling my arms around his neck, pulling him down to me. This close, I can feel how much he wants me; how much he needs me. Knowing I shouldn't, but that I'm going to anyway, I press my lips to his.

His whole body stiffens at first, but in the next instant softens, his arms come around my waist, deepening the kiss. I feel like I'm melting... melting into his touch. He shudders against me, and I swear I can feel his walls crumbling. All the tension, all the resentment and anger between us falling away, leaving only us standing in the room.

We kiss for what feels like an eternity, but still, it's not enough, and when his hands wander from my waist to my lower back and then fall to my ass, I almost burst with need. His touch is electrifying, it ignites something deep inside me. His fingers trail even lower until he is at the hem of the shirt brushing against my bare skin.

He groans when he makes contact with my flesh, and as if that was the final straw, the one that made him snap, he grabs onto me, his fingers digging into my skin. In one swift move, he picks me up. Instinctively, I wrap my legs around his middle, and my arms around his shoulders as he carries me like this to the bed.

Oh, my god, this is it. I'm going to lose my virginity.

I always thought I would be nervous and scared when it happened, but right now, I'm feeling none of those things.

All I'm feeling is lust and need as he gently deposits me onto the bed. Only then does he break the kiss. His eyes bleed into mine as he hovers over me. Indecision paints his features, and I know already that he's second-guessing this, us. Something overcomes me, and I know I can't let things end the way they did last time. Yes, this is wrong, but some of the best things end in tragedy. I know without a doubt, I will regret this, but I need him. I need this, and I need it now.

"Please..." The word comes out as a needy whimper. I want this so bad. I want him so bad. Apprehension gives way to something deeper, and I know he feels it. The connection between us, the heat. He wants to reach out and touch it, taste it, and I want to let him. Licking my lips, I gaze up at him through hooded eyes. Time stands still, as I wait with bated breath for him to make his choice.

I know the instant he's come to a conclusion, because like a rubber band pulled far too tight, he snaps and falls back on top of me.

His perfectly sculpted lips mold to my swollen ones, and his body weight presses deliciously against me, pushing me deeper into the mattress. Leaving me no way of escaping him. As if I would.

Nudging my thighs apart with his legs, I feel his hand snake between us. All he does is graze his fingertips over my drenched folds, and I mewl like a cat in heat. Breaking the kiss, he smiles devilishly against my skin, before starting to nibble at the flesh along my neck.

"I knew you'd be wet for me," he pants, as he gently rubs against my clit. I almost come right then. The rough pad of his fingers combined with his low husky voice vibrating through me has the power to coax the orgasm right out of me.

Raking my nails over his shoulder, I wish he wasn't wearing any clothes. Fisting the material in my hands, I'm about to pull his shirt off to make my wish come true when he brings one finger down to my entrance and dips it inside, slipping through the wetness with ease. He teases me, dipping in and out a few times before sliding it in all the way.

All thought evades my mind in an instant, leaving me with nothing but pure ecstasy as the tingling deep inside my belly gathers, building, and on the verge of exploding.

"Fuck, you're so tight," he growls, thrusting his finger inside while keeping his thumb on my clit. His finger feels so big, I can only imagine what it would feel like with his cock inside of me. Closing my eyes, I give in to the feeling, letting it overcome me. It rushes in like water, suffocating me, drowning me in its sweet goodness.

"This is mine." He hisses, biting along my collarbone. The sensation sends shivers down my spine. "Say it. Tell me it's mine. Tell me you won't let anyone else touch it."

Sweet baby, Jesus.

He's so intense, but I can't deny him. "It's yours, all of it. All of me. Only you."

I can feel the heat pooling in my belly. My climax is near, snaking up my spine, gaining speed with each thrust.

"Good girl," He purrs with approval and starts to fuck me with his finger, adding a second one to the mix, stretching me slowly as he does so.

With the added finger it doesn't take long before I'm exploding around him. Clamping down on his fingers, I stifle a whimper by sinking my teeth into my bottom lip. The climax is more intense than any I've ever experienced before. My whole body is on fire, every cell scorched by the flames, leaving behind my spent body in a pile of ashes.

Sebastian shifts on top of me and my eyes flutter open. His gorgeous face is closer now, and my heart skips a beat when I think he might kiss me again. He doesn't though. Instead, he hovers there, studying my face like I'm some fine piece of art.

I can feel his incredibly hard cock pressing against my inner thigh, telling me that he wants me just as bad as I want him. So, why doesn't he move? Why doesn't he take his clothes off and drive into me? Why doesn't he claim me like I know he wants to?

"I want you so bad, but we can't... we just can't," he answers my silent questions.

I want to object. I want to yell at him, shake him until he comes to his senses, but the truth is, he's right. We can't. There are a magnitude of things wrong with us coming together, but the biggest one is the fact that he's the dean, and I'm a student.

There must be some kind of rule against student and faculty relationships. He could get in serious trouble, not to mention all the people who would look down on us.

Even with all the endorphins still flooding my brain, dread and disappointment hang heavy in my gut. I don't know why I thought it would be different this time.

I should've expected it, because, of course, I knew all of this before. It's not like it's the first time I've thought about it. I've spent many nights since coming here staring up at the ceiling of my dorm room wondering if we would ever cross the line like this.

In every dream or thought, we put everything behind us. We did what we both craved. But this isn't a dream, this is reality. Still, it doesn't make it hurt any less. I can't help but want him, and I don't know how to make it stop. I have to find a way to make it stop.

AFTER A VERY AWKWARD, very uncomfortable drive back to the dorms, I spend the rest of the day in my room, recovering physically from being hungover, and mentally from the realization of what happened between us, and the fact that it can't happen again.

"So, are you ever going to tell me where you stayed last night?" D asks. I feel bad about not telling her, but I just don't think I should tell anyone, not even her. If the truth gets out, and Sebastian loses his job, I'll never forgive myself.

"Some guy, I didn't even catch his name," I lie. "I do know he wasn't a student here. He was at the party with a friend he told me."

"Sure, he was..." Delilah looks at me suspiciously. She's opening her mouth, no doubt in an attempt to dig deeper for information when my cell starts to ring beside me. Grabbing the buzzing device off my nightstand, I focus on the number. It doesn't look familiar, but it's local, so I answer it anyway.

"Hello," I say, giving Delilah an apologetic smile.

"Good afternoon, this is Ashley from the campus bookstore calling. I'm trying to reach Lily Kline."

"That's me."

"Hey, Lily, just wanted to let you know that all of your books just came in and are ready for pick up." *Books? What?* It takes a good second for it all to click in my mind, most likely from all the liquor saturating my brain. Sebastian told me he would buy me my books the other day. I just didn't think he would actually do it.

"Hello?" The friendly voice calls, and I realize, I haven't said anything in way too long.

"Ah, yes... yes, thank you. I will be coming by later to pick them up. Mhm... just double-checking, have they been paid in full or do I need to bring some money?"

"Nope, you paid everything online when the order was placed."

Yup, definitely, Seb.

"Okay, thanks again." I hang up the phone, and swing my gaze over to D. Her eyebrows are raised, and I know she is expecting an explanation for all of this sooner rather than later.

"What? It's just my book order."

D, blinks slowly, her button nose wrinkling as if she's smelt something bad, or worse my lie. "It's not the books I'm giving you this look for. It's because I know you're hiding something, and I want to know what it is."

"I'm not hiding anything." Getting the words past my teeth is hard. Delilah is my closest friend, and while I don't think she would tell a soul about Sebastian and me. I don't want to risk word getting out. Rumors spread like a wildfire on campus.

She gives me a look that says she doesn't believe me but doesn't push the issue. "Let's go get some dinner since you slept all day, and we can pick up your books on the way."

"That's a great idea actually, I could go for a big greasy burger right about now," I grin, my stomach feels a whole lot better now, but with that, hunger comes along.

She nods and starts putting her sneakers on when she turns to me again. "I'll leave you alone for now, but I know you're hiding something." Guilt settles into my gut at her words. I try to hide it with a smile, but I'm sure she sees right through it. To my relief, she doesn't say anything else though.

Not bothering to put makeup on, I pull my hair up in a messy ponytail, grab an old pair of jeans to throw on with a baggy sweat-shirt and slip into some comfortable flats. The bookstore, as well as the diner, are in walking distance, so we head out on foot, right after I'm ready.

We pick the pile of books up on the way. D looked at me funny when she saw that all of them were new copies and none of them used, but luckily, she stuck to her word and left me alone about it... for now.

With my heavy backpack full of textbooks slung over my shoulder, we walk into the diner. It's pretty crowded this time of the day, and I almost regret coming here. I don't want to be around this many people right now. I'm about to suggest we just do carry out when a whiff of fries and burgers tickle my nostrils, and my stomach growls in response. *Okay, I need food now.*

The hostess grabs two menus, and I watch her ponytail bounce from left to right as we follow her through the packed restaurant. We sit down in a small booth, and she takes our drink order before leaving.

Her body moves out of my line of sight, and my eyes meet a pair of hazel ones across the diner. There are four tables between us, but I feel like he is right in my face. For a moment, there is no one else in the room, just him and me. I don't hear or see anyone besides Sebastian across the diner. Our eyes stay locked for what seems like hours until he suddenly looks away and the spell is broken.

I blink, realizing how dry my eyes are. Did I blink at all the last minute? My eyes are still glued to Sebastian's face as I watch his lips start to move. It takes me another moment to realize that he is talking to someone. I swing my gaze to the person sitting across the table from him.

Jealousy slices through me like a hot knife as I take in the beautiful woman who is with him. She is smiling at him, showing off her straight white teeth, and dimples in her cheeks. She's only wearing light makeup, a casual dress, and high heels, but with her model-like beauty, she might as well have just stepped off the runway. Her long auburn curls fall down her back in smooth waves, and I'm reminded that I didn't even comb my hair.

"Okay, Lily," Delilah's voice drags me back to our table. "I'm not stupid, you know?" She lowers her voice, her eyes darting around the room to make sure no one can accidentally overhear us. "Clearly you have a thing for the dean and judging by the jealousy dripping out of you right now, there must have been something between you two."

Letting my shoulders sag, I slump down into my seat, feeling defeated. "It's so complicated, D."

So, fucking complicated.

7

SEBASTIAN

*I*t takes everything inside of me to look at Laura, who is sitting across the table from me. She's rambling on about budget plans, and faculty resources like she always does when we meet to talk business, but it's never annoyed me as much as it does right now. All I want to do is stuff a handful of that half-eaten salad into her mouth just so she will stop talking.

What makes the whole situation even worse is knowing that Lily is sitting ten feet away. What must she think, seeing me here with Laura? I want to storm over there and tell her that Laura and I are discussing school finances, and nothing more, but what's the point? I don't owe Lily an explanation. I'm not hers, and she is not mine. Even if this was a date, there would be nothing wrong with that. My head knows that, but my chest aches, and my stomach twists in guilt. I feel like I'm betraying her.

Laura excuses herself to go to the bathroom, and I use the alone time to glance over at Lily. She looks like she just rolled out of bed and stumbled over here, yet she manages to be the most beautiful woman in the room. She doesn't need fancy clothing and a layer of makeup to look stunning.

She hasn't looked back over here since she first got here. She is trying to ignore me, but I can see from across the room that I have an effect on her, just by being here, the same way she affects me. It's always like that when we are close to each other. Our bodies are like two magnets, constantly being pulled toward each other. We might be able to look away, but we can't ignore the gravitational pull.

A current ripples between us like an invisible live wire is hanging in the space separating us. The question is... how can I make it stop? How can I stop myself from needing the heat, the zing her touch brings? When she touches me, I feel alive, my heart beating for so much more than my own body's functioning.

"You okay, Sebastian?" Laura asks, sliding back into the booth. I blink myself out of the trance Lily's presence brings. "You seem distracted today."

"I'm good, just busy with all the new responsibilities that came with the job."

"I totally get it," she nods while checking the time on her watch. "Ugh, I got to go. Hubs picked up the kids from daycare, but he can't handle dinner and kids." She rolls her eyes. "Men, just don't know how to multitask."

"It's fine, thanks for meeting me after hours." I asked her to come here because I figured being alone with her in the office would be weird, now I'm second-guessing my decision. Having Lily seeing me here with her might be worse.

"Any time, Seb. I'll talk to you soon," she says, getting up from her seat. I slide out as well, giving her a quick hug. I've known Laura and her husband for a long time, we've worked together for the past few years, and we've all become friends somewhere along the way.

Grabbing two twenty dollar bills out of my wallet, I place them on the table before heading for the door. I look up and catch Lily storming through the restaurant toward the bathroom. Before I can even think about the fact that I am in a public place, and people could very well see me, I follow her.

Luckily, the bathroom is all the way in the back, and there is a hallway leading to it, so by the time I'm in front of the women's restroom door, no one in the diner can see me. I open the door and find Lily huddled over the sink, splashing water onto her face.

"What's wrong with you?" I ask as if I have no idea what's bothering her.

She turns off the water and straightens up. Pulling out two pieces of paper towel, she starts to dry off her face with her back turned to me. "Thanks for the books," she murmurs, ignoring my question.

This is about the books? Yeah, I don't believe that.

"Surely you aren't acting like this because I sent you books?"

With her back still toward me, she dries her hands or at least pretends to. I wait another moment before I've had enough. The need to see her face overwhelms me. Closing the distance between us, I grab her upper arms, twisting her around, so she's forced to look at me. Anger and defiance swirl in her icy orbs. She's not just angry, she's on the verge of exploding. Red hot jealousy is swirling just beneath the surface.

"Is she better than me because you can be seen with her in public? You wouldn't have to hide her, or your feelings for her." It feels like I've been slapped again. Her words sting, but more than that, I feel like an asshole seeing the hurt overtaking her beautiful features.

All I want to do is take her into my arms, and tell her she has nothing to worry about, that I don't care about Laura. I want to tell her how much she means to me, and that I can't stop thinking about her. But I can't. I won't. I might not want Laura, but I couldn't be seen with Lily in public. If I were to ever have any kind of relationship with her, she could never be more than my dirty little secret, and she is worth so much more than that. I can't do that to her. So, I do the only thing I can think of. I lie. It'll be easier if she thinks I'm with Laura. It'll be easier if I push her away.

"Yes, that's exactly why I'm with her because I would never want to be seen anywhere with you. You're a risk that I can't and won't take." I'm lying through my teeth, but it's this, or we keep dancing around each other. A never-ending merry-go-round of feelings we can never give in to. Her pretty blue eyes mist over before she wiggles out of my hold and pushes against my chest. Shoving me away with all her strength, she runs out of the bathroom, leaving nothing behind but her faint scent. I could've stopped her. I could've told her

I didn't mean anything that I just said. That I was lying, but what's the point?

I can never have her... *never* and leading her on, making her believe otherwise, it's not fair, it's not fair at all, and I refuse to do that to her. To myself.

~

I DON'T KNOW why but after, the encounter with Lily in the diner the other day, I thought that I would feel better. I thought maybe if I pushed her away, crushed every chance of ever having her, I'd start to get over her.

Pfft. That would be the case if I lived in a perfect world. I was wrong. Things seem to have gotten worse instead of better. Before she was a hunger I could sedate with a look or even an indecent thought, but now there's no calming the desire pulsing through me. I want her. It's like the temptation of getting caught, of risking it all only heightens my need for her.

Every moment of my day is spent trying not to think about her. A tension headache has taken up residence in my skull and doesn't have plans of leaving any time soon. Why the hell is this so hard? Doesn't my body get that I can't be with her? Is my brain the only rational part of me? Maybe sleeping with someone that isn't a student is what I need to finally get over her. I'm probably just pent up with need since I haven't had sex in like... way too long.

That's all this is... an itch to scratch, I'll feel better once I've screwed someone else... *Idiot.* I'm a damn idiot. Sleeping with someone else isn't going to fix this. If anything, it'll only complicate things. The mere thought of anyone but Lily beneath me makes me shudder.

Walking down the front steps of the admin building a soft feminine giggle filter's into my ears. It's almost nine at night, and it's not all that surprising for students to be out walking around, not with the building so close to the dorm rooms. Naturally, I ignore it, keeping my eyes locked on the concrete.

I've nearly reached my Jeep when I hear "*My roommate is gone, want to come up?"* it's not the words alone that cause me to look up with fire in my gaze, and anger coursing through my veins, but instead, the voice speaking those words.

It's soft and warm, and it belongs to a woman that shouldn't be inviting random guys to her dorm room. Squeezing my hand into a fist, I let the bite of the metal keys into my flesh calm me as I walk toward the scrawny guy who has his back to me, and Lily who has yet to notice me.

As soon as my eyes clash with Lily's, she smiles, her willowy frame swaying gently like a leaf caught in the breeze.

She's wearing a miniskirt that does little to cover her ass and a shirt that's showing off her entire midsection, and as I get closer, I see her eyes are glassy, pupils dilated.

"You want to fuck?" The guy slurs, leaning into her, a husky laugh piercing the air. "Because I'll fuck you... all over the dorm."

Like fucking hell, you will.

I know I have no right to be angry. That this is normal college behavior, but Lily isn't a regular college student. She might not be mine, but this type of shit isn't going to fly with me. I've barely got a leash on my rage when I reach the guy, placing a hand on his shoulder, I pull him backward none too gently. Air fills my lungs once there is an adequate amount of space between them.

Lily looks up at me, a pout on her glossy pink lips.

All I can think is. I'll deal with you next.

"What the—" The guy starts as he spins around, fists clenched, and ready for a fight, but he stops himself mid-sentence when he sees who I am.

"Go back to your own dorm. There will be none of that tonight. If I catch you around here again trying to get into the female dorms, especially drunk, there will be problems." I'm barely containing my anger now, the need to slug this fucker in the face, and tell him to never put his hands on Lily again is astounding.

I've never been this territorial, this jealous over someone. I pride myself on being a good guy, a gentleman, but none of the thoughts running through my head right now are very gentleman-like or good.

"Seriously?" Lily pouts, crossing her arms over her chest, pressing her tits together, and drawing my attention to them.

"Uh, yeah..." The guy takes a step back, and then another as he glances between us. "Sorry, Dean Miller. I'll, ummm, see you later, Lily." He calls before turning and running in the direction of the male dorms.

Over my dead body will you see her again. Watching as he runs like his life depends on it, makes me smile.

"You don't own me, *Mr. Miller.*" Lily shoves a finger into my chest. Being as short as she is, I have to look down at her, which, of course, gives me the perfect view down her shirt. Fuck, she's gorgeous, even in the obliterated state she's in. My cock hardens instantly, as if he has eyes of his own, and can see her.

"I'm an adult and can make my own choices when it comes to who I sleep with." She scolds, her eyebrows puckering together, anger or some form of it washing over her face.

"You are more than welcome to make adult choices when you're sober, but right now, you look to be three sheets to the wind, so all you'll be doing now is going to your room to sleep. Screw whoever you want, when you're sober." I damn near bite my own tongue off speaking.

"You're not the boss of me," she slurs and takes a step back. Twisting around to turn away from me, she almost trips over her own feet. Thankfully, I'm there and grab her by the arm to steady her at the last minute.

"You can't even walk without stumbling over your own feet, so it's very doubtful that I'll be letting you make *adult* choices," I growl, my tone almost animalistic. Why does she keep doing this? Looping an arm around her waist, I pull her small body into my side and make her walk next to me. "I'm taking you to your room where you will stay until you've sobered up, and that's the end of discussion."

Lily huffs defiantly next to me but doesn't say anything. I know I'm taking a huge risk walking her into the dorm, but what other choice do I have? Hopefully, no one will see us. It's late, and it's a school night so there shouldn't be a lot of people out and about.

"Don't you have classes in the morning?" I ask as we walk inside the dorm building and up the stairs.

"Yeah, so what?" she snaps.

"So what? You're kidding, right? When you're on a scholarship, grades shouldn't be a back-burner subject."

"Stop acting like you care," she growls, and struggles to break free of my hold, but there's no way in hell I'm letting her go, not until she's tucked safely in her bed.

I try not to let what she's said bother me, but all I can think about is what if something had happened to her. If she had gotten hurt thinking I really didn't care. It's an irrational thought, insane even, but I'm already bat shit crazy because of her.

Leaning into her, I inhale her sweet coconut scent letting it filter into my nose before saying, "If I didn't care about you then why am I risking my ass right now to get you into your dorm?" Lily stops dead in her tracks. We're almost to her room, but apparently, she doesn't care.

Looking up at me, she grabs a fist full of my shirt and pulls me down into her face. If we were caught like this, it would cost me everything, and yet, I can't seem to care right in that moment. My pulse thrums in my ears, and my eyes move over the bow of her kissable lips. Damn, do I want to devour those lips of hers.

Fuck me, I am so screwed.

"Because, you, Sebastian Miller, are stupid." She releases me with a shove, and just like that, the bubble surrounding us pops.

"If you're trying to insult me, it's not working. Now give me your keys," I order as we get closer to her door.

"Blah, blah, blah." She mocks but does pull her keys out. They slip through her fingers, and drop to the floor at her feet, landing with a loud clank. *Fucking Christ.* Reaching down, I grab them and walk the rest of the way to her dorm.

"I hate you. I hate you, but I want you too, and I don't understand it," Lily murmurs into my side, her hands clutching on to my arm. Voices fill the hallway followed by doors slamming down the hall. My heart sinks into my stomach, as my fingers shake while I try and get the key into the keyhole. This is it. Was it worth it? You risked it all for her.

Miss. Shit. Heavy footfalls pound against the carpeted floor. People are coming right toward us. Fuck, fuck, fuck. With sweaty hands, I'm certain we're caught, but then the key slips into the hole, and with a twist, and a step forward, we're in the room, the door slammed closed behind us. Air fills my lungs for the first time since I entered the building.

Beads of sweat slip down my forehead as I gently maneuver Lily to her bed.

"All I ever wanted was someone to care. Someone to help ease the pain in my chest. Being with you, near you, it makes it easier for me to cope. It makes the pain manageable."

"Lily," I sigh, settling down onto the edge of the bed. With both of us in here, it seems smaller. Her big blue eyes peer up at me, and without really thinking about it, I brush a few of the sticky blonde strands from her heart-shaped face.

"Sebastian," she says my name just like I did hers. Like a promise whispered in the middle of the night between two star-crossed lovers.

"I need you to stop doing this shit. Stop putting yourself in danger. One of these times, I won't be here to rescue you, and then what? What happens then?" I can't even think about something happening to her. Some stupid douchebag putting his hands on her. Her passing out and getting raped, or worse. "Do you want to get hurt? Is that it?"

The softest of smiles creeps onto her lips, and the need to pull up that tiny miniskirt and spank her ass consumes me. She needs to be taught a lesson, one that she'll actually remember, and I'm seconds away from doing just that when she opens her mouth and starts to speak.

"I want to hurt because I deserve to suffer. I'm alive, and they're all dead. All of them. They left me here...." Tears pool in her eyes, and my heart shreds into thin pieces at the sight. My stomach tightens, and I want to throw up. All the knives in the world could cut through my heart, and it would hurt less than it does right now, looking at Lily with regret, and tears in her eyes.

"They left me, Seb. I should be with them!" Her voice rises, and her clenched fists beat against the mattress. "I should have been in the car with them."

"No. No, you shouldn't." I can't help myself. Fuck the repercussions. Fuck everything. Tugging her toward me, I pull her into my arms, and she lets me, almost like she knows she needs me. My chest fills with an unknown emotion, and I squeeze her, wanting her to know I've got her without saying it.

"Don't talk like that. Don't act like your life is any less because you weren't in the car that day. It's not your fault, none of it is." The fact that she thinks this, that she feels like she's to blame, that she wishes she was in the car. It enrages me while only making me want her more. She needs me.

"I tried to end it... I tried to make it better." My arms tighten around her on instinct. She tried to end it? I stare down at her, her eyes flutter closed, and I know she's close to passing out, but I have to know what she's talking about. I have to.

"What do you mean you tried to end it?" My hot breath fans against her cheek, and I cup one of her cheeks in my hand, sliding my thumb along her plump bottom lip while I wait for her to answer me. Those lips of hers part, releasing a soft breath, but words never follow. Instead, she passes out in my arms. My hand remains on her face for a long time while I do nothing more than hold her to my chest, wishing that things could be different.

Temptation is a bitch. To want and need for something you cannot have, even worse. It's evident that Lily needs me, but how can I be there for her without crossing the line? How do I support her and care for her without giving in?

She wants me. I want her. All the rules say we shouldn't be together. That we can't. I've never wanted to say fuck you to the rules so badly. I look around her room, trying to look anywhere but at her face, even though that's all I want to take in. Half of the room's walls are covered with art. Drawings, paintings, and sketches, one more beautiful than the next. I knew she was here on an art scholarship, but I didn't realize she was that good. I make a mental note to talk to her art teachers and see how we can help her get noticed.

When she starts to lightly snore, and I've held her in my arms much longer than I should've, I tuck her into bed and press a kiss to her forehead. A whimper passes her lips at the loss of my touch, but she snuggles into the pillow a moment later. It's like I'm being pulled in two directions. The right one, and the one that my body wants me to give in to. Giving her one last glance, I slip out of her room, locking the door behind me.

Exhausted, and beat the fuck down, I walk out of the dorm trying my best not to draw attention. I've just reached the door, so close to escaping without a single soul seeing me when the door comes flying open, and a tiny woman comes rushing through it, her body slamming into mine without pause. My hands move on their own, grabbing onto her arms to steady her.

"Oh, my god. I'm so sorry." The woman's voice pierces my ears, and I realize then that I've heard that voice before. When she lifts her head, and her face comes into view, I damn near sigh in relief.

"Delilah?" Thank fuck, it's not someone else.

"Mr. Miller?" She squeaks, shock filling her eyes. Instantly, I release her. She sways on her feet for a moment before standing up a little taller. "What are you doing here? It's after midnight." Fuck. I didn't even think to look at the time before I left. I can't imagine how bad this looks.

"Uh, yes, there was... there... there was an issue in the dorms. I was just clearing it up. Ummm, have a good night," I lie, and watch as a smile creeps onto her face. If she knows I'm lying, she doesn't say anything.

When I finally get outside, I all but run to my jeep, adrenaline coursing through my veins.

The lies are piling up.

The temptation is too great.

I'm going to end up snapping, breaking straight down the middle. The only question is, will it be worth it? Is Lily Kline worth giving up everything I've worked so hard for?

8

LILY

One week has passed since the night that I passed out in Sebastian's arms. Delilah has asked me half a dozen times what happened that night, and even though I tell her nothing happened, she still doesn't believe me. I guess it's only a half-lie. Something happened that night, it's called, I spilled all my stupid beans, but it's not as juicy or fun as D is making it out to be.

"Come on, I have to go to class in ten minutes you could at least give me a little tiny piece of what happened? It's not like I'm going to tell."

Rolling my eyes hard enough to give myself a headache, I snap. "It's not like that, D. I mean it kinda is, but it's not. It wasn't... we didn't do anything that night."

D crosses her arms over her chest. "You can't say it's kinda like that, and then it's not. It's either fucking or not fucking. Which is it?"

My mouth pops open. "Neither. It's neither. Go to class. I have a headache, and I need to try and find a way to make this better."

"Well, a good start would be to just screw him. It's evident that you have chemistry."

How did I know she would say that? Like it's no big deal to sleep with the Dean of the university. Like it won't get him in trouble or cost him everything? Like it won't make people look at me, or call me names? As if screwing will make all of our problems go away?

"Chemistry doesn't make it okay, D. I'll explain more later."

Slinging her backpack over her shoulder, she takes a step toward the door. "Whatever, if you aren't going to spill, then I'm not going to risk being late for class."

"Good idea," I concur.

"Make good choices. I'll see you at dinner." She smiles and walks out of the cafeteria.

I clean up our table and bring the dishes to the conveyor belt before leaving myself. I don't have any more classes for the rest of the day, so I'm heading straight to the dorm, planning to relax with some painting, a tub of ice cream, and a glass of wine.

Fifteen minute later, I'm back at the dorm, and do exactly what I'd planned to do. Getting out my art easel, I set up my canvas before I line my paints and brushes. I get out a glass, and the wine bottle, as well as a tub of ice cream and a spoon.

There we go, the scene is set for a perfect afternoon.

Taking a few bites of the ice cream, I use the time to fill the canvas in my mind. As the cool sugary chocolate chip mint goodness melts on my tongue, I decide on a night-time skyline. Putting the ice cream down, I hold my full wine glass in one hand and my paint-brush in the other.

Starting with the outline, I carefully place each line, getting a feel for the entire composition. With each stroke of my brush and each sip of my wine, I feel the tension leave my body. *Home.* When I'm painting, creating this piece of magic, it's like nothing can touch me. Like I'm invincible. It doesn't take long to finish the painting or the bottle of wine.

I'm just adding the final details on the oversized moon hanging high above the skyline when a knock on the door rips my attention away from the canvas.

Delilah must have forgotten her keys again. I swear the girl would forget her head if it wasn't attached. Meandering off the bed with my almost empty wine glass in hand, I open the door. Ready to start making fun of D for being so forgetful, I open my mouth, but the words never come as the person on the other side of the door isn't Delilah at all, but one of the dorm monitors.

Her eyes instantly go to the wine glass I'm holding. *Shit.* Alcohol is a no go in the dorms, they even have you sign paperwork upon moving in stating that you understand that and agree to abide by the no drinking rule.

"Ms. Kline," the petite middle-aged woman tsks.

"Yes..."

"May I come in?" At her question, I open the door all the way and wave her in with my free hand. She crosses the threshold, and I feel compelled to slam the door in her face, but don't. Having a place to sleep is pretty high on my list. Once inside, she turns around, her eyes roam over the room. It looks like she's trying to find something, anything to write me up for.

When her icy gaze swings back to me, she asks, "Are you aware that alcohol is prohibited in the dorms?"

I can't help but roll my eyes at her. "Yes, I know, but do you know that this is college, and everybody drinks?" I immediately regret my words. Fucking wine. Curse you. It has words tumbling out of my mouth before my brain can catch up.

The woman's mouth pulls into a thin line. "That might be so, but your drinking must be pretty excessive if we have other students complaining about you."

What the fuck?

My eyes go wide at her accusation. I mean, yes, I've been drinking a few nights a week, but doesn't every other college student on the planet? I can't imagine anybody reporting me for it, and it's not like I'm loud and obnoxious when I'm drunk. This woman should go to the frat houses on a Friday night.

"Do you understand how serious this is? I could kick you out of the dorms right now, you know. We have a zero-tolerance policy." *Shit. Shit. Shit.*

"Please, it's just some wine. I'll pour it out right now." I don't think I've ever sobered up so quickly in my life.

"Calm down, I'm going to give you a warning this time." She pulls out a piece of paper from her purse and hands it to me. "I need you

to sign this form. It says that you understand that you are on proba-
tion and will be evicted if there are any further violations."

"Oh... o-okay," I stutter, taking the paper from her. I sign along
the bottom where it says *signature* and hand it back to her.

"There is a waiting list for these dorms, and when we have
students drinking, and acting out, it makes it very easy for us to
determine who to remove and who to keep."

"Got it." The warning couldn't be any clearer.

"Goodnight, Ms. Kline." She dismisses me and walks out of the
room like she was never here. I close the door behind her, and
then go, and crawl into my bed. Who would report me? Better yet
who has seen me drunk? The only person that mentioned seeing
Sebastian in the dorm was Delilah, and I haven't heard any rumors
being spread, then again, I probably wouldn't. It's not like I'm
hanging out with the popular crowd. This is nothing but another
piece of shit on an already shitastic day. Pulling the blanket up and
over my head, I squeeze my eyes shut, and wish for tomorrow
come.

SPOILER ALERT, the next day isn't any better. Walking into creative
writing, I can already feel eyes on me. Three girls are whispering and
giggling as I enter the room. I can only assume they're talking about
me since they're damn near staring craters through my face as I walk
by. Taking my usual seat toward the back, I pull out my notebook,
and pen, and prepare for class, ignoring their icy glares from across
the room.

I've just started writing my daily journal entry when a shadow
crosses in front of me, blocking out the light from above. Dropping
my pen, I look up and meet Arabella Hamilton's disgusted gaze.

"I bet you thought you were so cool trying to bring Kyle back to
your dorm with you?" My brows furrow in confusion, what is she...
then it connects Kyle... Kyle Weber, the guy I almost dragged to my
dorm room in an attempt to forget Sebastian. Disgusted with myself,
I think back to that night. I would have taken him up to my room if it

hadn't been for Sebastian. I would've given my v-card to some random guy for no reason at all.

"I didn't know he was with anybody..." I honestly didn't. He definitely didn't act like it, and he didn't say *I have a girlfriend*, which should've been the first thing he said if he was truly taken, right?

"Save it." She flicks her auburn hair over her shoulder, examining her nails as if they're more entertaining than me. "Everybody knows Kyle is *my* boyfriend. And I mean, everybody." She's talking slow now like I'm dumb or something, and if I cared, I suppose I'd be insulted, but I'm not. It takes much more than some mean girl spewing a little hate to break me.

"Maybe if you weren't so fucking weird you would know this because you would have friends to tell you not to touch another woman's man, and don't even use the excuse of being drunk." Ignoring her second comment, I stare at her perfectly painted face.

Crossing my arms over my chest, I say, "I have friends."

Arabella laughs, but it sounds more like a witch screaming into the night. "Your roommate doesn't count, idiot. She has to like you since she's forced to live with you."

Okay, that one stung a little, but it's not true, so it doesn't matter. D and I are tighter than pigs in mud.

Pursing my lips, I mumble, "Okay, I get it, I'm weird, and you love Kyle. I won't flirt with him again. Can we move on now?"

"Sure, we'll *move on*... might want to make sure you don't get caught drinking in the dorms again. Wouldn't want anybody to report you," she grins, and all I want to do is wipe that stupid smile off her face.

"This is college. Who reports someone for drinking? Literally, everyone is drinking. I mean Liam is passed out on the goddamn table over there." I point to Liam, who is one of the biggest partiers I know. He legit is at a party every night. I have no idea how he makes it to classes, let alone on time.

She shrugs, and the two girls flanking her do so too. "Don't know, don't care. All I know is that you better keep your hands to yourself, and your mouth off the beer bottle." She snickers all the way back to her seat, and I grab my pen, squeezing it between my fingers. I want to scribble all over the page, scream, throw something, do anything but sit in this damn room for the next hour with that witch and her fake ass friends, but there's nothing I can do.

All class period, I stare at the back of her head, telling myself it's not worth the trouble to toss my pen or maybe even the chair I'm sitting on, at the back of her head.

As soon as the professor excuses us, I start to gather my things and get up to leave. I'm walking down the center aisle toward the double doors when someone's elbow jabs into my ribs, knocking the air out of my lungs, and books onto the floor.

"Oh, sorry," Arabella giggles as she continues walking by me. It takes all my restraint not to grab her hair and pull her down onto the floor. The only thing keeping me from doing that is knowing that if I get into a fight, I can kiss my scholarship goodbye.

Her cronies follow behind her, each kicking one of my books across the floor as they do. "Oops," they cackle in unison. Luckily, we're in the back of the class, and no one seems to notice the scene unfolding, or no one cares.

I wait until the teacher, as well as most of the students, have left the room before I start to collect my books off the ground. One geeky looking guy ends up helping me pick them up, probably feeling sorry for me. I give him a grateful smile before he disappears from the room.

On the way home, I hold the backpack strap so tightly I think I might rip it in two with my grip. I want to punch something... or someone so badly. The anger inside of me building, ready to explode at any given moment.

It's not just the skank squad who has my fury at the tipping point. It's everything, everything combined, like a hundred small patches of fire have finally come together, and formed into one huge blaze, large enough to burn down half the rainforest.

All of the things I've been holding on to, suppressing, shoving deep, and trying to drown with alcohol are now bubbling up to the surface. I'm no longer able to keep it down and contained. By the time I get to the dorm, I'm basically speed walking. All I want to do is get to the room, lock myself in, and the rest of the world out.

Everything sinks a little lower when I enter the room and find that Delilah is not here. I don't know if that's a good or a bad thing. I don't want her to see me like this, but I could really use a friend right now. Anybody, but that's just it. I have no one. I'm all alone... *I have no one.*

Tears I didn't know I was holding back start falling down my face without permission, and the pain in my chest migrates down into my gut. I just don't want to be alone anymore.

I want to make the loneliness go away, the pain of losing them still hurts so bad, it feels like I just lost them yesterday, and I'm reliving the moment over and over again. My soul is shattered beyond repair. There's no saving me. Nothing can fix this kind of pain.

Not knowing any other way to make it go away, to numb the pain, I reach for the bottle of wine from beside my bed. Not even bothering to get a glass, I unscrew the cap and bring it to my lips. I tip the bottle back until the tangy alcohol fills my mouth. I don't know how much was left, but I don't sit the bottle back down until it's empty, the contents sinking heavily into my stomach, warming me from the inside out.

More. I need more.

Never before did I feel the need to use drinking as much to cover up my pain, to numb it. I thought I was done with this after my grandparents sent me to rehab. I thought I had gotten past this. Until I came to North Woods. Until *him.* I didn't expect him to be here, didn't expect him to be the Dean of the university. A bitter bubble of laughter escapes my lips, that would be my luck.

I hate myself a little more each day. I'm alive. I get to go to classes. Get to experience life, fall in love, get married, have kids. I get to do everything my sister never got to. My chest aches so badly it feels like something is trying to rip its way out, and the only way I can stop it is to get some more to drink.

There should be another bottle around here somewhere, but I don't remember where I hid it, so I start digging through the room, opening every drawer, every cabinet. Aimlessly, I tear the room apart, looking in every nook and cranny, getting more aggravated by the minute, the longer it takes me to find it.

Spinning around quickly, I knock over a side table, another surge of anger grips me, sinking its claws deep into my flesh. Fury overtakes me, and I kick the stupid table. The flimsy piece of plywood fly's through the air and crashes into the door with a loud bang. I'm too far gone to care though.

When I finally find the bottle of wine tucked under my bed, my dorm room is ripped to shreds, kinda like my heart, right now. Tattered. Bleeding. Broken. Ignoring the destruction entirely, I settle down on the bed, and unscrew the wine bottle, and start taking big gulps. I'm so enthralled by the alcohol that I almost miss the knocking at the door.

Annoyed by the interruption of my self-pity, I stomp to the door, and rip it open with an angry, "What?" The word gets caught in my throat when I see who is standing in front of me.

Shit. Fuck. I'm so fucked.

"Ms. Kline," the dorm monitor scowls at me. It's the same lady who wrote me a warning *just* yesterday. Her gaze drops to the wine bottle in my hand before she leans over to look past me, and into the room. "Pack your things. You are expected to leave the premise immediately."

"You can't...." I'm floundering, mouth gaping open like a fish caught on a line, "I have nowhere else to go."

"I guess you should've thought about that before you decided to break the rules. This isn't high school, and we're not your parents, Ms. Kline. We will treat you like an adult here because you are an adult."

Like a small child, I feel the need to stomp my foot and throw a tantrum, scream that I don't have parents anymore, but even I know that won't change anything. I've broken the rules and just like everything in my life, I will now have to live with the consequences.

"Whatever," I growl, heading for the closet. I'll just have to find a new place to stay. How hard can that be? I find my suitcase, and head over to the dresser stuffing my clothing inside of it, I throw a few more of my belongings haphazardly inside until it's full, then, I zip it up. Grabbing my backpack on the way to the door.

"Anything else I will have your roommate package up for you."

"Thanks..." I wait for her to move, and when she does, I bolt from the room. Halfway down the hall, I hear a cackling from a group of girls. I don't know why since I'm already in a heap of bullshit, but I turn around and look at them. Arabella and the slut barbie brigade are standing there laughing at me, while I'm forced to leave the dorms.

"Buh, bye." One of them taunts, waving goodbye.

"Bitches," I mumble under my breath as I descend the stairs, pulling the suitcase down the stairs behind me carelessly. I've got more important things to think about right now.

Like where the hell I'm going to sleep tonight?

9

SEBASTIAN

The last week has been just as bad as the week before, if not worse. Lily is now the last thing I think about at night, and the first thing that pops into my head in the morning. Her beautiful features are engraved in my mind. I find I even yearn for the way she smells, but most of all, I dream about holding her again, feeling her in my arms the way I did last week. I want that, her, all of it, so badly, I can feel the want and need burning through my veins.

Gripping the steering wheel a little tighter, I will the thoughts away and try to concentrate on the road ahead of me. There isn't much to focus on though. I've taken the short drive from campus to my house so many times, I could probably drive it blindfolded.

Reaching over to fiddle with the radio, I turn on some music, hoping for a welcome distraction. I only glance down to find the button for a second, but when I look back up, I notice a petite figure walking on the sidewalk, pulling a suitcase behind her.

Hmmm. I almost pass the woman, but quickly realize that her body looks very familiar. The way she walks, the curves of her figure, and the way her hips sway slightly with each step. It grips me.

Is that Lily?

No, it can't be. Why the hell would it be her? Still, the nagging feeling won't subside, so I slow the car down and pull over to the side of the road. I watch her approaching in the rearview mirror. She looks up and notices me in the car, stopping dead in her tracks. It's already dark outside but even in the dim light, thanks to the street-lamp above us, I know it's her.

What the hell is she doing?

Putting the car into park, I get out and attempt to rein in some of my anger. She's standing there like her feet are suddenly glued to the ground. I walk around the car and head toward where she is standing. Our eyes meet, and like a thunderstorm blowing in, I already know this is a recipe for disaster. She's been drinking. But that's not what worries me the most. No, what worries me, scratch that, what terrifies me, is the overwhelming sadness that is in her eyes. I've never seen her so sad, so broken.

Her emotions are right on the surface, and it feels like I'm on a cliff's edge, looking down. She wants to drop, but no way in hell am I going to let her.

"What the hell are you doing out here?" I ask, glancing down to the large suitcase she's pulling behind her.

"I'm going to stay at the motel for a while," she answers plainly as if that answer would be sufficient enough.

"What happened? Why are you not in the dorms? It's late, and it's not safe to be walking alone at night." Her eyes fill with tears at my question. Shit. "Get in the car, you're not staying at the motel."

"Where will I stay then? I can't go back to the dorms." For a long moment, we just stare at each other. *Where will she stay?* I don't even care about what she's done in that instant. I just need to get her safe.

"We'll figure everything out. For now, just get in the car, so we can go to my place. You need to tell me exactly what happened when we get there, so I can fix it... and I don't just mean the dorm thing." I don't need to explain anymore. She knows exactly what I'm referring to.

Nodding, she starts to walk toward my car. Her shoes drag across the sidewalk, and I grab her suitcase from her hand, and open the trunk, depositing the heavy thing inside. Obviously, this isn't a temporary situation. When I reach the driver's side of the car, she's already inside and buckled.

Slipping into the Jeep, I put it into drive and start toward the house. Now that we are confined in the small space, I can smell the alcohol on her, confirming that she's been drinking again.

Lily shifts uncomfortably in her seat. "Should you really be doing this? I don't want you to get in trouble for being *seen* with me in public."

Her dig at me doesn't go unnoticed, but I ignore it, deciding she's probably had a bad enough night already.

"Helping a student isn't going to get me in trouble. You have nowhere else to go."

"I can get a hotel room for a while. They rent by the week, and a bunch of other students do it."

"Oh, yeah," my eyes dart between her and the road. I'm angry and sad, but the anger takes precedence right this moment. "And how do you plan to get to and from classes? Are you going to walk?"

She crosses her arms over her chest, and looks away, "I'll do what I have to do. I'm sure some guy at the hotel would give me a ride. At least I can be seen with him, and don't have to remain hidden."

What does that mean? I don't understand. Surely, she isn't implying that she would use her body, is she? If she is, I swear to god things are going to end badly.

"What does that mean?" I ask, trying to hide the anger in my voice.

Her shoulders rise and fall in a shrug, and I swear if my hands weren't already strangling the steering wheel, and I wasn't driving a car, they may very well be wrapped around her delicate little throat.

"If you asked me to get into the car just so you could lecture me, you can let me back out. My grandparents are going to flip enough as it is when they find out. I don't need another *parent* giving me the tenth degree."

"I'm not going to lecture you." My voice softens as I speak, "I don't care about what happened. All I want is to make sure you're okay, and that you have somewhere that you can stay. Somewhere that I know you'll be safe and able to manage to get back and forth from classes."

Pulling into the driveway of the house, I put the Jeep in park and kill the engine. Lily doesn't make a move to get out, and I itch to take her into my arms and make all the hurt disappear from her face. It would be so easy to replace that pain with pure bliss.

"Let's... let's go in," I clear my throat, and adjust my already swollen cock while climbing out of the vehicle. This is a bad idea, the worst I've ever had. *Way to go, Seb.* I keep saying that but, I keep doing the same shit. Bad idea after bad idea. I'm just stacking the shit up like cordwood.

Grabbing her suitcase from the back, I walk around and meet her at the front of the car. Her eyes are cast down at the ground, and all I want to do is tip her chin upward, and tell her everything is going to be okay. But is it really? Will it all be okay? The reality is nothing has been okay for a really long time. Not for me, and apparently not for her either.

"Come on. I'll make us some dinner. You can take a shower and then we'll talk."

"There's nothing to talk about." Lily kicks at the pavement.

"There's plenty, now get inside." I don't know what compels me to do it, but I grab her hand and start walking toward the front door. Strangely, she follows, either because she doesn't want to lose my grip, or she decides there's no point in fighting me on it. Pulling my keys out, I unlock the door and shove it open.

I walk her to the couch and make her sit. Her face is almost stoic like she is trying to hide her emotions from me. When I let go of her hand, my own feels empty and cold.

"I'm gonna make some food. Just relax, unless you want to take a shower. You are more than welcome to. It's that's way," I say pointing down the hallway. "Clean towels are in the cabinet next to the sink. I'll be right back," I tell her, before heading into the kitchen. I decide on frozen pizza, and while that's baking in the oven, I cut up some veggies and toss a salad.

The entire time I'm cooking, I try to figure out how I'm going to talk to her, and what exactly I'm going to tell her, but come up empty. By the time I'm carrying two plates to the living room, I'm no closer to a solution than I was twenty minutes ago.

It looks like she hasn't moved an inch, she's still sitting in the exact spot she was when I left. Handing her the plate, I take the seat next to her, being careful to leave enough space between us, so our thighs don't touch. We both start eating, and I am more than glad she eats vigorously without needing to be prompted. She needs to eat, and not just because she's been drinking, no, she's so thin and could probably use some hearty meals here and there.

Finishing first, I set my plate on the table in front of me and lean back on the cushions. Lily does the same with her plate but remains sitting in the same position she's been in since she got here.

"What happened?" I ask.

"It's nothing that you can fix. I let everything get the best of me. I'm homeless with no job, nothing." Before I can say anything, she buries her face in her hands. She's falling apart, and I need to be the glue that keeps her together.

Inching closer, I say, "You're not homeless, and you're not alone. Maybe I can't fix it, maybe I can. I don't know because you won't tell me."

"The dorm has a no drinking policy. I was caught with wine twice now, this time was after being issued with a warning."

Fuck. "Shit, Lily... I don't really deal with the housing people. I'm not sure if I can fix that." They've already given her a warning, what more can they do? If they let her back in, it's going to look bad for the university, and if I stick up for her, it's going to look bad for my image. Zero policy is zero policy.

"I told you, you can't fix it."

"That doesn't mean I can't help you though. We'll find another place for you to stay." I try and soothe her with my voice. Yes, she made a mistake, but this is college. Who the hell isn't drinking in those dorms?

"My scholarship doesn't pay for anything besides the dorm, and I can't afford anything on my own. If my grades suffer, I lose the scholarship. I shouldn't have to choose between an education and a roof over my head." She sniffles, "Stupid wine and stupid bullies."

"What do you mean bullies?"

"Nothing... girls being girls. She thinks I was hitting on her boyfriend... called me out on it in front of her friend. It was really not worth getting upset about, but on top of everything else, it just got to me."

"We'll figure it out. Don't worry about it right now. In the meantime, you can stay here."

She looks at me like she is trying to figure me out before she asks, "Are you sure?"

"Positive," I answer without batting an eye. I know this is wrong, but I'm not going to let her stay at that motel.

She gives me a smile, but it doesn't reach her eyes, those are still filled with sadness. She breaks her gaze away and lowers her head.

"I'm not used to this," she says, looking down at her plate.

"To what?" I'm a bit befuddled by her response.

"Someone taking care of me like this. I'm used to depending on my own."

"What about your grandparents?"

"They tried their best, but it's been hard on them... I've been hard on them. Every time they do take care of me, it comes with a good amount of guilt, so I'd much rather take care of myself. At least then I don't have anyone saying *if it wasn't for me, you wouldn't have that.*"

"I'm sure they would get where you're coming from if you came to them about this, about anything that you're feeling right now."

She turns to me, her eyes are red, and tears stain her cheeks. She looks like a broken angel, cracked straight down the middle.

"All I am to them is a reminder of the daughter and granddaughter they lost. When they look at me, they don't see me. They see Amy, my mother, my father. They see an ungrateful brat that lived. My sister always was there favorite... now they're just left with second best."

"Stop it!" I snap, moving closer, because hearing her talk like that about herself, it tears me up inside. My heart aches for her. I can't let Lily go down this path of self-destruction. *I won't.*

"Why? You can't tell me that when you look at me, you don't see her too. That you don't wish it was me that died that night, instead of her."

Staring at her, I know I can't lie. When I look at her, I do see her sister, but not because I see her as Amy, simply because she's just as beautiful as her sister was.

Cupping her by the cheeks, I don't think about what I'm doing, I simply act. Leaning in, I breathe her in, letting her fruity scent fill my lungs.

"When I look at you, I see Lily. Lily is alive. Amy is dead. Yes, you look like your sister, but you're not her. You're you, and I've come to realize that."

She sucks her bottom lip into her mouth, and it looks like she's fighting off tears. I don't want her to swallow the pain down. I don't want her to have to bury it underneath a mask of anger and resentment. I want it, every burning ounce of it.

"Let it out, Lily. Show me all your broken, ugly pieces, and I'll help you put yourself back together. I'm not afraid. I've fought my own demons, and I'll help you fight yours."

At my words, she crumbles. All her perfectly built walls start to fall. Tears slip from her eyes and trail down her cheeks. Emotions she's probably held in for a long time, pour right out of her like an overflowing sink of water. Moving a hand to the back of her head, I bring her to my chest and let her bury her face there. Sob after sob punches the air, all pieces of me being rattled with the sound.

She cries for a long time, and I let her. Satisfied in holding her, I rub her back until the sobs become fewer and her whimpers quiet down. I keep holding her until the crying stops altogether, and her breathing evens out.

When I'm sure she is completely out, I shift her in my hold. Sliding one arm underneath her legs, I keep the other wrapped around her back. Picking her up, I carry her into the bedroom.

Careful not to wake her, I gently place her on top of the mattress before taking her shoes off slowly. Grabbing the corner of the blanket, I pull it up and over her, stopping only when I reach her shoulders. That's when she opens her still swollen eyes.

"Will you hold me for a little while longer?" Her voice is small and fragile sounding, and even though my head tells me to say no, the rest of me is saying yes. I slip out of my own shoes and slide into the bed next to her. She scoots over a little bit, but not enough to leave any space between us. I wrap my arms around her, and she cuddles further into my side.

"Thank you... for everything. For being there for me, for helping me, and for saying all the things you said earlier. It really means a lot to me to have you..." She suddenly stops herself as if she is regretting the last part.

"You do have me, Lily. Maybe not in a way we both want, but you do have me. You don't have to be alone anymore." She cuddles into me even more, nestling deep into my body, and I welcome it. I'm greedy with need for her, for her soft body to be pressed up against mine, for her warmth, her intoxicating scent. I want it all. Before I know it, her breathing evens out, and I find myself drifting off to sleep as well. A smile tugs at my lips, and I realize that this is the first time I've smiled, actually smiled, in a long time. That for the first time, I'm not going to bed feeling completely alone.

THE NEXT MORNING, I wake to coconut and vanilla in my nostrils. As I inhale deeply through my nose, the events from the night before come crashing down on me. Popping my eyes open, I find Lily, her big baby blues are open, and she's staring up at me with wonder in her eyes. Her hands trace over my chest, and even though there is fabric between my skin and her fingertips, it feels like they're burning through my skin, reaching deep inside me and tugging at the fragile remains of my heart.

"I'm sorry if I woke you, and for..." She pulls her hand back, and I want to tell her it's fine if she touches me, but it isn't. She's a student. I'm the Dean. We shouldn't be sharing the same house, let alone the same bed.

"It's okay, don't apologize. We're just... friends? Okay? We need boundaries. No sex. No kissing." My jaw aches as I say the words because deep down even if I don't want to admit it, I want all those things with her. The kissing, the sex, and every single thing in between.

Lily's creamy white cheeks, tint pink as I speak, "Of course. No sex. No kissing. Friends. Nothing more, nothing less."

She smiles at me, her perfectly straight white teeth appearing from behind her pink lips. Lips I wouldn't mind kissing right now. Fuck. My cock is hardening as we speak. Untangling myself from her, I tug my shirt down as if the fabric would be long enough to cover my growing erection. *Idiot.* At least I'm wearing clothes. Lily's eyes brighten as they move over me, inspecting my torso as if something is going to stick out to her.

"So, ahh, yeah." I get out of the bed and stand. Squeezing at the tight muscles of my neck, I say, "Let's have some breakfast, shower and then we can go and get the rest of your stuff from the dorms. Do you think your roommate has it all packed up?"

Lily nods, "Yeah Delilah is a bit OCD so she most likely has the room sparkling clean and all my shit stacked up on my bed."

"Good." There's a tense pause between us. It's not awkward, not really. It's just strange for me to wake up with a woman in my arms, even stranger for it to be a woman that I know I'll never have. "I'll go start breakfast. You can shower first."

Leaving the room before I end up saying something stupid, I head into the kitchen to make breakfast. Pulling out the eggs, cheese, and ham, I settle on making ham and cheese omelets. I also get the coffee pot going, because what is life without coffee.

A few minutes later, I have two steaming plates of cheesy, eggy, ham goodness. Placing the plates on the breakfast nook table, I walk back down the hall and toward my bedroom. I don't even think to knock before entering, thinking she must still be in the bathroom. However, I'm wrong, so wrong.

Entering the bedroom, I stop just over the threshold, the saliva in my mouth turning to glue, and my cock coming to stand at attention at the sight of a clean Lily standing in nothing more than a towel in my bedroom.

She glances up at me, her eyes darkening as if she has forgotten our agreement from just a short time ago. Strands of blonde hair stick to her shoulders, and water droplets glisten as they slide down the valley between her breasts, which are hidden beneath that stupid towel. I want to lick those drops off her skin, taste her, feast on her until she's nothing but a withering mess of arousal and need.

"Sebastian." Her perfect mouth opens, those lips of hers part slowly, and I can hear her saying my name, but I can't break my gaze. I can feel the need for her deep down in my gut. It twists and turns, digging its thorns into my stomach. Somehow, the hold she has on me snaps, and I force my gaze to the floor, my hands forming into tight fists.

This hold she has on me is both dangerous and intoxicating. It terrifies me and excites me all at once.

"I'm sorry. I should've knocked."

"No, it's okay," she mumbles, and slowly, I lift my gaze starting at her feet and moving upward, stopping to take note of the heat in her beautiful eyes. *No, Lily, no.* One of us has to be strong, and that person's not going to be me.

"It's not. I'll be sure to knock next time."

She nods her head as if she understands and I turn and walk out of the room, closing the door behind me, my stiff dick making it hard to walk. How the fuck am I going to do this? How am I going to live in a house with the one person I want, that I cannot fucking have?

When she appears from the room a few minutes later, my dick has finally deflated. Together we eat breakfast, mostly in silence. There's a heat between us that sizzles and zaps with each movement we make. I do my best to ignore it but haven't figured out how I'm going to get a grasp on my emotions, on my cock that seems to constantly be hard now.

"I'll need to swing by the grocery store, then we can go to the dorms, and then back here. I know it's not ideal right now, but like I said last night. I would rather have you here with me where I know you're safe than in some seedy motel catching rides from some random college guys." Lily nods through bites and sips of her coffee.

"Thank you, really, it means a lot to me. I know you're putting your neck on the line for me and I don't want you to think I don't appreciate it."

Taking a sip of my coffee, I swallow it and then shake my head.

"Stop, it's fine. If anyone asks, then I'll explain the situation. Until then, we won't tell anyone."

"Perfect." Lily tucks a strand of her damp blonde hair behind her ear, and I stare at her way longer than I should. This is going to end badly. I can already feel it. So why the hell aren't I doing anything to stop the inevitable.

Maybe because for the first time in forever, you're living.

THE DAY PASSES FAR TOO QUICKLY, and before either of us realize it, the sun is setting. Lily has classes tomorrow, and I have a full day of meetings. Sleep is something I desperately need right now, but something that I most likely won't get. Not with Lily under the same roof.

I do my best to ignore the far too short sleep shorts and T-shirt that she's wearing when she comes into the living room with her toothbrush in her mouth. Her golden hair frames her face making her appear angelic, and I look down at the couch, tucking the sheet into the cushions.

"Please don't tell me you're going to try and sleep on the couch," she mumbles around the toothbrush.

"That's exactly what I'm doing. You're the guest so you can have the bed." Tossing two pillows down, I grab the comforter and move it to the edge of the couch. Lily places both hands on her hips and stares me down. Her toothbrush is still hanging out of her mouth, her eyes are wide, and she looks different, happy.

She takes the toothbrush out before saying, "Technically I'm not a guest. I live here now. But besides that, you're like a whole foot taller than me. Let me take the couch. You'll be much more comfortable in the bed."

"No way, I'm not letting you..."

"I insist," she cuts me off. "Seriously, you won't even fit on the couch. How the hell will you sleep here without hurting your back?" She taps her chin. "Let me take the couch, or I'll revisit the motel idea."

"Lily," I warn my voice low.

Her eyelashes fan against her cheek as she looks at me innocently.

"You know I'm right, so just give in."

Releasing a loud sigh, I roll my eyes. She is right. I would be extremely uncomfortable on the couch.

"Okay, you win, you sleep on the couch," I say in defeat. Lily gives me a huge smile like she is proud of herself for winning our sparring match and disappears back into the bathroom.

I walk down the hall telling her goodnight through the closed door. She does the same, and I retreat into my bedroom, where I strip down to my boxers and crawl into bed.

It feels weird being in here while Lily is in the other room. Last night, I slept better than I have in a very long time, and I have a feeling that holding Lily all night had something to do with that. Now that she's out there and I'm here, the insomnia is hitting me hard.

Rolling over, I try and find a better position. I fluff my pillow and pull the blanket up over my back and close my eyes. Nothing. When that doesn't work, I roll over again, and again. Eventually, I end up on my back, staring up at the ceiling, my eyes wide open.

Almost an hour passes, and I still can't seem to fall asleep. Is she sleeping? I bet she's peacefully asleep already. I feel like my brain is one of those wind-up toys that just won't shut up. There's nothing that should be keeping me awake, and yet I can't seem to sleep. I consider getting up to take a shower, when the door to the bedroom creaks, opening just a hair, there's a pause, and then it opens more, just enough for a slim body to slip through.

Lily. She's sneaking in. She must not be able to sleep either.

It's dark in here, so I don't think she can see that my eyes are open. She tiptoes closer, moving with the stealth of a cat. My heart starts to beat faster with each step she takes toward me until she is right next to the bed. I don't move or make a sound as she carefully lifts up one corner of the blanket, and crawls into the bed, the mattress dipping a little with her weight.

I can't suppress a smile as she scoots closer, and closer until she is pressed right up against my side, her willowy arm snaking across my middle. My abs flex at her touch, and I can feel the heat of her touch in my groin.

She must be thinking she's so sneaky right now. Did she plan this all along? If she did, I can't be mad at her. I know I should stop whatever is going on between us before it bites me in the ass, but I'm at the end of my rope when it comes to pushing her away. So, I don't say anything when she drapes her leg across mine and buries her face into my bare chest.

It's not long until her breathing slows and becomes heavier, confirming that she is asleep. I, on the other hand, am beyond wide awake. It feels like I took ten shots of espresso.

Lily's leg moves up my thigh, a soft sigh passing her lips. I know she is sleeping and doesn't know what she is doing, but my dick doesn't realize that. He doesn't care. All he wants is the softness between her legs, and while I'd like to give us both a taste of that, it's not happening.

With her knee moving closer and closer to my cock, he decides to harden, and pretty soon he's so hard it fucking hurts. How the fuck am I supposed to sleep like this?

Screw this, I have to do something about the iron rod between my legs. As slowly as I can manage, I peel myself away from Lily, trying my best not to wake her up. Sliding out of the bed like a stealth ninja, I disappear into the bathroom.

Twisting the lock into place on the door, I turn on the shower and strip out of my boxers. My cock springs free, practically screaming with need, and I grip onto it as I step into the shower.

My hair isn't even wet all the way when I start pumping the angry beast. I've never felt the need to jerk off as much as I do right now.

Stroking myself like my life depends on it, I close my eyes, and bare my teeth, imagining the one person who makes me feel this way. The woman lying in my bed, on the other side of this door. The one I can't get out of my head... the one I can never have.

My thighs quiver, as my strokes grow faster and faster. Up, and down, up and down. I imagine this is what Lily's pussy feels like, her softness meeting all my hardness. We're a match made in heaven but forbidden as sin. Every muscle in my body tightens, and I groan so loudly I'm sure Lily can hear me. A lightning bolt of pleasure zings up my spine, the air in my lungs stills and my heart hammers furiously against my ribs as I stare down at my cock watching as the sticky, warm come erupts from my cock, landing against the tiled wall in thick ropes.

Fuck is all I can think as I sag against the tile.

I want her. I want her so badly. But having her, taking her, goes against everything I've worked so hard for. If only things were different. If we were different people... then I could call her mine.

10

LILY

*T*he next few days pass by in a blur. All my things are here now, and I've officially moved in with Sebastian. Well... really unofficially, since the only other people who know that I am here are; Rem, Jules, and Delilah. I had to tell D because I had to explain where I was living now.

We had to tell Jules and Rem because Sebastian can't always drive me back and forth to campus. Because A, we're on different schedules and B, we can't really be seen together.

So, Remington or Jules drive me to and from campus most of the time, but when Seb's schedule does happen to line up with mine, he parks his car behind a building or in a hidden corner of the parking lot.

There was an exciting playfulness about sneaking around the first few times, but that feeling died out quickly. I feel wrong doing it, not because I feel like I shouldn't be with Seb, but because it feels wrong that we are hiding. We are adults, and technically we are not breaking any rules. University policy prohibits student and faculty relationships, but we are not really in a relationship, at least not a sexual one.

After the night I snuck into his room, he let me sleep in his bed with him every night, but only to hold me, nothing more... much to my disappointment.

"What are you daydreaming about?" Delilah asks, falling into step with me.

"Nothing."

"Liar! You're probably dreaming about Dean Miller's abs," she giggles like a little schoolgirl.

I can't help but roll my eyes at her. "I shouldn't have told you about him. I should have made up some extravagant lie as to where I'm staying. I told you we are just friends. He is helping me out. No sex involved."

"That doesn't mean a girl can't think about abs," D quips. "Well defined, sweaty abs, rippling under that button-up shirt," she mimics a porn star's voice.

I shake my head at her and laugh. "You need to get laid. Go find a frat boy with sweaty abs, and no future."

"You know what, Lily. That's a great idea. I'll talk to you later." Delilah gives me a kiss on the cheek and darts off to who knows where. I keep walking toward the parking lot into one of the corners where Seb parks.

Today is one of the days I can ride back with him, and when I see him walking around the corner, my heart starts beating a little faster like it always does when I see him. He looks up and sees me standing next to his Jeep, his lips pull up into a smile, and suddenly, I feel two degrees hotter. *Get a grip, Lily.*

"Hey," Sebastian greets me when he gets closer. "How was your day?"

"Great. Yours?"

"Busy, and boring," he explains as he unlocks the car and we both get in. "Lots of developing recommendations for promotions, tenure, and compensation of faculty."

"Yes, that does sound boring."

"I was hoping we could do something fun tonight. Maybe watch a movie? Or get takeout, perhaps, both?" His question catches me off guard. We've been hanging out, but not like that. Usually, we eat together, but then I'll paint or do homework while he does something else. Watching a movie sounds a lot like something a couple would do, but I don't say that.

"Ah, sure," I say trying not to read too much into it. *It's just a movie, Lily.*

When we get home, Sebastian orders pizza before taking a shower. I change into my pajamas and cuddle up on the couch, waiting for him. The doorbell rings just as Seb comes out of the bedroom in a pair of shorts and a T-shirt. Rushing past me, he answers the door, and returns a moment later, with two pizza boxes in hand.

His hair is still wet when he sits down next to me, drops of water clinging to the strands, it looks soft, and I have the urge to run my fingers through it to see if I'm right. He puts the boxes on the table and props one of them open. The savory smell of cheese and Italian spices invade my senses, momentarily distracting me from the man I want to touch so badly.

He hands me a piece, and I lean back into the couch and start nibbling on the pizza while Seb starts the movie I picked.

"You picked *Guardians of the Galaxy*?" He quirks a brow.

"That's the one," I shrug. "I heard it's good." Also, it's an action movie, so there should be a minimum of romantic scenes in it. I don't need anything else to fuel my desire for him.

After we stuff ourselves with pizza, Seb reveals that the second box was holding brownies, which I happily accept when he offers. By the time we're done with dessert, the movie hasn't even run twenty minutes, and I've become painfully aware that I don't have anything else to do with my hands.

I feel so ridiculous even thinking about it, but I need to keep my hands busy because if I don't, all I'll think about is reaching over to touch Sebastian. I try so hard to concentrate on the movie but having him so close and not being able to touch him has me on edge. All I want to do is scoot over and climb onto his lap. I want to bury my face in the crook of his neck, to kiss his skin and feel his muscles flex beneath my hands. I want to know what he looks like when he comes. I want all of it.

Peeking at him out of the corner of my eye, I catch him shifting uncomfortably in his seat. Is he reading my mind? Or is he having his own indecent thoughts? The fire between us is smoldering, suffocating almost. If he can't feel the heat, then there's something wrong with him.

"How do you like the movie?" Seb suddenly asks.

"Huh?" I mumble a little flustered. How stupid am I? He asked how I like the movie, and all I say is, *huh.*

"Do you not like the movie?" he says, chuckling. "You seem distracted."

"I'm just tired," I lie. Sleep is the last thing on my mind right now. "Maybe I'll just go to bed. It's been a long week."

He frowns at me, the skin between his thick brows pinching, "Are you sure? I can find another movie? Or..."

I don't have the heart to tell him that being this close to him is doing crazy things to my lady bits. I know it's already hard for him to keep strong, and I don't want to make matters worse, but I can't be near him right now without wanting to climb him like a tree.

"No, it's okay. I'll just go lie down. You can finish the movie if you want."

"Okay," he says. I don't know if I imagine it or not, but I think he sounds almost disappointed. For a split second, I contemplate staying just to make sure he isn't upset, but then he shifts in his seat again. My eyes zoom in on his muscles flexing underneath the thin fabric of his shirt, and my mouth starts to water. Like literally watering, drool pooling in my mouth. *I've got to get out of here.*

"Goodnight," I tell Seb and scurry away down the hall.

"Goodnight," he calls after me.

Once I reach the room, I crawl into bed and cover myself with the heavy comforter. It feels cool against my heated skin at first, but not even a minute later, I feel like I'm burning up. There is a fire deep inside me, burning through my core, and I know there is only one way to stop the flames from burning me alive.

Glancing at the door, I contemplate going to the bathroom and using my fingers to make myself come, but I decide against it, knowing that I have plenty of time before the movie ends. No way will Sebastian walk in here any time soon.

Biting at my bottom lip, I trail a hand down over my flat stomach and into the waistband of my pajama bottoms. My fingers eagerly find my already swollen clit. I'm not surprised by the amount of wetness I find as they slide between my folds with ease.

Moaning softly, I start to rub small circles around the small nub. My hips lift out of reflex, and I spread my legs, wishing, dreaming that it was Sebastian's fingers, tongue or maybe even cock there. Moving faster and faster, I can feel the heat in my core tightening, my moans growing louder even though I try to hold them in.

I want to come. I need to come.

I'm so close, so damn close... Grabbing the pillow next to me, I bite into it, hoping it'll silence the screams that want to rip from my throat.

"Hey, you..." His voice crashes into me like a wave, toppling over my body, pulling me down, deep into the abyss. Pleasure courses through me as I come at the sound of his voice. It's embarrassing and crazy. I've been caught, but in that moment, I can't seem to care. Embarrassment has taken a back seat, while pleasure is driving me straight into uncharted waters. All I can feel is the euphoric bliss pulsing through me like a second heartbeat.

Slowly, like a feather, I float down from my high. I'm scared to open my eyes and look at him. Scared of what he might say or think or do. What if he's angry? What if he's disappointed? I can't think about any of those things. Otherwise, I'll lose it.

Remaining very still, I pretend that I'm not here. Maybe he'll walk away, and we'll never have to talk about what happened? *Fat chance.*

The bed dips, and my eyes flutter open all on their own.

Staring up into his hazel orbs, I can see it all. His want and need. The battle he's fighting to keep himself in check. I can see the resistance there, it's fading with each second, withering away. I pull my hand from my bottoms and wait for him to say something. Peeling the blanket back, his eyes collide with my fingers, fingers that are still glistening with my release.

Very gently, he grabs my hand and brings it to his mouth, his eyes darken so much that they appear almost black now. My body starts to tighten, like a spring-loaded coil, I'm seconds away from going off yet again.

Parting his lips, he sucks the two fingers I used to get off into his mouth. His eyes drift closed, and a groan that I can only describe as manly and deep—so deep—echoes through the room. He sucks on my digits, and I can feel that sucking motion in my pussy, and I want him there, tasting, feasting.

When his eyes pop back open, I know he's let go of his restraint. His walls are down. All I have to do is give him the word, and he'll take from me whatever I'm willing to give him.

"What did you think about when you were making yourself come?" He croaks, and I know this is where we fall together, where we break the rules and do the one thing we both said we wouldn't.

"You..." The word has barely passed my lips, and he is on me, his mouth slanting against mine in a kiss that is both pleasure and pain, longing and passion, fire and ice. He shifts his body, so he is above me, hovering over me like a protective blanket. I couldn't stop myself, stop this, even if I tried. One of my hands finds purchase in his hair while the other grips onto his shirt tugging him closer.

Fire licks at my skin. There's too much clothing, too much space between us. In a frenzy, I pull at his shirt, the kiss breaks and I tug it up and over his head. In return, he tugs on mine, and I let him take it off, exposing my bare chest.

His gaze moves straight to my chest, his Adam's apple bobbing as he swallows. Without blinking, he cups my breast in his hand and leans down, taking the pebbled nipple into his mouth. He runs his tongue over it, licking it like it's an ice cream cone before closing his lips around it and sucking hard. I moan loudly, arching my back, and pressing my breasts further into his face.

He releases one side just long enough to switch to the other, giving that one equal attention. I'm thrashing beneath him, withering in need. The feelings coursing through me are almost too much, and all he's done so far is suck on my tits.

My hands explore his upper body, my fingers running over every muscle, every ridge and dip I can find. I want to touch every inch of him, to embed the memory of this moment in my mind, to paint a picture of us coming together because I know it will never happen again. There is no forever for us, there is only now, and that's good enough for me.

Releasing my nipple with a pop that bounces off the walls, his hungry gaze works its way down my body. I'm still in my sleep shorts, but I figure it won't be that way for long. Trailing his fingers down my body, he touches me with a softness I didn't expect. I shiver. My stomach a ball of nervous tension. When he reaches the waistband of my sleep shorts, his fingers hook inside, and he looks up at me to make sure I'm okay with what he's about to do.

With a slight nod, I lift my hips as he pulls my shorts and thong off in one swoop, leaving me completely bare and at his mercy.

"You're so beautiful," he murmurs against my lips as he shifts above me, his lips pressing against mine tenderly.

"So are you," I whisper back, reaching for him. He pulls back, and spreads my thighs slowly, almost as if he's savoring his first glimpse of me completely naked.

Licking his lips, he says, "I'm going to taste you, eat you until I've had my fill and then I'm going to fuck you, punish you for driving me insane."

He gives me no warning as he pushes my legs back toward my chest and dives in. A gasp catches in my throat at the first lick, and then I'm not sure what happens. All I know is somewhere between all the licking, sucking, and biting, I come again and again. He's like a ravaged man enjoying his last supper.

When he finally comes up for air, sweat has formed against my brow, and my chest is heaving, my heartbeat whooshing in my ears. I watch him pull his shorts down, freeing his very large, very hard cock.

Looking down at me, he moves, his thick cock grazing my sensitive core and I groan at the sensation that ripples through me.

Gripping his erection, he gives it a couple pumps, and my eyes move toward the motion. I can't look away. I want him.

"Are you sure you want this?" he asks, his voice husky.

Could I say no? Yes. Do I want to? No.

"Yes, I want this. I want you." I answer as I reach for him, my fingernails raking across his chest. He hisses through his clenched teeth, and the muscles in his neck tighten at my touch.

"We shouldn't, we fucking shouldn't. We were doomed from the very start. All these rules, all this..."

I'm worried, he's going to stop, that he's going to break my heart all over again, but instead, he lines his cock up with my entrance and slams inside of me. One thrust of his hips and my virginity is gone. Tears spring from my eyes, and trail down the sides of my cheeks at the intrusion. Seb just stares down at me, his gaze burning into my flesh.

"Shit, did I hurt you?" he questions, a moment before I can see him put the puzzle pieces together. "You're a..." His eyebrows pinch together as if he's in pain. He moves to pull out, and I wince, wrapping my legs around him, holding him inside me.

"Yes, I am a virgin. Well, *was*. I was a virgin, but I'm not anymore. I want this with you. Please, don't stop. I wanted it to be you." Something happens then, it's like a switch goes off inside of him. He grits his teeth and starts to move, very slowly. His muscles tense, and his body shakes as he does everything he can, not to hurt me. But I don't want his kindness. I just want him.

Cupping him by the cheeks, I pull his face down to mine and press my lips against his. Then, I sink my teeth into his bottom lip and bite him. He groans, pulling out, before slamming back in. Pleasure and pain mix together, and with every thrust, the sting resides.

"Fuck me, Sebastian," I demand.

"I don't want to hurt you." He grunts, moving slow.

Panting, I say, "You won't. It doesn't hurt anymore. Please, I need this. I need you."

Swallowing, he nods and pulls away again, sitting back on his knees, he grips me by the hips, impaling me on his length. My mouth pops open as he swivels his hips, the head of his cock touching some place inside me that feels like heaven.

"Oh...oh..." I start to cry out, bucking my hips to meet his hard thrusts. In this moment, it's just us. Two souls healing each other. Two souls finding the will to keep going and becoming one somewhere along the way. Using his thumb, Sebastian draws tiny circles against my clit.

"Come for me, Lily. Milk my cock, take from me."

"Shit..." I scream as he drives into me again and again. The headboard bangs against the wall with each thrust.

Like a rocket, I go off, and I swear fragments of my body, my heart, go with me. Every muscle tightens, and I clamp down on his cock, squeezing the life out of him. The contours of Sebastian's face look pained, but I can't tell because his grip on my hips turns bruising as he buries himself deep inside of me, again, and again.

Two more thrusts and he closes his eyes, throwing his head back, he lets out an ear-piercing roar, that I'm pretty sure everyone in a five-mile radius can hear. Then he stills and starts to come, his sticky seed filling me. It occurs to me then, as warmth radiates through me that we didn't use a condom.

Damnit.

He must realize it too, because when he turns his head back to me and opens his eyes, they are filled with shock, even within the aftermath of his climax.

"Shit, we didn't use a condom." Panic seems to grip him, replacing the calm, relaxed demeanor, that masked his face a short while ago.

"It's okay... I mean, I-I should be okay. I just had my period. So, it's unlikely that I would get... you know..." I stumble over the words before trailing off, unable to even say the word *pregnant*.

Sebastian shakes his head, "It's not okay. It was a reckless choice. One that could end up hurting both of us."

I know he is right, and that he didn't mean it in a hurtful way, but I can't help feeling the sting from his words. It's like he slapped me with them. He regrets what we did, and that part probably hurts the most.

Immediately, I'm reminded of what we are to each other and how wrong this was for us to do. Nothing will come of it. I'll never get to be his girlfriend. I'll never be more than a dirty little secret to him. He's the Dean. I'm just a student. Never mind the other things stacked against us. We were fated for this. Fated to never have a chance.

Without thinking, I crawl from the bed and find my shirt and sleep shorts. I tug them on, wincing at the uncomfortable state of my body. Seb stares down at the bed where I was just lying. I can see the wheels turning in his head.

"We... this was..." He stumbles, trying to find the right words to say, but I know what he is thinking... *a mistake*. He wants to say this was a mistake, and I can feel my heart breaking in my chest. The only thing I can think to do is break his heart before he can break mine. I'm tired of always being the one who gets left behind.

"If you're going to say this was a mistake, then you're right. This was a huge mistake."

"I... I don't... fucking Christ, Lily, that's not what I meant." He reaches for his boxers and slips into them. Suddenly, the room feels smaller, colder. He's taking up all the space inside my heart, and I can't risk getting attached, wanting more, because he will never be able to give that to me. Stupid. I was so stupid.

"I'm not sorry for what just happened between us. I'm just... I'm confused right now. I forgot the condom, and it was your first time and..."

I can't do this.

Swallowing down a sob, I shake my head, and hold up a hand telling him I'm done listening. "It doesn't matter. I'm sorry it happened. It was a mistake. All of this has been a mistake. Me staying here. This. Us."

Squeezing my eyes shut, I will it all away.

"Lily," he calls my name, his voice is soft, and floats through me like wisps of smoke, and the overwhelming need to cave for him is consuming, but giving in will only lead to more pain, and I've hurt myself enough tonight.

"No, just, please go... actually no, I'll go, this is your place after all."

"No." Sebastian's authoritative voice cuts through the air, and my eyes open at the sound. That beautiful face of his is twisted with agony, he's staring at me like I'm a puzzle he can fix, or figure out, but he can't. "Stay. I'll leave. I'll go stay with Remington but let me tell you this now. We are not over, Lily Kline. What happened tonight, was meant to happen, it was inevitable, and you know it. There was no escaping us coming together. I just..."

"Please go," I whimper, feeling the tears sting my eyes. I will not cry in front of him. I won't. He stands there for another long second, maybe thinking I'll change my mind, but I won't. When he realizes that, he gathers up some clothes and a few other things, before going to the door. He stops there, hovering, waiting for me to tell him to stay, but I won't. I can't. Sebastian Miller was never meant to be mine. He was always hers, and he always would be.

11

SEBASTIAN

"Are we going to talk about why you showed up here last night at eleven or..." Remington's voice trails off. There's a pounding behind my eyes that seems to get worse with each word that comes out of his mouth.

I don't want to talk about last night. About how amazing it was. About how I fucked it all up by opening my stupid mouth.

"What happened, Seb?" Jules asks next as she sits down at the table, a cup in her hands.

"Not you too." I sigh and thread my fingers through my hair in frustration.

"If you would just spill the beans, we wouldn't have to gang up on you."

I let my hand fall to the table. "Can't I just come over without there needing to be a reason?"

Remington rolls his eyes, "You can come over whenever you want. It's just you don't, and then randomly you show up late at night, out of the blue, annoyed and cranky. That's not normal, and since I'm not a complete asshole, and I care about you, I want to make sure you're okay."

"I'm fine. I've told you that ten times now, and yet you keep pushing." My gaze collides with Remington's. He looks like he doesn't believe me, probably because I'm lying, but that's none of his business. None of this is.

Jules interjects probably sensing a fight brewing. "Because deep down, you aren't. What's going on, Seb? Is it Lily?" Every muscle in my body tightens at her name. My thoughts swirl with images of us from last night. Her beautiful flushed face, the way she came to life at my touch. It was amazing, it was forbidden.

Rem notices the knee jerk change in my temperament and grins, "Yup, definitely Lily. What happened?" He leans in, perching his chin on his hand, staring intently at my face.

"Seriously? It's not some soap opera episode. I'm not hiding anything exciting. Lily and I had a fight. She was going to leave, and I told her I would leave instead. Then I left. End of story."

"If it's not that exciting, then why don't you tell us what the fight was about?"

Swallowing thickly, I reply, "It's nothing."

"Doesn't sound like nothing." Rem's grin widens, and I know he's just goading me, trying to make me mad but I'm already pissed off at myself. I don't need to be lectured further by my brother, who isn't exactly the best at making choices.

Still, I feel the overbearing need to speak about what happened. I have no worries about them telling anyone, so why haven't I said anything? *Cause I'm a coward.*

Sucking in a sharp breath, I say, "We had sex. Then I made the mistake of saying something without really thinking."

"Was it *I love you?*"

"No," I growl, "It wasn't. It was something else. Something that I feel she took out of context." Jules reaches across the table and places her hand against mine. Her touch is comforting, it always has been. Since the beginning, Jules has been like a little sister to me.

"What did you say? What happened?" she asks, with real concern etched into her features. Staring at her, I wonder how my asshole brother got so lucky. Jules is one of the kindest, sweetest people I know.

"I was... my emotions were running high and well, I didn't know that I was her first until it was too late, and to make matters worse...

after that, I started to say something about us being a mistake. I stopped, but it was too late." I pause, a horrid pain slicing through my chest at the memory. "She gave herself to me, and then, I opened my stupid mouth and all but pushed her away."

I didn't sleep a wink last night, and not because I wasn't tired. I was fucking exhausted, but I couldn't stop thinking about Lily, about the hurt in her eyes when I said those words. When I opened my mouth after the best sex, I'd ever had in my life.

"She gave you her virginity, and you said it was a mistake?" Jules asks with a wince.

I nod. Jesus, why does it sound so harsh with her saying it.

Jules frowns, "Did you tell her that you didn't mean it?"

"Of course, but it was too late. She pretty much shut down and pushed me away. Physically and mentally."

The truth is, things are complicated between Lily and me. We both want each other but are fighting the current that's bringing us together. I wasn't lying when I told her what happened was inevitable. We were going to collide, and we had, and it was amazing, but the aftermath of it all was catastrophic. I don't want to hurt Lily. I don't know what to do.

There is no undo button, there is no way I can forget about what we've done. And I definitely don't want to either. Lily is unforgettable.

"What are you going to do?" Rem asks, breaking the silence.

"I don't know. I'm going to try and go back to the house in a little bit and see what happens. Hopefully giving her the night to herself and time to cool off will encourage her to listen to my apology."

"Well, good luck with that," Rem tells me, earning himself a jab in the ribs by Jules.

"It will be fine, Seb," Jules tries to calm me down. "Just go talk to her. Explain it like you explained it to us. She'll understand."

God, I hope so. I really fucking hope so.

～

I turn the lock hesitantly, and push open my front door slowly, not because I am scared to see Lily, but because I'm scared she won't be here. She was so upset when I left last night, and the worst thing she could do to me right now is just leave.

I want to talk to her, I want to make this right, and if she left, ending things the way we did, I would be devastated.

Holding my breath, I walk into the living room. Only when I see her sitting on the couch, her legs drawn up to her chest, do I fill my lungs with air. *She is still here.*

"Hey," I greet her, throwing my keys and phone on the side table.

"Hey," she answers, her voice quiet and timid, unlike her normal self.

"I'm glad you're still here. I was worried you would leave or something," I admit.

"Where else would I go?" Her question stings. Is she only here because she doesn't have a choice? Does she feel like she is stuck here with me? Shoving those questions to the back of my mind, I take a deep breath and start talking.

"Listen, Lily, I'm sorry about last night. I didn't mean to say that it was a mistake..."

"Can we please just forget about it?" She interrupts me.

"Forget about it?" Is she serious? I can't just forget one of the best nights of my life. "I don't want to forget about it."

"Well, I do, and I think you should too," her voice is stern, or at least she tries to keep it that way, but I know Lily too well. I notice the slight tremble in her voice and the way she nervously plays with the hem of her shirt. *She is lying.*

"Lily—" I start but she cuts me off once again.

"Please, let's just forget last night happen and go back to how we were before."

I take a moment to weigh my options, and I come to the conclusion that if this is what I have to do to keep her here, then I'll do it.

"Okay, fine... we'll forget last night happened," I say, the words leaving a sour taste on my tongue.

"Thank you," Lily mumbles.

I give her a small nod and turn around, heading for the shower, when the doorbell rings. *Who the hell is that?*

"Are you expecting someone?" I ask Lily.

When she tells me no, I spin around. A little annoyed by the unannounced visitor, I walk back to the front door and open it.

"Hey, bro," Lex greets me, brushing past me and into my house before I can invite him in or even say hello.

"Ever heard of a phone?" I basically growl at him. "You know, to call and tell people that you are coming by their house?"

"Jesus, what's with you? We're family, we come by whenever, no formal announcement necessary." He walks through the house and into the living room with me right behind him. When he gets there and sees Lily sitting on the couch, he stops. "Oh... I get it now."

"Hey, Lex," Lily greets my brother, ignoring his remark.

She gets up to give him a quick hug before they both take a seat on the couch.

"I didn't know you were here." Lex's gaze swings between us. "I hope I'm not interrupting anything?"

"I've actually been staying here, because... well... I kind of got kicked out of the dorms for drinking," Lily explains, and Lex starts to bounce with laughter.

"No way? You got kicked out for *drinking*? I always thought drinking was part of the lesson plan in college."

Lily smiles, "Not quite. Also, they gave me a warning, and then I got caught the very next day."

Lex laughs even harder at that. "I didn't know you were that rebellious," he quips, and there is something so playful almost flirty about his tone, it has my insides twisting with jealousy. If Lex wanted Lily, he could have her. That's the fucked-up thing about our situation. Everything is stacked against us. There is a bright neon light blinking the word forbidden above us. It'd be so much easier for her and Lex.

"So, Lex, how come you dropped by?" I ask, trying to get his attention away from Lily.

"Just wanted to stop by and see you, I guess," he shrugs, his playfulness gone in a flash. Looking at him, I can tell something is off. He's haunted by nightmares, by the things that happened while he was overseas. He doesn't want to talk about it, never has, but someday he will. He'll have to, or it'll eat him alive.

"If you want to spend some quality time together, I was just about to go to the gym. Want to come with? The gym on campus is pretty nice," I offer.

"Yeah, let's do it. I wouldn't mind letting off some steam. Maybe even punching something...probably you," he smirks.

"It's settled. Let's go see if the Marines made you tougher or if you still cry like a baby when I beat your ass."

"You wish," Lex snorts, and suddenly I'm actually glad he came over. Maybe this is exactly what I need, a little one on one time with my brother and a good workout to clear my head.

"You want to come?" Lex asks Lily who immediately shakes her head.

"No, no... I have some schoolwork to take care of, you guys go ahead."

"Okay then, let's head out. See ya, Lily," Lex says and gets up. Brushing past me, he heads out the door not waiting for me.

"Bye, Lex," Lily calls after him, smiling. Then her gaze swings to me, her smile fading quickly. "Bye," she whispers.

"Bye. I'll be back in a little bit," I tell her. She nods slightly and forces her lips to curl up into a slight smile. *So much for everything going back to normal.*

When I walk out, Lex is already sitting in his car, waiting for me. As soon as I get in, he speeds off. We're barely on the road when the questioning starts. "So, you and Lily, huh?" Those thick brows of his bounce up and down.

"It's not like that..."

"Bullshit! You don't have to tell me about your love life, or lack of one, for that matter, but don't fucking lie to me," Lex warns, and I'm surprised at how fast his mood has changed. Something is definitely going on.

"Fair enough..." I hold up my hands, telling him with my body language to calm down. "It's complicated, and I'd rather not talk about it right now."

Lex sucks in a deep breath, almost as if he is trying to calm himself down, and I'm not sure what to do or say. This isn't Lex. It's unlike him to be moody. I think on how to approach the subject, while we make a stop at Lex's place so he can get changed.

When he gets back into the car, I ask, "So what's going on with you?"

Lex shrugs, and for a moment, I think he isn't going to open up to me, it wouldn't surprise me, he's always kept to himself, I'm about to push the issue when he opens his mouth to speak.

"I'm having a hard time adjusting to civilian life, I guess. I thought it would be different, easier, that's all." Lex's admission shocks me, to say the least, but that's not the feeling overwhelming me right now. That would be guilt. Guilt for not checking in on my brother more. How did I not know about this before?

"I'm sorry," is all I can manage to say.

Lex shakes his head as he shifts to drive. "Don't feel sorry for me."

"I don't. I mean, I'm sorry for being a self-absorbed asshole. I should have spent some more time with you. You've been home for a month, and we've barely hung out. That's on me."

"It's okay, Seb, I know you're busy with your new job. Seriously, don't beat yourself up. This is not on you. It's something I have to deal with myself. Plus, it's not like I've been alone. I've been spending a lot of time with Dad and Rem."

"So, what did you mean by 'you thought it would be different'?"

"I guess, I just thought everything would go back to normal when I got back home. I thought I would go back to normal, but I feel... different."

"Have you thought about talking to someone, like a therapist?"

"I don't need a fucking shrink," Lex says, his tone defensive.

"Okay, I get it. No shrink. At least come to me when you need to talk to someone."

"What do you think this is, idiot?" Lex points between us, making me laugh this time. He shakes his head, just as we pull into the gym parking lot. "And you're supposed to be the smart one out of us three."

I'm not so sure about that anymore.

12

LILY

*T*aping my foot, I wait behind the admin building like I usually do. Seb is a few minutes late, but I'm not going to call or text him to see where he's at. I don't want to seem like the angry, pushy girlfriend who needs to know where he is every five minutes. I cringe at the thought... *girlfriend*. As if. That'll never happen.

We've barely talked since that night. The past few days have been tense between us. My chest aches being close to him, my hands itching to reach out and trace his body. I'm pulled toward him, drawn to him in every way. When he enters a room, I can't look away. I try to forget what happened between us, try to tell myself that it was just sex, but of course, that's a lie. It was so much more than *just* sex. We both know that.

Five minutes turns into ten, then twenty, and I'm starting to get aggravated. Where the hell, is he, and why didn't he tell me that he was going to be late?

When it's thirty minutes after the time we normally meet, I've had enough. I don't care if I seem like an angry girlfriend. I'm not going to wait around at his beck and call.

With my head held high, I waltz around the admin building and through the front door. Most of the offices are already empty, the lights turned off, with everyone gone. Everyone but Sebastian. Picking up speed, I keep walking to Seb's office until I come to a sudden halt a few doors down from his.

"Oh, Sebastian," a female voice fills the hallway. A voice that is definitely coming from his office. "You know I don't mind a little overtime if it means helping you out."

The door opens all the way, and a beautiful woman steps out.

It's the same woman he was with at the diner. Red hot jealousy burns like a wildfire through every inch of my body.

"Still, thanks for doing this," Sebastian says, walking out behind her. The next instant, he looks up, his eyes colliding with mine, all while I stand there like an idiot. Then he breaks eye contact and looks back at the other woman. "I'll talk to you soon, Laura."

"Sure thing, Seb," she says and starts walking down the hall. She gives me the friendliest smile when she passes me, completely unaware of how uncomfortable I am. I wait until she has disappeared around the corner before I look back up at Seb.

"I'm sorry, I'm late. Honestly, I didn't realize how late it was until a minute ago. I was about to call you."

"You don't owe me an explanation," I force myself to say, even though it kills me to do so.

Seb gives me a disbelieving look. "Will you come in for a few minutes. I have another stack of papers to sign, and I don't wanna make you wait in the hall."

"Sure," I say when really, I want to say no. The jealous rage festers just beneath the surface, like an evil little beast it sits on my shoulder whispering questions in my ear that I have no business asking.

Why was he meeting with that woman again? Who is she? Does she like him?

Following him into his office, I flop down on the couch, trying my very best not to remember the very indecent things that happened on here. When I was on my knees in front of Sebastian, with his cock in my mouth. Heat builds within my core at the memory and my pussy throbs remembering the feel of his smooth skin, the way he smelt, the way he looked, how bright his eyes were as he watched, trapping me in his gaze.

Shit, I'm not supposed to think about that, or any of this.

"Is everything okay, Lily?" Sebastian asks, and I swear it's like he can read my mind. Like there is this imaginary string tethering us to each other. He knows me almost better than I know myself, and that's terrifying.

"Yeah. It's fine. I'm fine, I mean." I correct myself, my voice cracking at the end. I don't want to give away how jealous I am of him moving on, or the possibility of him moving on, but I can't help the way I'm feeling. It's like I know I can't have him, but I don't want anyone else to either.

"Are you sure? You seem a little... off."

"I'm fine," I snap, lying once again, and it's even harder to say it this time because deep down inside I'm not fine. I'm falling for Sebastian Miller, falling helplessly for a man that I cannot have.

Sebastian's gaze hardens as he places his pen down and shoves away from his desk. My eyes are glued to him as he walks across the room, closes the door, and clicks the lock into place.

"What are you doing?" I croak, my skin growing hotter. It feels like I have a damn fever, but I'm not sick. Unless you count being in love an illness.

He doesn't say anything and instead walks toward me, his eyes never leaving mine. I feel like I need to stand up, so I get on my feet. He's all man, and I can't help but drink him in, admiring the way the suit he's wearing hugs every inch of his toned body. I've been starving for him for days, for his touch, for his cock.

Stopping in front of me, he reaches out and gently pinches my chin between two fingers forcing me to look at him.

"To me, you are irreplaceable. What happened between us, it was meant to happen, and it will happen again, and again, because you, Lily, are a drug I can't quit. That I don't want to quit."

Swallowing around the knot that's formed in my throat, I try and gather the words I've been wanting to say.

My lips tremble, and I can feel my core pulse, the promise of pleasure flickers in his eyes.

I need him. I want him.

"I want you. I want you so much it hurts to be away from you, but..." I try and jerk out of his hold, but he squeezes, pinching harder.

"What... tell me, Lily. Tell me what you want?" Sebastian leans in, the words are nothing more than a breath against my lips, but the urgency behind them is clear. He's so close now that if I moved just a smidge, we would be kissing.

"I want you, but I don't..." His face falls, and I start to talk again, "I don't want to be your dirty little secret. Something you're forced to hide. I won't be that girl, Sebastian."

A smile curve's his lips, and his eyes light up, "You aren't a secret, Lily. You're the sun, and the moon, you're the goddamn stars in my galaxy. You're happiness and sadness. You're perfection and chaos. You're mine. You're not your sister, you, Lily, are never forgotten, always sweet, always kind, and I'm going to prove to you just how much I want you and no one else."

Tears fill my eyes at his words, and before I can muster up a response, he's kissing me. He breathes life into me, filling my soul with a fire that will never be extinguished. Clawing at each other's clothes, my mind registers the sound of buttons flying, landing somewhere off in the distance, and fabric tearing but I'm too far gone to care.

Like a storm of pent up anger and need, we collide, the air sizzling. Sebastian has me naked and pinned to his desk in seconds. I can't help myself. I'm starved, ravaged with need. I bite at his bottom lip hard enough to draw blood and earn myself a throaty growl of approval.

He picks me up slightly and makes me sit on the desk, my naked ass on the edge of the wooden surface. His fingers run over my thighs and land on my knees, where he stops to push my legs apart. The cool air meets my heated folds, and I am reminded of how wet I am.

Sebastian steps around me, and in one swoop of his arm clears the entire desk. Papers, pens and other knick-knacks falling to the floor and all I can do is giggle.

That giggle dies when Seb positions himself in front of me again, his eyes as dark as the night sky. With his pupils blown out, he looks almost dangerous, a little unhinged, and my core tingles at the thought of him losing control and taking me here right now. There is something so exciting and sexy about this. Like he has to have me right this second, and there is nothing that's going to stop him.

He steps between my legs, fitting there perfectly. He takes my lips one more time before gently pushing my shoulders down, making me lie flat on the desk. His fingers fumble with the zipper of his slacks, freeing his steel hard cock in record time.

My legs are still spread, giving him a prime view of my glistening folds. I want him to see, to know how much I want him. His fingers trail over my center, and I almost come right then.

Our gazes collide. "You're so wet, Lily," Seb points out the obvious.

"You're so hard," I retort with a grin.

"What a pair we are," he grins back. "Perfect for each other in every way. I'm going to fuck you now, right here on my desk. If you don't want that, then you need to speak up now."

If I don't want that? It's all I've been able to think about.

"Please fuck me, Sebastian," I whimper, and that's all he needs to hear.

With a growl that sounds more animal than man, he lines himself up with my core. The tip of his cock brushes against my entrance, the anticipation killing me. I want him inside of me. Need him inside of me. Right, the fuck, now. With a knowing grin, he rubs himself up and down my slit, spreading my juices across my folds and the head of his cock.

A deep throaty moan escapes me when he grazes my already swollen clit, but that feeling is nothing compared to the mind-blowing pleasure that takes root inside me when he returns to my entrance and enters me in one hard thrust. My entire world falls away and comes crashing back together again. I know, because of Sebastian, I will never be the same person again. He's touched me in a way that I'll never ever forget. A way that has changed me.

With a possessive hunger for more, he pulls out and thrusts back in, grinding me on his cock. All I can feel is him, all I can breathe is him. Keeping one hand on my hip, he moves the other to my shoulder, leaving me nowhere to escape. Then he makes good on his promise to prove to me just how much he doesn't want me to be a secret.

Staring deeply into my eyes, he starts to fuck me, "I don't care who hears us." Thrust. "I don't care what they think." Thrust. "I don't care what they say." Thrust. "All I care about is you." Thrust. I'm swimming in a pool full of pleasure, and I don't want to get out. I'd drown in it if I could.

"I want you..." I pant, between thrusts, the sound of our bodies colliding fills the air, while the smell of sex meets my nostrils. It's exotic and tantalizing. What we're doing is forbidden, but it feels right, and I believe him when he says he only wants me and no one else.

Leaning forward, he swivels his hips and captures my lips with his teeth. He nips, sucking at the flesh to soothe the bite he left behind.

"You'll always have me." He grunts, sweat beading on his forehead.

I don't want what we're doing to end. Not ever. But I can feel my core tightening, with every deep thrust, the head of his cock touching something heavenly inside of me.

"Fuck, I need you to come, Lily. I need to feel you squeeze my cock until there is nothing left inside of it. Come for me, baby, come..." Sebastian's chest heaves as he speaks, his fingers biting into my flesh as he thrusts faster and faster. There will be bruises left in his wake, but I'll relish seeing them on my skin because only I will know who put them there and the power that that person holds over my heart.

"Sebastian," I cry out, arching my back off the desk. Pleasure floods my veins as I start to come. It isn't just my body shaking, but my entire begin. Every muscle in my body tightens, every cell zings, and my mind hurdles into nothingness as I let all the feelings overtake me.

"Fuck, Lily, fuck..." Sebastian pants into the crook of my neck as he grinds deeply inside of me, his cock seeming to grow. I feel fuller, so full, but also loved, so loved.

"I'm coming... I'm fucking coming..." His teeth grind together, the words barely passing his lips as he empties himself deep inside of me. My chest heaves, the pounding of my heartbeats filling my ears, and all I can do is smile as I look up at him, watching as pleasure overtakes his features. He looks even more like a god with his teeth sunk into his bottom lip, his eyes squeezed shut, and his cheeks flushed pink.

A second later, he sags against me, catching part of his weight on his hands. His hot breath fans against my sweat-slicked skin and I shiver.

"Shit, I'm sorry. I forgot a condom again." He whispers against my skin. "I'll be sure to be more careful next time."

"Next time?" I blink. Everything comes back to me. Us. How we can never be together. How wrong it is that we keep doing this. I want Sebastian, but I'm afraid, so fucking afraid and I don't know if I'm willing to let go of that fear.

Sebastian pulls back, his eyes are soft, and I can see the feelings he has for me written clearly across his face. With his hand, he cups my cheek, and without thought, I nuzzle into his touch, not even realizing how much I need it.

"When your sister died, I vowed to never love again. I promised myself that I would never move on, that no one would ever take up space in my heart like she did."

His confession shocks and saddens me all at once. He loved her so much that he didn't think he could ever be with anyone again, at least not like this.

"Then... why? Why do this with me?" Tears sting my eyes, and I want to tell him to get off of me. To go to fucking hell but I just don't have the strength.

"Because I love you, Lily. I love you, and it's taken me this long to realize it, but I do. At first, I thought it was just the fact that you looked so similar to your sister, but I knew even then that it was more. I was attracted to you the instant you walked into my office. Every waking minute I'm thinking about you, and every day, I wonder if you're thinking about me the same."

Gulping, I nod because I'm afraid that if I try and speak, the words won't come out. Not after what he just confessed.

He loves me... he said he loves *me*.

"Lily," he says my name so softly, I want to weep at the sound. "I love you. I want this. I want to try. Can we try? Can we see what happens?"

"Like... date?"

Sebastian nods, and my eyes bug out of my head. "I'm... I'm not sure..." before I can finish answering him, my cell phone starts to ring. He pulls away even though I can see he doesn't want to, leaving me just enough room to escape him. I take it and slither off the desk, grabbing my skinny jeans off the floor and tugging them up and over my ass by the time I reach the couch.

I can feel Sebastian hovering over me. His presence is like the sun. Always moving, always there even when it's not.

"This isn't over, Lily. No matter what you say, it isn't. I'm not going to let your fear rule us. I want you, and I know you want me. The answer to our problems is sitting right in front of us."

Ignoring my phone for a moment, I whirl around, "You're the Dean, and I'm just some troubled student who can't get her shit together." All over again I'm alone, the walls are closing in around me. Sebastian is here, but he's not mine. He can't save me. "Then there is our age difference and our pasts, everything is stacked against us. We will never work. We've been doomed from the beginning." I don't know how or why I say the things I do, but I do. I think it's time he realizes how much is stacked against us.

Sebastian's brows pinch together, "I want you, Lily, and I won't give up. Not until we try." He pauses, his pink tongue darting out over his full bottom lip. "I don't know how we will make it work, but we will. We'll never know unless we try." The determination in his eyes isn't wavering, telling me all I need to know, and my knees go weak, realizing how much he truly wants me, wants us.

Still fear of the unknown threatens to swallow me whole. Can we do this? Really, do this? Be more than just secret lovers screwing behind closed doors? I don't want to be his secret, but I don't want to give up this chance to be together. Is being with Sebastian worth it, even if it is in secret?

"I... I want you, but..."

Sebastian shakes his head, "No buts, Lily. It's just you and me. Don't let the fear win."

As afraid as I am of being with him. I'm more afraid of being without him.

"You're mine, Lily, and I am yours." He oozes a confidence I wish I had. "We'll figure this out. I might not know everything but what I do know is that I'm not giving up on you. On us. Please, just give us a chance. I want this. I want you. We might not be able to hold hands and kiss on campus, but we can tell everybody we trust. We can go on dates in the town over, we won't have to hide everywhere or forever, just..."

It hits me then, right in the gut.

I'm falling in love with him.

Nope, not falling.

I am in love with him.

13

SEBASTIAN

I watch Lily as she nervously wrings her hands in her lap while we wait for Rem and Jules to get to the restaurant.

"You sure this is not going to be super awkward?" She whispers across the table like it's some kind of secret.

"Why would it be? It's not like Rem and Jules didn't know already," I try to soothe her. "Trust me, they are perfectly fine with us dating. Jules was basically jumping for joy when I told her."

Lily arches a brow. "And Remington?"

"Well, he's not really the jumping for joy kind of guy, but he slapped me on the back and handed me a beer, which is pretty much the same." I look up and spot Rem and Jules as they walk into the restaurant hand in hand. "Here they are."

Lily stiffens beside me, and I wonder why she is so damn worried about this? They walk up to our table. Rem nods his head toward me, and Jules has a smile so huge it fills her whole face. *Yeah, she is definitely happy about this.*

Lily stands up as Jules comes straight for her, wrapping her slender arms around her, engulfing her in a big hug. When they release each other, Lily looks around and meets Rem's eyes. He gives her a welcoming smile that I hope soothes some of the worry. As soon as she realizes that Jules and Rem are really okay with this, she relaxes. I can see the tension drain from her body, her shoulders drop and her back becoming less like a rod.

Jules comes around and gives me half a hug as well before we all sit back down.

"I'm glad we get to do this," Jules chimes, just as the waitress comes around and takes our drink order.

"Me too, I was a little nervous," Lily admits. "I didn't know what you would think about... us."

"Lily, we are nothing but happy for you. There is no reason why you two shouldn't be together." Jules beams.

"Well, the university policy disagrees with you," Lily points out.

"It's a stupid policy, made up by some asshat paper pushers. Fuck them," Rem chides.

"It's not that easy. If they find out, Sebastian will lose his job and me my scholarship," Lily says a sadness in her tone. The risk is there, in every single thing we do, but risking everything for love? Yeah, it's worth it.

"Well, you never have to hide from us. We are happy Sebastian finally came to his senses. I mean, we could see he was head over heels for you from ten miles away. It just took him a bit to see it." Jules says, giving me a sweet smile.

"Yeah, he is stupid like that," Rem chuckles. "Glad you came to your senses, big bro."

Rem is interrupted by the waitress coming to drop off our drinks and take our food order. When she leaves again, I elbow him in the side for his little show of calling me *stupid*.

"What was that for?" he grumbles.

"For calling me stupid." I take a pull from the beer I ordered. Lily and Jules break off into conversation about classes, and how things have been going for each of them. Listening intently, I find nothing but joy in seeing Lily smile and interact with my family. It makes my heart swell, my thoughts shift. This is us. We're really doing this. Really a couple. My face slices in two with the smile that overtakes it.

Moving my hand beneath the table, I find Lily's hand and inter-twine our fingers. She pauses mid-sentence, and I notice the slight intake of breath before she starts to breathe normally again. All she's worried about lately is showing any type of PDA, but I want her to know that I don't see her as a secret. Deep down, I want to scream to the world, she is mine, but I have to find a way to do that without jeopardizing everything we have.

"Have you noticed a change in Lex at all?" Rem asks interrupting my thoughts.

"A little, why?"

Rem shrugs, "He just hasn't been himself. He flies off the handle at small things, and one day, I swear he was going to have a panic attack over the microwave going off."

"Maybe he's got PTSD?" I take another swig of my beer, "I've noticed he's become a little hot-headed, but nothing insane. Maybe we should sit down and talk to him together?"

"Yeah, maybe," Rem nods, "I just feel like a shit brother for not being there for him. Like yeah, I have my own stuff going on, but I should put more time into hanging out with him, and shit. Hell, I don't even know where he's staying right now."

The ache in Rem's voice tells me all I need to know. I've heard that guilt-laced tone a time or two before, and whatever he's thinking, he's blaming himself for.

"I went by his apartment the other day. It's down by Milton Road," I say, hoping to put his mind at ease.

"Well, I haven't been invited over there," he murmurs, sounding a tiny bit offended.

"A door goes both ways, Rem, you can open or close it, but if it never moves there's always going to be a door between you."

Rem snorts, "Thanks for the analogy."

Rolling my eyes, I bite back a smart-ass remark. The waitress returns with our food, and we eat mostly in silence. Lily is all smiles, her pink painted lips are tantalizing, beckoning me forward, and leaving me with indecent thoughts. Shit, all I want to do is take her across the table and screw her into oblivion.

Rem must be able to read my facial expressions because a tiny bubble of laughter passes his lips, earning us both a confused look from Jules and Lily.

"What's so funny, you two?" Jules asks accusingly.

"Nothing." I shake my head, fighting off a grin because of my brother's stupid face.

"Everything, baby, everything..." He says, leaning into Jules, his lips brushing against the side of her throat. She emits a tiny squeak, and a blush creeps up her cheeks.

"Stop it, Remmy. We're in a restaurant!" She pushes him away, but even I can tell she's not immune to my brother's advances. There's a reason he used to be considered the biggest manwhore on campus.

Lily squeezes my hand, and though she's smiling, I can see the sadness lingering in her eyes. To be able to do what Rem and Jules are doing right now.

Leaning into her, I lick my lips, my eyes dart between her eyes and those pink pillowy lips of hers. I'm consumed with the need to kiss her, "We don't have to be so careful here."

I don't even give her a chance to respond before my lips descend on hers. There is nothing like kissing Lily. She whimpers into my mouth, and I swallow up whatever it is she wants to say. Nipping at her bottom lip, I wait for her to let me deepen the kiss, but she presses her lips into a firm line, making it impossible for me to enter that perfect mouth of hers.

Giving up, I break the kiss, it's best not to tease my already steel hard cock.

"Sebastian," Lily pants, her chest rising and falling rapidly, her creamy white cheeks, a dusky pink as she scans the restaurant like someone is going to jump up and point a finger at us.

"Yes, Lily," I grin, my heart racing in my chest. I haven't felt this alive since I was a teenager. Jules and Remington are smiling from ear to ear, their happiness for me only adds to my own. I'm an over-flowing pot of joy right now.

The waitress stops by the table, dropping off the check. Lily tries her best to put a smile on, but I know what I just did is eating her up. We pay, and soon it's time to leave.

"We have to do this again!" Jules announces as we all get up and head for the door. "I've missed going on double dates. Everyone is always busy."

Taking Lily's hand into mine, I pull her into my side, "Of course, we will do this again. We'll go on so many double dates, you'll get tired of us."

"Doubt that'll ever happen. Jules loves you, probably more than me," Remington frowns, making a puppy dog face at Jules who merely rolls her eyes.

"I am the better brother, so I'm not at all surprised by that," I say with a laugh. Rem grunts in response, and as we trail around the corner, I almost run headfirst into someone.

"I'm so sorry..." I start, but the words lodge in my throat when I realize who it is that I just about ran over.

Clark Jefferson and his girlfriend, Emerson stare at me for a second, before shifting their gaze down to mine and Lily's joined hands. I can feel Lily trying to disappear into my side, probably wishing the floor would swallow her whole.

"Sebastian..." Clark swallows thickly, and I can see he's trying not to make this awkward but is there really any way not to. He's seen me with my cock out and my pants down around my ankles. He's seen me, the Dean of the university, getting a blowjob. Yeah, there's no way around this.

"Clark, Emerson. It's nice to see you."

"Emerson!" Jules squeaks with excitement as she engulfs Emerson's tiny frame in a hug. Emerson looks like she wants to run away. Through it all, Lily remains at my side, unspeaking, unmoving, like a statue.

"Dude, Clark." Rem greets him, and I swear I've never felt so out of my element in my entire life. Rem and Jules have no idea what those two have seen us do, so when Jules glances over to Lily and sees her standing there like a ghost, her eyebrows go up in confusion.

"Well, um, we were just leaving..." I force my mouth up into a smile. Clark nods, and Emerson gives me a shy smile, her eyes not quite meeting mine. Tightening my grip on Lily's hand, I pull her around Clark and Emerson, and toward the door. Rem questions me with a raised brow but thankfully doesn't ask anything.

Rem and Jules say their goodbyes and promise to meet up sometime soon. Once out of earshot Lily whispers, "Do you think they remember me?"

All I can do is nod my head. I can't lie to her. It's not like we were doing something wrong, not really. Once outside, it feels like I can finally breathe, and I suck all the air I can into my lungs. I've just exhaled the breath when Rem comes walking up to me.

"What the hell was that? Why were you acting so weird with Clark and Emerson?"

Knowing damn well that I can't lie to Rem, at least not successfully, I say, "They saw us... *together*, on campus."

Rem's mouth pops open, and his eyes narrow. He's going to say something smart-assed, and then I'm going to punch him.

"You know Clark isn't going to say anything, he is like family now. You can trust him."

Okay, so I don't have to punch him. At least not yet. I'm about to tell him that we'll talk about this later, that I don't want to talk about this in front of the girls. I don't want Lily thinking crappy about herself or...

"They caught us having sex in Seb's office." Lily blurts out like it's no big deal. Like a fish out of water, my mouth opens and closes, and then opens again. Did she... seriously?

Rem and Jules just stare at us wide-eyed for about three seconds before they break out into the loudest fit of laughter I've ever heard. Jules holds her stomach like she is trying to hold it together, and Remington wipes tears from his eyes.

"You should've seen your face. You looked like a dead fish." Remington mocks, making a sad attempt at mimicking my facial expression from a moment ago.

"It's not funny, asshole." I slug him in the arm before averting my gaze to Lily to see if she's okay. She looks, well, a little less worried and less like she's carrying the weight of the world on her shoulders.

"It kinda is." Rem snorts.

"No, it's not. What if someone else had found us that night?" I question annoyingly.

All he does is shrug, "They didn't. It was just Clark and Emerson. No need to get your panties in a bunch."

Shaking my head, I swallow down all my anger. I don't have the patience for this right now. Rem doesn't understand what's at risk for

Lily and me. He doesn't know the danger that being together brings, and yet still here we are standing outside a restaurant together like two lovers. I want this with her, and only her. In that moment, all I can think is, if it's worth it, I'll find a way to make it work. I'm not giving Lily up. Not ever.

We part ways from Rem and Jules, and as I'm walking around the car to climb into the driver's seat, my phone goes off. Without looking at it, I reach into my pocket and turn it off. I'm pretty sure I know who that is, and I can't talk to the lady at the gallery right now, not with Lily here. I want to make sure I got her the gallery spot first before I tell her about it. Nothing like getting her hopes up just for them to be crushed later.

Climbing into the car, I wait until Lily is buckled up before pulling out of the parking spot. While driving home, I realize how happy tonight has made me. It wasn't anything crazy, just a simple dinner with family, but somehow it was so much more.

Seeing the carefree smile on Lily's face after we got all the awkwardness out of the way, how she enjoyed herself, felt good, and sharing her with the world, being able to kiss her and show everybody that she is mine, it felt better than I ever could've imagined.

"I'm gonna hop in the shower, and then we can crawl into bed," Lily yawns as we enter the foyer giving away just how tired she is.

Once she disappears into the bathroom, I fish my phone out of my pocket and turn it back on. Excitement bubbles to the surface. I can call the gallery back now and surprise her later.

My excitement fizzles to disappointment as soon as I look at the screen and realize that it's not a message from the art curator like I had thought, but a text message from an unknown number. Opening the message, my heart sinks into my stomach, bile rising up my throat. There are two pictures in that message, both of them are of Lily and me; one of us kissing, and the other is of us entering the house together.

My hand squeezes the phone tight enough to snap it when I see the message attached to the pictures.

Unknown Number: **Wonder what the University would think if they saw these images?**

The need to type out a reply, to scream at this person for threatening Lily, for threatening me pulses in my veins. Without even knowing them, I want to hurt them. To make them pay. But that won't happen, not with these pictures dangling over my head. I have no choice. I have to play nice. With shaking fingers, I type out, *what do you want?* Instead of the lengthy, anger riddled message, I want to. Then I slide the phone back into my pocket and hope like hell I can keep this hidden from Lily because if not, I'll most likely lose her forever.

14

LILY

"*W*hy are you peering down into your iced coffee like it killed your cat or something?" Del questions as she shoves down into the seat beside me. Meeting up in the library to study is the easiest for me. Studying at home is boring, and studying when Sebastian is home isn't really studying, not when all I want to do is climb him like a mountain.

Tapping my pen against the wooden surface, I answer, "Just thinking..."

"About?"

"Stuff."

"What kinda stuff? Butt stuff? Or stuff, stuff?" Del wiggles her dark brows, before tossing a few strands of her dark brown hair over her shoulder. No matter what, she always finds a way to cheer me up.

"Just *stuff*." I shrug, unsure if I want to really get into talking about mine and Sebastian's relationship with her. Delilah and I are good friends, but I don't want to burden her with my insecurities or problems.

Delilah's lips form into a pout, and she leans into my face, real close, almost like she's examining me. "Does this have something to do with that hot mountain of a man, known as the dean?"

I hate it when she calls him that. Or Mr. Miller. Or Dean Miller.

"Maybe, but I think it's all in my head..." I chew on my bottom lip, "Yeah, it's probably nothing." It has to be nothing because there is literally no proof of any wrongdoing. The only noticeable thing is that Sebastian is acting different, but I can't really pinpoint how. He's the same, nothing's really changed not in the sense of him being close or caring for me, but more in the sense of uneasiness. He seems anxious, and almost angry sometimes, and it seems to come out of nowhere.

Del's gaze widens, "Oh no, do you think he is cheating on you? Because if he is...I'll help you dispose of the body. I know a really..."

"No. Stop." I shake my head, grinning. Delilah is too good of a friend. "I really don't think that's it. He wants to spend every minute of the day with me and, though, I don't have a lot of relationship experience, I feel like if he were cheating that wouldn't be the case. I don't know. I just feel like he is worried about something."

"Hmm, sounds like you need to talk to him. Figure out what's going on. I've dealt with cheating men before but to be honest, beyond that, I don't have much more experience and definitely not with a guy like Sebastian."

Puzzled by her explanation, I ask, "What do you mean, a guy like him?"

"Like a guy who has his life together," Del giggles. "I've dated more of the, I'm taking a year off college kind of guys."

"Those are the guys you should be dating, silly. You're in college. Now is the time to be dating douchebags, assholes, and fuck boys. Not when you're thirty and looking for a man to settle down with, to get married and have kids."

Del shrugs, "Yeah, I guess you're right, but if that's the case, maybe you should be taking your own advice. Maybe Sebastian is too serious? Maybe that's the problem?"

I think about what she's said before I shake my head. "No, I don't think so. For being the dean, and having all that authority, he's really laid back."

"I'll bet he is..." Delilah giggles again while opening up her textbook.

"Are you always such a child?"

"Yes, yes, I am." She answers before diving headfirst into a stack of notes. While Delilah might be childish on the outside, laughing and teasing, she takes her academics serious.

With the fun over we reroute our attention back to our books, trying to at least get a little more studying in. I've just finished a chapter of biology notes when two girls sit down at the table next to us. Jesus, there is an entire row of tables ten feet away, but they have to sit right on top of us. I try not to be bothered by it, but cripes.

I catch one of them giving me a friendly smile, out of the corner of my eye. I'm pretty sure her name is Ana, and I share a class with her, but I can't remember which one. Probably one of the boring ones. My guess being math or social studies. Classes I spend time thinking about art, instead of what's going on in class.

"Did you hear the rumor about the new dean?" Ana whispers to her friend, but she might as well be yelling it with how close they're sitting to us. My ears perk up at the mention of Sebastian. I know it's rude to eavesdrop, but I can't help it. Del's eyes snap up, and she gives me a knowing look, before directing her gaze back down to her books.

"The one where everyone keeps saying he is super hot?" The other girl giggles, and suddenly, I have the urge to accidentally drop my book on her face. Wonder if she would think he was still hot then?

"Well, that is no rumor, have you seen the man's abs?" Ana retorts. "I'm talking about him banging a student."

"No way!" The other girl practically shouts, and Ana reaches out, covering her mouth with her hand.

"Shut up. You're going to get us kicked out." Ana pulls her hand away, and the girl frowns. Ignoring her friend, she continues, "I heard someone saw him with a student. Like them getting into his car and him taking her to his house."

My throat tightens, and my heart beats so fast, I think I'm on the verge of a heart attack. This can't be happening. This is my worst nightmare brought to life.

"Who is the girl?"

I wait with bated-breath for Ana to say my name but a second ticks by and then another before I see her shrug her shoulders.

"No clue. Whoever saw them was too far away to make out who the girl was."

"Boo! That's too bad."

"I know, I would love to know who she is, so I can ask her how she got him and if she is willing to share..." Ana winks at her friend, and I can feel the bile climbing up my throat. I'm going to vomit all over the place if I don't get out of here. I can't listen to any more of this.

"Ready to go, Del?" I ask, already gathering up my books and notes, while stuffing the papers in between the pages. I can't do this. I can't.

"Yes," Del says a little louder than necessary and the girls beside us look at us like we've grown a second head. Shoving my shit into my backpack, I wait as long as I can for Del who is slower than the ice age, might I add, before I start walking away. I'll just wait by the circulation desk for her.

As I walk, my heart sinks lower and lower into my belly. Tears prick at my eyes, and I blink them away. I cannot. I will not have a mental breakdown in the university library over this.

"Hey! Wait up," Del calls from somewhere behind me, and I stop, my shoes squeaking against the linoleum. My chest rises and falls, but it doesn't feel like I'm getting any air into my lungs. Del comes to stand in front of me. Her face is a blur, tears fill my vision, but I can still make out the mixture of fear and sadness reflecting back at me.

"It's just a rumor, Lily. No one knows that it's you." She whispers, her voice soft.

"I... I know...it is." All I can focus on is getting away from everyone. Everything. I can't handle this right now. "I... I have to go. I'm sorry."

"Lily, wait..." Delilah calls, but I'm too fast. Wiping at my tear-stained cheeks, I rush out of the library. I have no idea where I'm going to go. Pulling out my phone, I dial the first number I can think of.

"Lily. Hey, what's up?" Jules' sing-song voice fills my ears melting away a thin layer of my anxiety.

"Can you... I don't mean to inconvenience you or anything, but I need a ride back to Sebastian's place."

"Oh, my god, stop it, Lily. You're not an inconvenience. You're basically family. More like a sister than a friend."

"That means a lot to me. I'm just feeling crappy today, and I want to go back to the house and sleep for a while." *Forever.*

"Yeah, sure, where are you at?"

"Umm, I'm near the library. I'll wait for you out front."

"Okay, see you soon." We both hang up at the same time.

Heading back toward the library, I find one of the benches out front and sit down. My head falls into my hands, and I suck oxygen in through my nose to ease the ache that's forming in my chest. I thought the anxiety attacks were gone. It's been so long since I had one.

As I sit, waiting, trying to calm myself, my thoughts run rampant. This was a mistake. If anyone finds out that it was me... my stomach twists, and twists and all the anxious anxiety I've been feeling ripples through me.

I love Sebastian, truly I do, but we can't keep hiding this. We can't keep pretending like what we're doing is okay, when it isn't. Love is a risk I'm willing to take, but to stay with him, one of us will have to make a sacrifice.

AFTER JULES GAVE me a ride home, I took a shower and then a nap. Waking up, I felt a little bit better but still not one hundred percent. In my mind, all I can hear is Ana's voice. All I can see is my name sprayed on the walls of the school. It kills me that we're doing all of this in secret. The one thing I never wanted to be is the one thing I've become. I won't be his dirty little secret. I won't. Something has to change.

Trying my best to get my emotions under control, I make myself a cup of coffee and sit down in the living room. I should paint or draw, or do something, but I can't. Five minutes later, I hear Sebastian's jeep pulling in the driveway.

As soon as he enters the house, a calm overtakes me. It's like his mere presence has the power to soothe any ache or pain from my body. The front door opens, and I hear him depositing his stuff on the dining room table.

"What's going on, Lily? I'm worried about you, baby." He practically growls as he stalks into the living room and over to where I'm sitting on the couch. When I look up at him, there are tears in my eyes.

Stupid emotions. His hazel eyes soften further, and he looks at me like I'm a piece of glass that's about to shatter, and maybe that's because I am. I'm about to break, and I don't know if Sebastian will be able to piece me back together again.

Without even a second thought, he takes me into his strong arms, pulling me into his chest. My hands fist at his shirt, and I inhale deeply into the crook of his neck. We've done a lot of things. He's seen me in a couple of low times, but he's never seen me this broken. Carefully, he sits on the couch, never letting me go and positioning me on his lap.

"What happened? Are you okay? I will kill whoever hurt you. I swear to God." Though I don't think Sebastian would ever hurt a fly. I know he means it. The warmth of his body seeps into me, and I lift my head from the crook of his neck and press my lips to the throbbing pulse beneath the surface.

I can't give him up.

"Tell me what happened, Lily, because I'm about two seconds away from losing my fucking mind." Sebastian tenses, and that angelic jaw of his turns to stone.

"Earlier, I was in the library with Delilah, we were studying, and…" I don't know why it's so hard to talk about. Why the words get caught in my throat, but they do.

Those hazel orbs I love so much flicker with rage, "Who hurt you?"

"No one hurt me," I answer finally.

His shoulders sag with relief, but the tension in his body isn't gone just yet.

"If no one hurt you, then why are you crying?" His voice is low and reaches somewhere deep inside of me. It causes an ache, a different kind of one, to pulse deep in my core. One of his hands comes into view as he cups me by the cheek and forces me to look up at him. "What happened, Lily?"

Licking my suddenly dry lips, I spill the beans, "There's a rumor. Someone said that they saw us together."

"What?" Sebastian blinks, and his eyebrows shoot up his face.

"Okay, bad wording. The rumor is that you're sleeping with a student. The person spreading said rumor doesn't know who the girl is, but that doesn't matter. Someone saw us together. Someone knows."

The way Sebastian is looking at me right now has me confused. He looks, well he looks like he's not all that concerned, and that bothers me. It bothers me a lot.

15

SEBASTIAN

I don't know what's worse, seeing Lily cry over this or knowing that I've kept the secret of someone knowing from her. Guilt from the secret I'm keeping burns through my veins. I can feel the words pricking against the tip of my tongue. I want to tell her that I already know but telling her won't make things better. Not now.

It'll just push her away, and I can't lose her. Not now, not ever.

"It's going to be okay, Lily. I promise you that nothing bad is going to happen," I try to soothe, knowing damn well, that it's a lie. I can't promise her that we are going to be okay. Not when I have no idea what's going to happen. This lie, the blackmailing, the rumor. It could all blow up in my face. It could cost me so much more than just Lily.

Lily stares up at me, her crystal blue orbs hold my gaze and remind me of the ocean. I want to dive right inside them.

"You don't know that. If someone finds out, you'll lose your job."

My lips tip up at the sides, "I don't care anymore, Lily. It's just a job. I can find a new one somewhere else. I cannot find a new you."

Her eyes grow to the size of tennis balls, while tears slip from them and down her cheeks, but I don't think they're sad tears. There is happiness lingering in her eyes, a happiness I'll do anything to keep there, forever.

"You... you, would be okay losing your job for me?" She chews on her bottom lip, a nervous tick of hers, I've discovered. I'm mesmerized and feel the need to bite that plump bottom lip too.

"If it came down to it. If it was a choice between you or my job, then yes. I would choose you, and I wouldn't care one bit about what anyone had to say about it." I answer wholeheartedly, tucking a few strands of golden hair behind her ear.

"But you love your job," Lily points out.

"I do, but I love you more." I've been thinking about it a lot over the last few days. I've paid my blackmailer five thousand dollars to make the pictures disappear, to save my job, and to protect Lily from any type of heartache. In the end, I know this can't last forever. I'll have to come clean soon, but before I do, I need to make certain that Lily knows I'd risk it all to be with her. I would give up my job right now, to make certain that she was mine forever.

"I love you too," Lily whispers before pressing her lips against mine. Turning in my lap, she straddles me, wrapping her thin arms around my neck, beckoning me closer, and deepening the kiss. Her sweet coconut scent entraps me. I love everything about this woman. Every. Fucking. Thing. Whimpering, she grinds herself over my already hard cock, causing pleasure to ripple through my body. It's like I'm the lake and she is the rock skipping across the surface.

Fuck. I need her. I've never been so consumed by a person in my life. Yeah, I loved Amy, but it was never like this. It was never explosive, with a need that gripped me by the balls and refused to let go. Gripping her by the upper thighs, I stand up and carry her to our bed. I let myself fall back onto the mattress with her body still wrapped around mine. She kisses me wildly, moaning into my mouth while grinding her hot pussy onto my still clothed cock. There's too much fabric, too much shit in the way of our bodies.

When I can't take the teasing any longer, I flip us over, so she is lying on the bed, and I'm hovering above her. Keeping eye contact with her, I start to undress her, tugging at her leggings, and ripping her panties off before taking my own clothing off. She giggles and rolls her eyes as I toss everything to the floor.

"You're such an alpha." She grins from below, and I have half a mind to prove to her just how alpha-like I can be.

"I want you so bad," I groan into her open mouth as I lean forward to steal a kiss. "I want every single part of you. I want to devour you, feast on you for hours, to taste, and lick, to fuck, and keep you tied to this bed, so I can do whatever I want to you, whenever I want to do it."

"Take me," she pants, the blue in her eyes darkening like a fast-approaching storm, at my words, "I'm all yours. Take me. However, you want."

"However, I want?" I question a grin on my lips. I don't think she knows what she is asking for.

"Yes... however, you want."

"If that is what you want, then I need you on your hands and knees right now." As I say the words, I look deep into her eyes, looking for any sign that she might be second-guessing what she just offered, but all I see is red hot lust and maybe a smidge of curiosity.

Moving, so she can roll over she crawls up onto her hands and knees like I've instructed. With her back slightly bent and her ass jutted out, I get a perfect view of her sweet little pussy. Her arousal glistens against her folds, and the muscles in my belly tighten at the sight. She peers over her shoulder at me with come fuck me eyes, a waterfall of golden blonde hair hanging off the sides. Beautiful. Perfect.

The battle for control that I'm grappling with snaps and I climb up onto the bed situating myself behind her. My eyes lock on her pretty pink pussy, and her puckered asshole, that I know has never been fucked.

Every virgin hole on her body will belong to me someday.

"What are you going to do to me?" she whispers, her voice hoarse.

"Whatever I want..." I speak through my teeth, before leaning down and giving her pretty pussy a generous lick.

Lily mewls against the sheets, and I do it again just to hear her sweet voice. Gripping her by the thighs, I spread her legs further apart, and bury my face in that spot that was made especially for me. She tastes sweet and tangy, like salt and honey. I need more, all of it. Unable to hold back, I start to tongue her pussy, moving in and out with shallow little thrusts.

"If you keep doing that I'm going to come," she pants into the sheets, and all I do is grin against her folds as I continue to feast on her. I move my attention to her clit, spreading her folds with my fingers to find that hard little bud.

"Don't move or I'm going to spank you."

Lily grunts and I can only imagine the look on her face right now.

Bringing two fingers to her entrance, I enter her slowly, all while imagining it was my cock entering her, instead of my fingers. Lily greedily pushes back against my fingers wanting more, needing more, but I'm not ready to give it to her yet.

I stop moving my fingers and using my other hand, land a hard slap against her right butt cheek. There's a pink handprint left in my wake, and I can't lie and say I'm not satisfied with how pretty her ass looks with a splotch of pink on it. My mark.

I wait for her to say something, to do something, to tell me to stop, but she doesn't. Instead, she moans, she fucking moans. It sounds like sin and fucking joy, and I swear, I come a little right then.

"You like that? Having my fingers stuffed inside your pussy while I slap your ass? You want me to keep doing it? You want me to make you come?"

"Mmm, yes..." She whimpers, half into the sheets, half into the air. I don't even respond. Instead, I get to work, leaving the two fingers inside, while alternating between each ass cheek, soothing the sting away before landing another slap.

Her tight little muscles squeeze around my fingers, and I mutter a low fuck beneath my breath at the feeling.

"I'm coming." She gasps, as her body shakes, tremors of pleasure working their way through her.

"Squeeze my fingers, gush that come all over my hand," I order, pumping in and out of her a few more times to elongate her orgasm. Pulling my fingers from her cunt, I bring them to my lips and lick them clean.

Her arousal glistens against her thighs. She's so wet, so fucking ready for my cock and I need her. It's like I'm sick, dying a slow and painful death and she's the only antidote.

"Ride my cock," I order as I throw myself back onto the bed. Moving slowly, Lily climbs over on top of me. As soon as her fingers grasp my cock, I hiss.

"You're so big and gorgeous..." Lily's voice is shy and innocent, and it would be a lie to say, I don't love it. I love everything about her, but I love that I get to be the one to corrupt her.

"You're so fucking beautiful, and you're all mine," I growl, my hands moving to her hips to help her. The head of my cock brushes against her folds and my pulse pounds loudly in my ears as she lowers herself. My eyes drift closed as pleasure consumes every cell in my body, her tightness swallowing every inch of my cock.

Opening my eyes, I look up at her, she looks like a fucking goddess. My goddess, my world. She is the sun, the sky, the moon, and I'm caught in her orbit, forever stuck. She is my reason for breathing, my existence.

My thoughts shift the moment she drops her tiny hands to my chest, her nails sink into my flesh as she starts to ride my cock, up and down, up and down. I'm caught in a trap, unable to pull my gaze away. Pink cheeks. Swollen lips. Hooded eyes filled with simmering heat in them. Those golden locks of hers fall down her back like a cascading waterfall. Her slick heat consumes me, and I can't stop myself from thrusting upward, needing to hit that sweet spot at the back of her channel that makes her legs shake.

We move like this for a while, both of us rocking each other closer and closer to the edge of the cliff. Digging my fingers into the supple flesh at her hips, I drive into her. My thighs burn, and her slickness covers my lower abs as I fuck her, owning and worshiping her body all at once.

"Sebastian," she whimpers, her movements grinding her pelvis against me.

"Fuck, yeah, baby, come, come all over my cock," I demand, loving the way she looks as she brings herself to climax on my cock.

As soon as she starts to fall apart, I start to fuck her again, my hips piston. I thrust harder and harder, my jaw clenching as I plow through her squeezing cunt. It doesn't take but a few thrusts for me to shatter.

My cock twitches as hot sticky come erupts from deep within my balls and into her tight hole filling her until there isn't room for anything else.

Lily sags against my sweaty chest, and I lift my arm, draping it across her back, holding her close. It takes us both a while to catch our breaths, and the entire time all I can think about is doing this forever with Lily. Putting a ring on her finger and watching as her belly swells with my children.

I want it all. Forever. I almost laugh. Not all that long ago, I did everything I could to forget her, but now I'll do anything I can to hold onto her, to keep her as mine.

"I love you, Sebastian," Lily whispers into my chest, and I press a kiss to her sweaty forehead. She doesn't have to tell me. I already knew.

I knew when we first started this cat and mouse game. I knew because I, too, was falling for her, and I was afraid of what it meant. For us. For me.

"I love you too, Lily, and nothing is going to change that. I don't care if I lose my job. I don't care if I have to give everything up for you. All that matters is that I have you. That I don't lose you."

Lifting her head from my chest, she stares up at me, "You'll never lose me, but I don't want you to give up everything you've worked so hard for. I'm not worth all of that. All the years of work."

I want to be angry at her. I want to tell her she is wrong, but I don't. Lily doesn't understand how deep my feelings for her run, the things I'll do, the things I'm doing now to protect her, to protect us. There isn't anything I won't do to make sure we stay together.

Call me obsessed, call me crazy, but I won't give Lily up. Not without a fight.

"You're right, you're worth more, so much more."

She doesn't respond, but I can see that she wants to disagree with me. Instead, she rests her head back on my chest and lets me hold her and kiss her, all before we make love again.

16

LILY

A few days have passed, but I still can't let go of what Sebastian said. It gnaws at me like a cancer, overtaking every single free second of my life. I can't do this to him. I can't let him risk his job for me.

He loves his job. He loves being the dean and running the school, so the very thought of him giving it all up to stay with me is frightening. He might not think so now, but I know if he loses his dream job because of me, he will eventually resent me for it.

The thought is so frightening that I feel the need to put some space between us. I need to clear my head. I need to find a way to make him understand this. I just can't let him give everything up for me. I have to come up with a solution without him being a part of the equation right now.

The sleek cell phone weighs heavily in my hand as I contemplate my next move. I pace the floor, trying to find a solution that doesn't involve me leaving. I don't want to go. I don't want to hurt him by leaving, but I need to get away.

My head hurts as I think long and hard about what I'm about to do. I can't let him give it all up for me. I can't. I would never be able to live with myself. I'd feel guilty forever. The battle within me ends with my finger pushing the green call button on my phone.

The screen lights up as the phone dials my grandpa's number. Two rings later, my grandpa's deep voice fills the speaker.

"Lily, girl, is everything okay?"

"Hey, Papa. I'm okay. Just missing home. I was wondering if you could come and pick me up, and I could visit for the weekend?"

"Oh," is all he says, and the longest minute in history passes. Nervously, I chew on my lip, waiting for his response. "Uhh, sure, yeah, sweetheart. I'll come and get you tonight. I can be in North Woods by five. Do you want me to pick you up at the dorms?"

I nearly sigh with relief. I really thought he was going to say no. "Yes, that's perfect, thank you. I can't wait to see you." I'm a little surprised by how true this is. I might not have always had the best relationship with my grandparents, but it doesn't mean I don't miss them. They've been the only constant in my life since I lost my parents and my sister.

Familiar sadness engulfs me at the thought, and I start to feel guilty again. I have to stop doing this to myself.

"See you soon, Lily," my grandpa says as he hangs up the phone. I stare down at the screen for a long minute before putting the phone in my pocket. I know Sebastian isn't going to like this, not one bit, and I consider lying to him, even just leaving but decide against it. He would be pissed, and the last thing I need is him scouring the earth searching for me.

I'll just tell him and let the pieces fall where they may.

TWO HOURS LATER, Sebastian arrives home. I have half an hour before I need to be at the dorms and I'd rather not spend it fighting with him. As soon as he crosses the threshold, he presses a kiss to my lips and deposits his phone, wallet, and keys onto the counter.

"I'm going to take a quick shower, then we can talk about what-ever it is that you wanted to discuss." The grin he gives me causes an entire kaleidoscope of butterflies to take flight in my stomach. How am I going to do this? I can already feel myself being pulled toward him, his gravitational pull too strong for me to fight.

I must be wearing my emotions on my face because Sebastian asks a moment later, "Is everything okay? Would you rather we talk now?"

No. God, no. I need a minute to breathe.

"No. No, it's okay." I respond and nervously tuck some hair behind my ear.

Sebastian looks skeptical, "Are you sure?"

"Yes, go shower, you stink," I snicker, and squeeze my nose shut, wafting my hand in front of it.

Sebastian rolls his eyes and starts down the hall, "Whatever. I do not."

With him out of sight and earshot, I lean against the table. It physically hurts me to think about leaving him, about how he's going to react when I tell him what I'm going to do.

The sound of the shower carries down the hall. At the same time, his phone starts to go off. Ignoring it, I walk into the kitchen for a bottle of water. It's probably Remington, or Lex. Walking back to the table, his phone continues to vibrate, and my annoyance over it mounts.

Who the hell texts that many times? I don't want to be that nosy girlfriend that goes through her boyfriend's shit. Sebastian has never done anything to make me feel like he would step out on me, that doesn't stop me from grabbing the phone though. Whoever is messaging him must really need him. The phone lights up in my hand, a message appearing on the screen.

UNKNOWN NUMBER: If you expect me to keep what you two are doing a secret, you'll need to pay me more than ten thousand dollars.

It takes me a moment to digest what I just read, but once I do it's, like I'm a plane nose-diving toward the ground. My heart sinks as I stare at the screen, reading the message ten more times before dropping the phone onto the table.

My head is swimming with questions, and none of them are good. *Someone is blackmailing Seb?* Because of me, us? Why wouldn't he tell me, or go to the police? He said he didn't care if he lost his job, but now he's paying someone off to keep us a secret. Confusion.

Dread. Anger and sadness. They all blend together. Why would he do that? Why would he pay someone off?

My head starts to pound, my mind feels like it's overloading. Like it's about to explode, and all I can think to do is run, to get out of here. I don't allow myself to think on it a second longer, afraid I may change my mind. Running into the bedroom, I grab the bag I've already packed out of the walk-in closet and speed walk out of the house, closing the door gently behind me, even when I want to slam it.

Once outside, it feels like I can breathe easier, but my heart and my head still ache. Walking aimlessly down the road, I turn off onto a smaller side road, and then another, and another, in hopes Sebastian won't be able to find me if he comes looking.

When I come to a small park within the neighborhood, I text my grandpa the address, asking him to pick me up here instead.

Twenty minutes later, the familiar station wagon pulls up in front of me, and my grandpa greets me with a weathered smile. His salt and pepper hair looks the same as the day I left. I'm so happy to see him that I almost cry. I open the door and slide into the passenger's seat. I throw my bag into the back seat before hugging his side and letting him kiss me on the top of the head like he's always done.

"Hey, sweetheart, you doing okay?" his gruff voice asks.

"Better now, I missed you," I admit while buckling up.

"We missed you too, sweetie, but I have to be honest, I'm surprised you do. I thought once you were in college, we would hardly ever hear from you, let alone see you," he chuckles, but I know his statement is true. Guilt and sadness overcome me at his words, and I know he is right. I certainly wasn't planning on coming back besides maybe Christmas and Thanksgiving, and even that was questionable.

I've never quite accepted living with my grandparents, and they never quite accepted that I was still here when their beloved daughter wasn't. I've heard *your mother would've never done that* one too many times not to know they resent me for being here when she isn't.

"I guess it took me to get away to realize how much you mean to me."

My grandpa clears his throat, clearly uncomfortable with the sudden emotional turn the conversation has taken. "So how are your grades?" he asks, desperate to change the subject.

"I'm passing all of my classes," I say, keeping out the part that I'm only barely passing some of them.

"Well, that's good to hear. We were worried about that. You know you haven't always been great with your academics... not like your mom was." *And there it is.* Just like that, I'm reminded why I couldn't get out of my grandparents' house fast enough.

Swallowing my pride, I don't answer with a snarky remark like I want to. Instead, I smile and try to forget that he said it in the first place. I sink back into the seat and try not to think about anything at all. Not about my grandparents, not about my parents and sister dying, and definitely not about Sebastian, the blackmail, and the fact that he could lose everything because of me.

"DINNER IS READY," my grandma's voice booms down the hall.

"Coming," I call back, but continue mixing the red and black on my pallet. I make a few more strokes on the canvas before depositing my brush into the water-filled mason jar. I step back and take in the now painted canvas.

With all my art stuff around, my room looks more like an art studio than a teenage girl's bedroom. I guess not much has changed. I'm perfectly fine with it though. I love the smell of the paint, the way the brush feels in my hand. My most favorite thing is being able to manipulate the paint to bend it to my will and create a world exactly the way I want to.

Painting gives me a sense of control that I've never had at any time in my life. I control the brush and the paint, no one else interferes, and when I mess up, I let the paint dry and paint right over it. Life doesn't have do-overs like painting does. Life is hard.

Before I leave the room, I open the drawer of my desk to look at the phone inside. It has been ringing non-stop since I arrived here. Most of the phone calls have been Sebastian, but there are plenty from Del, Jules, and even Rem tried calling a few times.

I only answered Jules and Del once and only to tell them I'm okay and safe. I didn't want them to worry or file a missing person report or something. Other than that, I ignored the plethora of missed calls and messages. I need time to think, to breathe. I don't want to let Sebastian sway my choices. I know he loves his job, and I know he wants me to stay in school, but I don't know if that's feasible.

After discovering that he's paying someone off to hide us, to keep us a secret, I'm not just sad, but angry. I don't want to be a secret anymore. I don't want to hide what we're doing.

Which leaves me with only one option.

Closing the drawer, I make my way through the house and into the dining room.

"Wash your hands, child, your fingers are covered in paint," my grandma orders.

I do as she asks without complaint and dry my hands with the dishtowel. Then I walk to the table which is already set. My grandma is a little different than my grandpa. While my grandpa does throw jabs at me, I can tell he loves me. My grandmother, on the other hand, is closed off. She's never said she wished I was in the car that day, but she doesn't have to.

Sitting at the table across from Grandpa, my grandmother makes my plate and hands it back to me like I'm a small child.

"I see you're still doing that painting stuff."

Stabbing at a green bean with my fork, I say, "Yup."

"That's a nice hobby to have, as long as it doesn't interfere with your schoolwork. You know that's the most important thing, right? You can't make money with art."

The metal of the fork bites into my flesh. "So, you've said."

"It's the truth. You need a steady income and painting isn't going to give you that. Plus, no one is going to take you serious with that kind of career."

"Actually, that's what I wanted to talk to you about...or at least get your advice on." It's a stupid thing to ask because I already know they're both going to tell me I'm an idiot for even considering dropping out to pursue art, but like the sadist I am, I ask anyway.

"Well, what is it?" Grandma questions, impatiently.

The tension grows thick between us, the words hanging off the edge of my tongue.

Setting the fork on my plate, I look up at both of them. The only two family members, I have left. The only two people, I have to look to for advice.

"I'm thinking about dropping out of college and doing something with art. I would really like to get an apprenticeship..."

"No," my grandma cuts me off, her voice stern. "Your parents would never forgive us for letting you drop out to pursue something like *that*. Did you ever hear of the term starving artist? That term didn't come out of thin air."

"I just don't think I'm cut out for college," I whisper.

"Of course, you are, you just need to get this art nonsense out of your head and concentrate on your studies. You need to think of the big picture here. Where would you live if you dropped out of school now? Would you come back here?"

I shrug, "I was thinking just until I find something..."

"Lily," my grandma cuts me off once more. "You know we loved having you here, but you can't stay here forever. You know, we don't have the money for an extra person to be living with us, and you're an adult now. You need to grow up and take care of yourself."

"It would only be for a short while..."

"Enough, you're not dropping out of school to chase after some ridiculous dream of becoming an artist. If you do, then you'll lose our support completely."

She's not serious, is she? Looking at her, I can see that she's more than serious, in fact, she looks like she's ready to tell me to get out right this second, and the fact that she said *our* tells me that they've already talked about this. Anger burns through me like a wildfire moving through the forest.

"If my parents were still alive, they would support my choices. They'd want me to follow my dreams. They wouldn't treat me the way that you both are right now."

"You're wrong. Your mother would never have allowed you to pursue art. There is no money in art, and without money, you cannot live. I'm sorry, child, but I will not allow you to live under mine and your grandpa's roof while chasing some dream that's never going to happen. I've already told you. If you drop out, any support we've given you is gone."

Emotions clog my throat, and I have to blink to fight back the tears. For years I've wished my parents were alive, but I've never missed them more than I do right now.

I need support, love, and I'm not going to find any of those things here. Coming here, back to this house, back to them, it was a mistake. Shoving from the table, I nearly knock the chair over as I get up.

"Where are you going?" my grandmother asks, her voice edging on anger.

"Leaving. Coming here was a mistake. I don't know why I ever thought to come back here. Maybe I was hoping you guys would show that you cared about me for once and didn't see me as the only reminder of your daughter, of the three people you lost."

"We don't see you like that," Grandpa adds, but it's too late because I know deep down, they do. I'm a screw-up, a reminder of three lives that no longer exist and as long as I stay here, that's all I'll ever be to them.

"It sure feels like that," I accuse, turning and storming out of the room. Taking two steps at a time, I rush up the stairs and into my room. I'm a burden to everyone. I can't stay here. I can't be a reminder. Coming here was supposed to help things, but it seems it's only made them worse. With tears in my eyes, I get my phone out of my desk. There's only one person to call, and that's the one person I ran from, the one person that I need, the one person that I know will support whatever decisions I make.

With tears sliding down my cheeks, I dial his number. He picks up on the first ring as if he was doing nothing more than staring at the screen, waiting for me to call.

"Lily," my name comes out in a sigh. The sound of his deep voice filtering into my ears is already calming me. "Are you okay? Please tell me you're okay?"

"I'm-I'm okay. Can you come and pick me up?" I croak while attempting to hide that I've been crying. I don't want or need anyone to feel bad for me, least of all, Sebastian. He's already got enough on his plate when it comes to us, and I don't want to burden him anymore.

"Of course, where are you? I'll leave right now."

"I'm in Blackthorn, at my grandparents."

"Okay," I can hear the jingling of keys and the closing of a door which tells me he's already walking out of the house. "I'm leaving now. I'll see you soon."

A car door opens and closes, and the roar of his engine fills my ears.

"See you soon," I whisper before hanging up.

I want to say I love you to him, I wanted to tell him how much he means to me, but it feels like if I do, it'll only make letting go of him that much harder. I'm a mistake. All I do is hurt the people around me. I'm a burden to everybody. I shouldn't be alive right now, and I shouldn't be living my sister's dream, sleeping with the man that she loved for years. I'm going to cost him everything. I'm going to ruin everything simply by existing.

Everything is falling apart, and I wish so badly that I was that canvas across the room. That I had the power to let myself dry so that I could paint myself a new past, a new beginning, and a new ending. A better ending.

17

SEBASTIAN

*S*he called. She fucking called. It's all I can think about as I drive two towns over to Blackthorn to get her. I don't care how far I have to drive to get to her. All that matters is having her in my arms again. I break about every speed limit there is just to get to her faster. I was so fucking worried when she was just gone. My mind was wandering to the worst possible case scenario. I couldn't get what she had said to me that night in her dorm room out of my head.

"I tried to end it."

She sends me the address in a text, and I use the GPS to find the way. The closer I get, the better I feel, even though my heart is pounding against my ribcage like it's trying to break free and take flight.

When I finally turn onto the road and see her standing on the sidewalk, it feels like a huge weight has been lifted off my chest, and I can breathe again at last. Stopping right in front of her, I put the car in park and get out. Practically, running around the car to get to her. Before I reach her, I take in her face.

It's red and blotchy giving away that she's been crying. Guilt rears its ugly head. Had she not found those texts, maybe none of this would've happened. Instantly, I'm overcome with the need to make her feel better, to tell her everything is going to be okay because it is.

Wrapping my arms around her, I pull her into my chest and bury my nose in her hair. Coconut, and vanilla with a hint of paint. She doesn't fight me, in fact, she does the same, dropping her bags onto the concrete, so she can wrap her arms around me. I sigh, feeling as if all the missing pieces in my life are coming back together once again.

"I'm so sorry, Lily. I'm so sorry," I repeat, holding her tighter, vowing never to hide anything from her again. These last couple of days have shown me just how hard it is to live without her. I can't eat. I can't sleep. I can't do anything without her. She is everything to me and losing her again is not an option.

"Don't be. I'm the one that's sorry," she murmurs, and when I pull away to look at her face, I find she's crying again. There's a pressure that appears in my chest as I look at her. I don't want her to cry anymore, not ever, and least of all, because of something I did. Brushing away the tears with my thumb, I press a kiss to each rosy red cheek. Damn, I've missed her.

"I'm sorry," she sniffles again, all the emotions crashing into me at once, "I'm sorry that you're being blackmailed. That I hurt you by leaving. I just needed some space, but it was a mistake to come here. Everything is a mistake. I'm a mistake." I can see her falling apart, and it's tearing me right down the middle.

"Stop you're not a mistake, and you have no reason to be sorry. I love you. I love you so fucking much. None of this would've happened had I been honest with you. Had I told you the truth about the blackmailing, but I didn't want you to worry, or leave, but it seems the opposite happened." I tuck a strand of hair that's stuck to her tear-stained cheek behind her ear.

"I was so fucking worried about you," I admit. "Do you remember what you said to me the night you were drunk, and I brought you to the dorms?" She thinks for a moment before she shakes her head slightly. "You told me you'd thought about ending it all. What did you mean by that?"

More tears run down her face, and I almost regret bringing it up, but I need to know what's going on in her head. I need her to be safe, even from herself.

"I can't believe I told you that... You don't have to worry though. I haven't had those thoughts in a long time, and I never acted on them, but in the past, it did cross my mind that everybody around me would be better off with me dead."

"Don't ever think that, Lily. I wouldn't be able to go on without you. I need you to promise me that you will never hurt yourself and if you ever have those kind of thoughts again you need to tell me immediately so we can get you help."

"I promise," she answers right away, sounding determined and sincere. "I swear, I haven't thought like that in a while, but if those thoughts ever return I'll talk to someone." I feel like a weight has been lifted off my chest.

I don't want her to cry anymore. I want to share the good news that I received over the weekend, the news, I had been waiting to hear for the last week.

"Can we go?" she finally asks. "I already look like a hot mess standing out here. I don't want to have another breakdown where the rest of the world can see."

Releasing her, even though, I don't want to, I nod, and gesture for her to get into the car, while I grab her bags. She moves slowly toward the door, and by the time I'm in the driver's seat, she's just buckling her seatbelt.

"Are you hungry?"

"Yeah. I kinda walked out on dinner, so I could go for something to eat." She gives me a sad smile that damn near breaks my heart in two. I don't say anything else as I drive us through the drive-through at McDonald's. Once we have our food, I park in the parking lot and roll down the windows. Lily sips on her strawberry shake, her eyes trained on the windshield. I wonder what she's thinking. I'm smart enough to know why she left, and I want to make sure she never does again. She's everything to me, and she needs to know that.

"I know now isn't the time to do it, but I can't stand the sadness in your eyes, and I have to do something to make it better."

She shifts, looking away from the windshield and at me.

"I have something I want to tell you too." She pauses, and those bright blue eyes of hers meet mine, "I didn't leave because I don't want to be with you. I left because I didn't want you to have to give everything up for me. I was trying to come up with a solution that worked for both of us. I was going to drop out of classes and wanted some advice, but my grandparents weren't the kind of people I should've gone to." A frown pulls at her lips, "They told me that if I drop out of school, I'll lose all of their support." She snorts, "As if they were all that supportive, to begin with."

Reaching out, I place my hand on top of hers. I just need to feel her, to touch her, to know that she's actually here with me.

"I didn't think you left or were leaving me, but I freaked out knowing you'd seen the messages. I was just worried..." I sigh, "I may have lost it a little bit. But as I sat there in the living room all alone in the dark, I started to piece it all together. I knew you were feeling guilty, and that you were upset. I knew that you were worried about being a burden when you're truly anything but that to me."

"I thought..." Lily looks down at my hand on hers and then interlocks our fingers. Shame fills her face. "I just don't understand why you didn't tell me. Why did you keep this from me? Don't you trust me?"

The sadness pours out of her like a sink that's overflowing, "I trust you with my life, Lily. I was just scared, and I didn't want you to worry or feel guilty." In that moment, I feel like a pile of shit. "All I wanted was to make it go away as fast as possible, and I thought that paying them off would do that. Of course, I thought about telling you and going to the cops. But I decided against all that because I didn't want everybody to find out about us that way."

Lily's lips form into a frown, "I knew you were worried, but I would like to worry with you next time. This concerns both of us after all, and we're together, which means your worries and fears are mine too."

"I won't keep anything from you ever again," I promise her.

"So, what are we going to do about it now? Go to the police?"

"We can, but I don't know what they could do. I already put some cash in an envelope and dropped it in the park's trash can. I haven't heard from whoever this fucker is since then." Lily nods, and I continue, "I really don't want to think about it right now though. All I want to do is enjoy having you back and make sure you know that I won't ever keep something like that from you again. When you left it almost killed me."

"Me too." She whispers. "I missed you every day."

"I'm pretty sure I missed you more, and I have something else I want to tell you."

"What do you mean?"

For the first time in days, I smile, "I may have used my status as the Dean of the university to pull a couple strings at the brand new gallery in town."

Those big eyes of hers seem to get bigger as she realizes what I've done. "You got me a spot for one of my paintings?"

"One?" I snort, and my grin grows at the same rate as her eyes widen. "You've got your own exhibit."

"What?" she squeals, jumping in her seat and almost knocking her food off her lap. "Oh, my god, Sebastian. Are you serious? You're lying right now. You have to be."

"Very serious," I tell her, taking in her wide smile and the bright sparkle in her eyes. "I was waiting to hear back from them before I mentioned anything about it. I didn't want to get your hopes up if it didn't work out."

"Oh, my god. Oh, my god." Her chest rises and falls rapidly, and I can hear her breathing from across the seat. "I can't believe this. How did you do it?"

"All I did was send them a few pictures of your paintings. They loved all your stuff and can't wait to have you. Your exhibit is in two weeks."

That does it. The cheeseburgers on her lap fall to the floor as she basically crawls across the center console and into my lap.

"Two weeks?"

I nod, joy consuming me. This makes all of it worth it. I would rather have not had her leave and been able to explain everything to her, but, at the very least, I was able to fix this. I was able to make it so we can be together without being a secret.

Lily runs her fingers through my hair, and pulls my head into her chest, squeezing me tightly. Fuck, I could die a happy man right now.

"Holy shit. I have a ton of work to do. A ton of things to paint, and..." She releases me only to bring her lips to mine. She kisses me like I'm the air she needs to breathe. Of course, my cock starts to come to life with her tight little body rubbing against me, and her pink lips on mine. I would kiss her all day and night if I had the time.

"Thank you, thank you so much. You're the only one that believed in my art. That believed in me." Tears glisten in her blue orbs, and I'm so tired of seeing her cry. I only want to see her smile. I only want to see her face filled with ecstasy as I bring her to climax on my cock, fingers, and tongue.

"I love you, Lily. I love you so fucking much, and I'm so happy that you're happy, but if you keep wiggling that ass of yours against my cock, I'm not going to be liable for what I do."

Lily's movements come to a halt, and she pulls back, a sly little grin on her lips. I look her up and down, her adorable button nose, delicate throat, and cheeks that are tinted a light pink. *You're corrupting her, Sebastian. She was a virgin when she met you.*

"What do you want to do, Mr. Miller?" The way her tongue flicks over her bottom lip as she says my name has me envisioning a whole lot of things. I've missed this, her, all of it. She's never leaving again, never. I don't care if I have to tie her to the bed.

"Do you want the PG-13 version or the R-rated?" I cock a brow and let one of my hands trail over her shirt covered chest. I can feel her hardened nipples through the thin fabric of her bra. They're begging to be released, to be sucked on. Jesus, she wants me to fuck her just as badly as I want to. "We need to get home, like right now... right now. Sit back down in your seat and buckle up," I order. My cock presses against the zipper of my jeans in protest.

Not yet, asshole.

With a displeased whimper, she follows my directions and crawls back into the passenger seat, pulling the seat belt over her body and clicking it into place.

"You didn't want to fuck me in the McDonald's parking lot?" Lily asks as I start the car. She's looking at me with a mischievous glint in her eyes, so I know she's only egging me on.

"No, I wanted to do so much more than fuck you in the parking lot. I wanted to do things to you that would scare all the families away." Lily shifts in her seat, her thighs rubbing together, telling me that she is turned on by my words. "You want me to show you what I had in mind?"

"Yes," Lily says breathlessly, and for the second time today, I break every speed limit on this damn road until I pull up into my driveway with tires squealing. The need to feel her naked body underneath my own is so overwhelming, all the worry and heartache from this weekend seem a million years away.

I lead her into the house, the house that's only ever felt like a home since she's been living here with me. Bringing her to the bedroom, I slowly strip off her clothes, before stripping out of my own.

With her naked body sprawled out on my bed, her golden blonde hair framing her head with a crown of gold, she looks like a goddess. *My goddess.*

"Do you have any idea how beautiful and sexy you look right now?"

She nibbles at her bottom lip and shakes her head softly. "But I do know how handsome and sexy you look right now." The giggle she emits goes straight to my groin.

"Is that so?" I tease as I crawl up and over her wriggling body.

"Yes, that is very much so, Mr. Miller..." And that's all she can get out before my lips clash against hers and I try to tell her with my body what words couldn't...that I'm sorry, so fucking sorry. I should have never kept anything from her. I love her more than life itself.

Until now, sex with Lily has been passionate, raw, and sexy. This is all of the above, but still, it's different, because it's more. This is lovemaking... two people coming together, forming one soul. I can feel her becoming part of me with every second that passes, and while it terrifies me, it excites me at the same.

Taking her slowly, I thrust into her deeply, so deeply that I can't tell where she starts, and I begin. All I can do is claim her, worship her as she should be.

"You're so deep," Lily whimpers as I kiss against her jawline.

"Am I hurting you?" I stop mid-thrust, praying like hell that I'm not. It would pain me to stop right now, but I would.

Her eyes shine brightly in the dim lighting of the room, "No, it feels good, it's just different." I get the feeling she can't put into words how what we're doing feels because neither can I. All I can do is continue to thrust, grinding my body into her center, swallowing every whimper and cry.

We go like this for what seems like forever, me rocking into her, feeling the beat of her heart against mine. Sweat dribbles down my back, and forms against my forehead, my muscles straining with the slow strokes. My body begs me to fuck her, hard, deep, fast, but my mind, my heart, it knows better. It knows that the reward, though, it may take more time, will be far greater if I do it this way.

Lily's nails sink into my arm, and I hiss through my teeth, keeping my rhythm the same.

"More, please, more," Lily pants, as she tries to lift her hips to gain more friction, but I ignore her pants, and instead, kiss her, continuing my leisurely strokes.

Slowly, I up my pace, but only a little and just enough to set her off into a spiral of pleasure.

"I'm... I'm..." She's so caught up in the pleasure, her mouth forming the perfect O that she doesn't even finish her sentence.

Instead, her channel tightens around my length, squeezing the fuck out of me, making it damn near impossible for me to move in and out of her. Gritting my teeth, I hang on to the last shreds of patience I have, and fuck her, letting the pleasure build at the base of my cock. When I finally fall apart, coming like I've never come before, Lily is right behind me, my name nothing more than a hoarse scream on her lips.

Collapsing against her, I barely catch myself before I crush her with my body. We're both sweaty, our chests heaving as we try and catch our breaths.

"That was..."

"Amazing?" I turn and grin at her.

"Yes, but it was different, it was..." Lily looks unsure of how to explain herself, and I get what she's saying, I don't understand it either. There are no words to describe what just happened between us. All I know is that she touched something deep inside of me, something that no one has ever touched before, and because of her, I'll never be the same. There is no life after Lily. There is only her. Only us.

I can't believe it. I just can't wrap my mind around this. It's amazing. I'm standing in the center of the gallery looking at the many paintings displayed all around the walls... but these aren't just any paintings, they're mine. My paintings are on the walls, being sold, and displayed to everyone.

"Everything looks great," Sebastian whispers into my ear, his arms wrapping possessively around my waist.

"Stop," I order attempting to push him away even though I really want to do the same to him, "People are going to be here soon. Other students, and you know, your staff."

The gallery is still empty, but hopefully, it will be bustling with people when the doors open. Even if it isn't, I'll mark this day down as a success.

"Okay," he pulls away with a frown. "I'll save it all for later." Even though we've been having sex every night, I feel like we haven't touched in months. It's how I always feel about him now. It's like I can't get enough like I'm always starving for more.

The sound of high heels clicking against the gallery's pristine hardwood floor meets my ears, and when I look away from the wall, I see Margret, the gallery's manager walking out of the back room. Actually, not walking, more like runway strutting.

"Lily, darling! Everything looks wonderful," she exclaims, waving her hands dramatically through the air. That is how I would describe her entire personality and personal style, *dramatic*. From her hair to her shoes, she reminds me of a peacock, always having her beautiful feather train on full display.

"Thank you, Margret, it means so much to be here and have my paintings displayed in your gallery," I tell her wholeheartedly. She has no idea how much this... her support really means to me. Some commotion in the back room draws our attention, and for the slightest moment, I worry that something might be wrong.

"That must be the catering service," she chimes and walks back, swinging her hips like she is walking down the catwalk. "Corbin, please watch the paintings," she calls walking a little faster. I turn and meet Sebastian's eyes, both of our lips turning up into massive grins.

"Is it bad that I want to take you back into one of the studio rooms and have my way with you?" His words cause a rush of heat to pulse through me.

"Sebastian," I warn knowing if he touches me, I'll end up giving in to him. I'm drunk on him. High off his love, and his touch all but short circuits my brain. I haven't dropped out of classes yet, but if I have my way, I will soon. I'm tired of school, I want to concentrate on my art, and I'm tired of sneaking around.

"Yes, I know. I'll behave myself, but it doesn't mean I'm not going to be thinking about stripping you down when I get home."

Shaking my head, I ignore the heat that flames my cheeks and walk over to a different set of paintings to put some space between us. I can practically see Sebastian grinning out of the corner of my eye. That bastard. He knows what he does to me.

It doesn't take long before people start to file in, Jules, Remington, and Lex are the first people to walk through the door, they all showed up to show their support, and the gesture isn't lost on me. Especially knowing that my grandparents are not going to come. Trying to force the thought away, I turn my attention back to Jules.

"Congratulations, Lily," Jules beams with excitement as she wraps her arms around me, "All these paintings are gorgeous."

"Thank you." I'm not sure if I'll ever get used to all this praise.

"It'll be nice to have an artist in the family," Remington says next, also giving me a hug. I don't respond because what the hell do I say to that? I'm not really part of their family, but they have been treating me as such since I came back to North Woods. Still, Sebastian and I aren't going to get married anytime soon. That is unless Rem knows something I don't.

Jules elbows him in the side and rolls her eyes, "Don't worry, he's just making plans inside his head for his brother."

"Take a look around and let me know if you see anything you like. I may know the artist and could possibly get you a discount," I wink as I'm walking away. Jules gives me a tiny wave, and I meander around the room, conversing with the other guests. I do my best not to get jealous when a group of female professors walk in and greet Sebastian.

All I want to do is scream he's mine when I recognize one of the women, it's the woman I've seen him with twice now. The last time I saw her was the night in his office, and even though that night ended well, the sting of jealousy remains.

She innocently places her hand on his arm, and it takes everything in me not to walk over there and remove it. I can't wait till the day that everyone can know that he's mine and I'm his. As if he realizes she's touching him, he takes a step back, putting some space between them. I can feel eyes on me, and when I look up, I find Sebastian staring at me. The heat in his gaze is enough to burn me to the ground.

My core tightens. *Stop staring at me.* I will my gaze to say, but instead, I'm sure I look like a doe waiting for the hunter.

The night carries on, and more and more people fill the gallery, looking at my paintings in awe. Soon all the paintings that adorned the walls of the gallery are sold, and I'm left standing in the middle of the room, my entire face filled with wonderment.

"Lily, love, it seems as though you are a hit." Margret smiles, showing off her perfectly straight white teeth, a flute of champagne in her hand.

"Thank you, Margret. I'm a little shocked. I can't believe it if I'm being honest." And I can't. I went from being told there was no money in art, that I would never make it, to selling every single painting in one night.

Margret rolls her eyes, "Please, I knew the moment that I met you, you were destined for great things. When Mr. Miller showed me one of your paintings, I was... I cannot even describe it. You literally gave me goosebumps."

I'm not sure what to say. In fact, I'm a little speechless.

Thankfully, my brain connects the dots, so I'm not standing there like a mute unable to speak, "Thank you. Thank you so much. I've always been told that I would never be able to support myself with my art, and while I'm not doing this to make money, I truly love painting, to be able to do this for life, for a job, it would be nothing but a dream come true."

She smiles against the flute of champagne, "Is that so?"

I nod, "Yes, it's my dream. My biggest goal."

"Hmmm," she purses her red lips, "what if I told you that I had a spot for you. A full-time apprenticeship?"

Shock fills my features, and the swooshing of blood fills my ears. She didn't just say what I think she did, did she?

"What?" I ask, even though I'm pretty sure I heard her correctly.

"Full-time paid apprenticeship. It's yours if you want it."

"Really?" I lift a hand to my chest. My heart feels like it's going to burst right out of my chest. Margret nods her head and smiles.

"Is it really so hard to believe? You sold every single painting tonight and brought in many new customers. I would be stupid not to bring you on."

"I...." I'm floundering, my lips aren't moving, and I probably look like a fish plucked out of the water, gasping for air.

Placing a hand on my shoulder, she leans in with a smile, "A thank you is sufficient enough, darling. I'm more than excited to be working together. I already know there are great things to come from our joining."

"Thank you," I whisper graciously.

"You're welcome, now go celebrate and do whatever it is that you college kids do." She moves her hand from my shoulder and waves it in the air, in a get out motion.

"I was going to stay and help you clean up."

"No need, child. We have a cleaning company that will do that for us. Go enjoy the rest of your night. I'll call you tomorrow, and we'll talk about all the details for your apprenticeship," she says, before giving me kisses on each cheek.

She turns around and heads to the back room. Only then, do I realize Sebastian has been standing a few feet away. I look over my shoulder, and our eyes meet. "Did you hear?"

He nods, a massive grin on his lips. I spin around all the way and fall into his arms. We are the last two people left in the gallery, so we don't have to hide our affection any longer.

"Let's go home and celebrate," Seb suggests, tugging me toward the door. "I always wanted to bang a famous artist."

We leave the gallery laughing, hand in hand, we walk to Seb's car, and I can't remember the last time I was this happy. Maybe not ever. Once in the car, I turn to Seb.

"So... I've been thinking," I start while Seb pulls into the road. "I want to drop out of school, and before you say anything, I will tell you that I have been thinking about this for a while. This is not a spur of the moment thing. Honestly, I never wanted to go to college anyway. I only went because of my grandparents. This is what I've been wanting to do, and getting this position just sealed the deal for me." The words pour out in a faster than normal tempo, and when I'm done, I find I'm sitting there waiting for him to respond.

All my life, I have been a disappointment to people around me, never meeting anyone's expectations. I don't want Seb to be disappointed in me too. If he was, it would crush me.

"Lily, if that's what you want to do, then I will support your decision one hundred percent. I'm so proud of you," he tells me, and I can't stop the tear from trailing down my cheek.

"Really?" I gasp, and it feels like I can finally breathe like I've escaped the suffocating pressure on my chest.

"Really... although, as your dean, I should probably advise you against dropping out," he chuckles. "You know education is impor-tant, blah blah blah..."

"Dean Miller, is that what you tell all your students?"

"No, just the ones I'm in love with."

"I love you too." *So, so much.*

19

SEBASTIAN

"So, things are good now? You're officially together?" Rem asks before taking a drink of his beer. It's guys night, him, Lex and I are chilling at his house eating pizza and drinking beer like a group of frat boys.

I nod, "Yeah, we're together, and it's serious, and we don't have to worry about hiding it or someone seeing us."

I can't believe how much better I felt once Lily dropped out, not that I would've cared if she had stayed, college just wasn't something she ever wanted to do. Painting was her dream, and I was going to do everything I could to help her achieve her goals. But I'm not going to lie, being able to kiss her in front of everyone, being able to touch her and say this is my woman, it's been amazing.

"I can't believe you're boning your dead girlfriend's sister," Lex says, careless to Amy's memory. I try not to let it bother me, he doesn't understand, and he's going through his own shit, but it hurts a little.

"Don't be a dick," Rem grumbles, staring Lex down.

"Sorry," Lex says a moment later, "my heads all over the place. I didn't mean to be a dick. I'm happy for you and Lily."

"Thanks, brother. Now we just gotta find you a woman."

"Yeah, no." He shakes his head and takes a drink of his beer,

"Women are too much fucking work, and right now the only thing I need to be working on is myself."

"Right, but I don't think I've seen you with a girl..." Rem taps at his chin, "Well, I haven't seen you with a girl in forever."

Lex rolls his eyes, "Don't need a girl."

"Oh, wait, there was that one girl, what's her name, Tina, Talila?"

"Taylor, and she's not my girl. She's Shawn's little sister, and I wouldn't touch her even if I knew her brother wouldn't chop my balls off for doing it."

Rem smiles, "That sounds like interest, or at least like you've thought about it."

"Seriously?" Lex's face turns serious, "I like my balls too much."

"Yup, definitely sounds like you've thought about screwing her, doesn't it, Seb?" Rem asks, trying to sway me into this teasing argument.

"No comment," I mumble while grabbing a slice of pizza from the box in front of me and take a bite. Being the middle brother always means I'm the one to break the tie or break up the argument between the two of them.

"Come on, Lex, just admit it. Just once." Rem's voice rises with each word.

"No."

"Yes." Rem mocks.

Lex squeezes his beer bottle and looks like he's grappling with his thoughts, "Okay, okay. I have. But I'll never cross that line. I value my life too much, plus Taylor is young, a little naive, and way too good for an ass like me."

"Lily's ten years younger than me, but that hasn't changed anything."

"It's not happening, and I only admitted it so he would shut up." Lex points to Rem who is smiling like a kid on Christmas morning.

"I wouldn't admit anything to him, especially if you want him to shut up, because all he's going to do now is talk, talk, and talk."

"For fuck's sake, seriously?" Lex growls with frustration.

"Yup, now you have to explain." Rem settles into the couch, staring up at our older brother like it's storytime. I swear now that he's settled down with Jules and let go of all his anger, and pain he's more of a kid than an adult. Sometimes, I wish he would go back to being the lost kid that needed guidance. *Sometimes.*

"There is nothing to explain, Rem," Lex's face pales, and we can tell right away that he's hiding something. Before Rem or I can say anything, the front door opens, and Jules walks in, a couple shopping bags in her hands.

Her big blue eyes land first on Rem, and then on Lex and me.

"Shoot, it's guys night," she mumbles under her breath as she closes the door behind herself. "Sorry, I totally spaced it. I'm just going to go crawl into bed." An apologetic smile appears on her lips, but she looks too exhausted to look happy.

"You're welcome to join us, babe," Rem offers, getting up off the couch. She lifts a hand as if it's a stop sign.

"No, no. I'm not feeling well, and I wouldn't be very good company. You boys have fun and drink some beer for me."

When she disappears down the hall, I turn to Rem, "Is she okay?"

Rem's jaw clenches, his eyes fall closed for a minute, and he looks like he might be contemplating something.

"Yeah, she's okay, she's just..."

I stare at him, waiting for him to spill the beans.

"Well?" Lex says with the same level of impatience.

Rem leans in like he's telling us a secret, "She's pregnant." Shock is the first thing I feel, followed by excitement, and then shock again.

"We don't know when she's due or anything yet. She's just been really tired, and suffering from some pretty bad morning sickness."

"Well, holy fuck, you've been chipping away at me looking for secrets when you've been holding one in all night."

Rem shrugs, "You never asked, so I had no reason to tell you anything."

"You're such an idiot," Lex laughs and throws his pizza crust at him. "Is Jules okay with you telling us?"

"I hope so, if not, then I guess I'm in trouble." He shrugs. Holy shit, my little brother is going to be a dad. I never thought the day would come.

"How do you feel about becoming a dad?" I ask, seriously curious about what's going through his head right now.

"Honestly, I don't think it's hit me yet. It's so surreal, I don't really know what to think. I always thought you and Lex would have kids first. I always envisioned myself being the cool uncle for a few years before I had my own kids, but now... it's just crazy to think I'll have kids before you guys." Rem shrugs, a grin growing on his face, "I guess it was meant to be this way. I've always been better at everything, even at making babies."

I roll my eyes at his statement, what a typical Rem saying. "If you haven't told Dad, then you need to do that asap."

"Yeah, I know. I was gonna call him tonight but then you two idiots showed up."

"That sounds like our cue to get out of here. Come on, Lex, we'll leave Jules and her baby-daddy be," I motion for Lex to get up before looking back at Rem, "You call Dad, and then go rub Jules' feet or something."

I get up, and Lex follows suit. We say our goodbyes and head out. The whole way home, I let the news sink in. Rem and Jules are going to have a baby. A freaking baby, a little human that Rem is going to be responsible for. Thank fuck he has Jules. I can't imagine him raising a baby on his own.

Dropping Lex off at his place, I watch him stumble to his door and drop the key twice before finally opening his door. He must sense me laughing at him because right before disappearing inside, he holds up his middle finger, sending me into a fit of laughter. Driving home, I realize how happy I've become in the past few weeks.

Everything is going better than I ever thought possible with Lily. Rem and Jules are in a great place, and Lex seems to be adjusting a little better. Life is good, and there is nothing that could sour my mood today.

For the past couple of weeks, I've been looking at houses, somewhere that Lily and I can grow together when we're ready to. A place for her to paint. That has enough room for all of her supplies. A place that is *ours*.

Pulling into the driveway, my phone starts to buzz in my pocket. I consider ignoring it, too eager to go inside and see Lily, but then I pull the thing out and look at it anyway. Instantly, my gut twists and bile burns up my throat.

Unknown Number: How much more are you willing to pay to keep your dirty relationship a secret?

That sick feeling that clings to my bones gives way to anger that boils just beneath the surface. I read every single word twice, and before I can really think it through, I'm typing out my response.

What secret? I have nothing to hide. Lily is an adult and not a student anymore. So fuck you.

Unwilling to deal with any more of this tonight, I hit the send button and power down the phone, hoping and praying that after what I've just said that will be the end of it.

Sighing, I realize I'm going to have to tell Lily. I don't want to talk about this with her, not with how great everything has been lately, and not when all I want to do is tell her about the house I'm planning to put an offer in on, but I promised her I wouldn't keep anything else from her and I'm not about to break her trust again.

With a heavy heart, I walk to the front door, preparing to tell her about the message. As soon as I enter the house, I hear the low humming of music and find her sitting cross-legged on a bar stool, a paintbrush in her hand. Closing the door gently behind me, I take a moment to stare at her, drinking her in. God, she's beautiful, and completely mine.

As if she can sense I've entered the room, she twists around, her eyes finding mine immediately. Those big blues of hers twinkle with joy. She smiles, perfectly straight white teeth appearing from behind her soft pink lips.

"I didn't even know you were home; you were so quiet."

"Sorry," I murmur. Setting my keys down on the table, I slip out of my shoes and take off my jacket, draping it over the back of one of the chairs. When I don't return her smile, she gets up, the sound of her paintbrush falling into the water sounds like a pin dropping in a silent room.

"What's wrong? Did something happen?"

Fear, or maybe even dread, drips from her words.

Taking her into my arms, I bury my head into the crook of her neck and hold her close to my chest. She smells like a tropical island, like rainwater and coconuts. Her scent calms me and reminds me that everything is going to be okay. I'm not afraid of losing her again, we're stronger than that now, but I'm tired of dealing with this person, tired of living in the past.

Pulling away, I look down at her. She has white paint smudged against her cheek and red paint on her hands. She looks like a true artist.

"The blackmailer messaged me again. It sounds like they want more money."

Lily's gaze widens, "You didn't give them any, did you?"

I shake my head, "No, of course not, but I'm getting tired of being reminded of this. We're moving forward and whoever this person is, is trying to make it, so we don't. I just want them to go away. They're ruining everything."

Lily takes my face into her hands, forcing me to look at her even though it's the last thing I want to do. I'm ashamed and angry that we're still dealing with this. She shouldn't be reminded of this over and over again.

"Everything is going to be okay. We have each other. Try to ignore it. Maybe with no response, they'll take the hint."

I didn't want to shoot her down, but that happening was very slim. Whenever money was involved, people would do some crazy things.

"Maybe, or maybe they'll try harder. Maybe they'll continue pushing until they get what they want." Anger was pulsing through me, burning like a raging wildfire.

"Stop, don't let them get to you," Lily whispered, her lips pressing against mine in a faint kiss. There was nothing like kissing her, nothing like making love when you loved the person you were doing it with.

My hands move to her hips, and I pull her closer, feeling all her soft curves. My cock already growing hard, begging to be inside her, even though I had just had her this morning.

"Whoa, before we lose our minds, and our clothing, tell me what the surprise is." Lily grins, and it hits me then. I almost forgot to tell her about the house with the studio.

"I know it's a little soon, and maybe you'll say no, I don't know."

Lily's face turns serious, "You aren't going to ask me to marry you, are you?"

Chuckling, I ask, "Would it really be that bad?"

She blinks slowly, "No, but I don't think we're ready to get married yet."

"Are you ready to move in together? To buy a house together?"

Shock replaces the seriousness in her eyes, "You aren't being serious, are you?"

"Yes, yes, I am." Lily doesn't respond, so I take that moment to explain. "I want to put an offer in on a three-bedroom house on the outskirts of town. It has a nice studio above the garage that you could use as your paint room, and I think the quietness of the country would help so that you could paint without distraction."

Her big blues glisten with unshed tears, "You didn't have to do all of this for me." She croaks, her throat tightening with emotion.

"I know, I didn't," I soothe, taking my hand and running it down her long blonde locks. "But I wanted to. You mean everything to me, and your dreams are mine. I want everything you want for yourself, and I want you to be as happy as I am."

"I am happy. I'm so happy it's almost crazy how good life has been. I'm always waiting for the other shoe to drop, for someone to pinch me and tell me this is nothing but a dream."

Leaning into her face, I whisper, "It isn't a dream. This is our new reality, and I can't wait to make a future with you." Pressing a gentle kiss to her button nose, I wait for her to respond. When she doesn't, I go to pull away, but only make it about an inch before her lips collide with mine.

She kisses me like I'm water, and she is fire. Like we're trying to extinguish the sparks forming between us before we get burnt. The kiss grows more possessive, and it doesn't take long for both of us to lose our clothes.

Bending her over the couch, I sink two fingers into her to ensure that she's ready for me. Warm, wet, and tight, my cock whimpers with jealousy as I finger fuck her a few times.

"Stop teasing me," she pushes back against my hand, and all I can do is grin as I pull my fingers out and replace them with my cock. The first stroke inside of her is like heaven. The second is like I'm being brought back to life, and the next are a blur as I fuck both of us into oblivion, making certain we forget about everyone and everything but each other.

20

LILY

With a steady hand, I place the final stroke carefully on the canvas, before stepping back and taking the finished piece in. It's perfect... and I'm not only talking about the painting, I'm talking about everything in this room. My own personal workspace, a place that is mine and mine alone.

The large open space is flooded with light coming from the huge slanted windows in the roof. Walls are lined with shelves that hold all my supplies; a vast selection of paint, different sized canvas', and every shape of brush you can think of. *My happy place.*

We moved into the new house only a month after Seb showed it to me. He sold his house quick enough for us to buy the new one.

Sometimes, I can't believe how lucky I am, it still feels like a dream.

I dropped out of school, and everything else fell into place. No more hiding, no more sneaking around. We get to be a normal couple like I always wanted.

Even my grandparents finally came around a bit. They are still not sold on the whole dropping out of school thing, but they seem more interested in my art and even impressed that I got a paying job doing it. A well-paying job, I might add.

Grabbing all my dirty brushes, I walk over to the small side table to start cleaning them, when a wave of nausea overcomes me. My fingers dig into the edge of the table, and I close my eyes for a moment waiting for it to pass like it always does. Sebastian insisted on me buying the more expensive paint, and even though the quality is much better, it seems to be more potent in the odor department.

The smell of paint has never fazed me before, but thanks to the new paint, I have to air out the room more often now, to not be bothered by it. Shaking the nausea away, I finish cleaning the brushes before scrubbing my hands clean. When my fingers are free of the various blues and purples, I dry them and make my way downstairs to the kitchen.

Seb is at work, and as usual, I spend most of the day painting. By the time I'm done for the day I'm famished and today is no different. So, I head straight for the fridge. I open the double-sided, stainless steel doors and stick my head inside.

A whiff of last night's lasagna tickles my nose, and instead of enjoying the savory smell like I expected, I'm surprised to find my stomach churning, the sour taste of bile on my tongue. Clamping my hand over my mouth, I will the vomit to stay down as I run to the bathroom.

Only when I'm kneeling in front of the toilet, do I lift my hand and empty the entire contents of my stomach into the white ceramic bowl. Vomit turns into dry heaving, my whole body convulsing as it tries to purge whatever the hell is bothering it.

What the hell? I was fine a minute ago.

When I'm done throwing up, and my breathing has calmed down, I stand and clean myself up before wiping everything down with some Clorox wipes. I close the plastic box and set the wipes back under the sink, but before I close the cabinet, my eyes catch sight of the box sitting next to the cleaning supplies... *my tampons.*

Within seconds, everything clicks into place.

The sensitivity to smell, the sudden vomiting... it hits me then that I haven't had my period since before we moved into the new house.

Oh, my god, I think I'm pregnant.

For the longest time, I just stand in the bathroom staring at the closed pack of tampons, wondering how I didn't think of this before. We've had plenty of unprotected sex, and sex equals babies. Everybody knows this, so why is this such a shock for me? It's like my brain has suppressed that part completely.

Holy shit, I might be pregnant.

After I finally snap out of the trance-like state I'm in, I pull out my phone and check the time. Sebastian shouldn't be home for another two hours. I contemplate calling Jules and Delilah to come and pick me up to take me to the store but decide against it.

I might not have a car here, but there is a little corner store within walking distance, and I'm hoping they have a pregnancy test there. I'll try that first before bothering anyone. Plus, I don't know if I'm actually pregnant or not. It could be nothing more than a scare, and I would hate to bother someone for something like that.

Ten minutes later, I'm dressed and out the door, speed walking down the sidewalk to my destination. I enter the store, and the bell above me chimes loudly.

"Hello," a middle-aged woman greets me with a big smile.

"Hi," I murmur, lowering my head. I don't know why, but I suddenly feel like a teenager buying condoms and lube.

"Can I help you, dear?" the lady asks.

"Mhm... no, I'm just looking around." *Ugh, this is ridiculous.* "Actually, I'm looking for a pregnancy test," I admit.

"Okay, that's aisle five, next to the pads and tampons."

"Thank you," I say and give her a thankful smile. Making my way to aisle five, I pass a woman pushing a cart. There is a little boy sitting in the cart, he eyes me curiously and then smiles a toothless grin.

I can't help but smile in return. My thoughts swirl as I reach the aisle. Could I handle having a baby? Sebastian has mentioned wanting children, and while I want children as well, I think if this pregnancy test is negative, we need to sit down and discuss our future.

Stopping in front of the pregnancy tests, I scan the boxes. There are at least five different tests, some off-brand, and a few that say you can test ten days sooner. *What does it all mean?*

Maybe I should call Jules? She just found out she's pregnant if anyone could tell me what test to get it would be her. Tapping my foot against the floor, I contemplate calling her, before deciding against it completely. Instead, I grab a couple different tests and walk up to the checkout. The lady who greeted me earlier checks me out without question, and I pay, telling her goodbye. On my way out, I spot the bathrooms and make a beeline for them, deciding to take the test here rather than at home.

My hands shake as I enter the stall and lock it behind me. Ripping open two of the boxes, I set the tests on the toilet paper box. Then I do my business peeing on each test before placing it back on its box. When I'm finished, I wash my hands and walk back into the stall, pacing the floor while I wait for the three minutes it says it takes for the test to work.

I'm a ball of nerves as I wait... what will Sebastian think? What if it's negative? What happens then? My throat tightens as I stop pacing and walk back over to where the tests are sitting. Maybe I should've done this at home. I'm close to having a nervous breakdown, and the last thing I want is for someone to see me fall apart in the grocery store.

Reality crashes into me like a car hitting a brick wall as my gaze bounces back and forth between the two positive pregnancy tests.

One positive could still mean it's wrong, but two, there is no way around it.

Bringing a hand to my racing heart, I try and calm myself. Thump, thump, thump. It feels like my heart is trying to take flight.

I'm pregnant. I'm having a baby. I'm having a baby with Sebastian Miller, and we aren't married, and our relationship is brand new and... I force air into my lungs to stop myself from going into a full-blown panic attack.

Tears well in my eyes and my hand moves from my chest to my stomach as if out of instinct. Okay, I'm having a baby, *we're* having a baby. Everything is going to be okay, everything. I'm terrified of what's going to happen next, but that doesn't mean I'm not filled with joy. There is a tiny little baby growing inside of me. A special piece of both Sebastian and I and there is nothing more precious than that.

For some reason, it hits me then, all of the pain over losing my family crashes into me, and suddenly it feels like I've lost them all over again. The wound pulsing and bleeding, as fresh as the day it happened. I wonder what my mother would think of me now. Would she be proud? Would my sister be happy that I found love, that Sebastian found love? I try not to dwell on what she would think, fear of disappointing her being my biggest fear.

It's okay, everything is okay. I repeat to myself.

Wiping the tears from my face, I gather up the tests and put them in the plastic bag along with the other two tests that I'll take late for Sebastian. Then I leave the store and head to the house. Walking down the sidewalk, I find myself smiling. I'm going to be a mommy; Sebastian is going to be a daddy. Jules will be an aunt, and Rem and Lex uncles.

With every step I take, I calm a little bit more. Nearing the house, I round the corner and crash into a woman who looks as if she's in a hurry. Opening my mouth, I go to apologize, but the words never come out. Before I realize what is happening, she has moved around me and is covering my mouth and nose with a cloth and wrapping an arm around my middle, pulling me back against her chest.

Confusion and fear rush to the surface as I struggle against her hold. There's no point in fighting though, the more I fight, the harder I breathe, and it only takes a few breaths for me to discover I'm fading, the darkness circling in around me with every inhale I take. My last thought before it all falls away is that Sebastian never got to find out about our baby. He never got to know he was going to be a father.

21

SEBASTIAN

*L*ike every day when I get home, I chuck my jacket and deposit all my shit on the table. Fuck, have I missed my woman today. Calling out into what appears to be an empty house, I say, "Baby, you better be naked and ready for me because my cock is hungry and he's coming for your pussy."

I expect to hear a giggle or a, *seriously,* but instead, I'm met with nothing more than silence. A second passes, and then another, and before I can think about it, I'm climbing the stairs up to Lily's studio. Inky fear fills my veins when I find the studio empty, the entire room clean, every item in its place.

Where is she?

Would she leave again? I don't even want to think about that. The idea of losing her makes me rabid, it makes me... I can't even think about it, it hurts too much. Walking back down the stairs, I check the rest of the house just to be sure, then I pull out my phone and call her. My hands shake nervously as the phone rings, and rings, and rings, each ring pushing me closer and closer to the edge of insanity.

Something had to have happened, there is no way she would just leave, that she would just walk away without talking to me first. Panic doesn't even begin to describe the level I'm at as I pace the floor, dialing her phone over and over again.

I leave a message, and then another, and another pleading with her to come home. My fear turns to anger, and the two mix together, my emotions becoming the catalyst to send me over the edge. What have I done? I thought everything was good. I thought she was happy. We bought a house together, and I was preparing to propose to her, wanting to make her forever mine and now this.

Slamming down onto the couch, I hold my head in my hands and tug on the longer strands of hair, willing an answer to appear in my mind. It's then that my phone starts to ring, the sound piercing through the hazy fog surrounding my mind. Scrabbling, I grab the device, my eyes scan the name on the screen.

Lily. Sighing in relief, I press the green answer key.

"Baby, are you okay? What's going on?" I expect to hear Lily's sweet voice, but instead, I hear another, one that turns the blood in my veins to ice.

"Sebastian, I'm so glad I was able to reach you."

Laura? Why does Laura have Lily's phone?

"What's going on? Why do you have Lily's phone? Is everything all right?"

Laura chuckles, but it's not the soft laugh I'm used to hearing from her, no this laugh is humorless, dark. "You haven't figured it out yet? I thought the dean would be smarter than that?" What the hell is she...

Like a bucket of ice water raining down on me, I realize just what's happening now. Laura is the blackmailer. Laura is the one who saw us together, the one who...

"Put Lily on the phone, right now. This isn't a game, Laura." I try and hide the fear from my voice. I don't want this bitch knowing how scared of losing Lily I am.

"You're right, it isn't a game at all, and if you want to see your precious girlfriend alive, then you'll do as I say. Otherwise, I won't have a problem slitting her throat and watching her bleed out."

My tongue seems to swell at her confession, and I barely get out my next set of words without biting it off. "What do you want?"

I can practically see the smile on her lips, "Ten thousand dollars. Then I'll let her go. Meet me at the abandoned offices near Riverside park at five, and we can do the exchange. If you call the cops or anyone follows you, I will know."

I don't hesitate in answering her, "Okay, fine, just, please... please don't hurt her." My stomach knots, my insides twisting until there is nothing but a painful ache in the pit of my gut.

"Oh, don't you worry. As long as you bring me the money your bitch and that baby inside of her will be unharmed."

"Baby?" I gasp, giving my shock away.

"Yes, baby. It seems like the stakes have gotten higher. Be here, or I kill them both." Before I can say anything, the line goes dead. My heart sinks into my stomach, and a wave of nausea overtakes me. A baby. I'm having a baby. Lily is pregnant, and Laura has her in her clutches. *Laura?* How the fuck can it be her? I never considered the blackmailer to be her. I think back on how long I've known her; she has always been a friend, and so was her husband. Could he be involved in this too?

For a second, all I can do is stand there and think of all the ways I've let Lily down.

I have to save her and our baby, but how? I'll give Laura every dime I have if it means keeping Lily safe, but how can I trust anything she says now? I've been so wrong about this woman that I thought was my friend, and if she is capable of blackmailing and kidnapping, then I don't want to think about what else she might do. It feels like I'm going to pass out, everything coming at me all at once.

No! I have to devise a plan, come up with a way to save her, to save our baby.

MY HANDS ARE DRENCHED in sweat, and I worry that the bag filled with cash is about to slip out of them. I grip onto the strap of the bag a little bit tighter as I walk into the abandoned office building Laura has sent me to.

A million scenarios race through my mind, and most of them are not good ones. Most of them end with Lily getting hurt or worse. If anything happens to her, I will never forgive myself. I will never get over it. I know I will not survive this kind of loss again, not when I barely survived it the last time. I have to save Lily and our unborn baby.

My heavy footfalls echo through the empty halls, and I strain my ears to hear anything else besides them, to hear any sign of Lily being here. A sign of her being okay. Please let her be okay. Please let this all work out. I called the cops right before arriving and told them to give me a ten-minute head start. Explaining the situation to them was terrifying.

Grinding my teeth together, I continue walking down the hall until I hear what sounds like muffled crying. Instantly, my slow walk turns into a run, my eyes darting to the doorway of every room I pass.

"I don't know what he likes about you," I hear Laura's venom-filled voice ahead and stop when I reach the door. I find Laura staring a scared Lily down, her blonde hair sticks to her tear-soaked cheeks, a thick piece of duct tape over her lips. There's a tiny cut above her right eye, and her hands are bound with what looks to be rope.

"Aw, look who's joined us?" Laura snickers and looks from Lily and up to me. A glint of metal catches in the light and dread consumes me. She takes the knife and tips Lily's chin upward with the blade, forcing her to remain looking at her and nowhere else.

"Here's your money, give her to me, please," I try and hide the fear pulsing through my veins, but it's impossible.

"You are so stupid, you know that? I've been hitting on you for years, scheduling our meetings so that we can be alone, and you never took the chance. Idiot. We would have been good together. I figured you just didn't want *any* woman," she giggles, "I thought you might be gay. But then I saw you with this skank... when you could have had *me*."

"So, this is all over you being jealous?" I probably shouldn't taunt her, okay I *definitely* shouldn't but I also need to keep her talking.

"More like offended," she quips. "I mean, come on, look at her. She has nothing on me."

She has everything on you.

Laura twists the blade in her hand, digging it a little deeper into Lily's skin. Not enough to draw blood, but enough to make Lily whimper. The sound pierces my heart like a hot dagger stabbing through the center. On instinct, I take a step toward her.

"Don't fucking move!" Laura growls.

"It's okay," I assure her, lifting my hands up to show her my palms. I feel like I'm trying to calm down a bull that's seconds away from charging.

"Take another step, and the blade might slip," she threatens, and my blood runs cold. She's not giving me any sign of keeping her end of the deal by letting Lily go, so I do the only other thing I can think of.

I decide to use her words against her, use her feelings for me against her.

"You know if you had told me that you wanted to fuck things might be different now."

Immediately, Laura's posture changes, it's like she perked up as soon as I said the word *fuck*. "What do you mean?" she asks curiously, the anger in her face slowly receding.

I shrug, "Of course, I thought you were attractive and don't think that I haven't thought about bending you over my desk a time or two," I lie, unable to look at Lily as I try to concentrate on Laura only. Lying is hard, and it's even harder when the words you're speaking are daggers to the heart of the woman that you love.

"Then, why didn't you?" At her question, she drops the blade from Lily's throat. *That's it. Come a little closer.*

"I didn't think you were into me. You were married with kids. What was I supposed to think?" Laura's face softens further, and it looks like she actually believes what I'm saying, "I guess I'm not good at picking up cues. You should have come out and said it or grabbed my dick or something like that, then there wouldn't have been any confusion."

Her cheeks redden at my suggestion. "Maybe it's not too late. Maybe we can still be together. Just you and me. You know we would be great. There would be no hiding our relationship."

Not a chance in the world.

"You're right. We still can. We can take the money and leave town... you and me," I coax, and she takes another step closer, and my eyes dart to the knife that's still in her hand. I need to get that knife, which means I need her to get just a little closer.

"What about her?" Laura spits out and motions toward Lily, who is now shaking on the floor. I only briefly gaze at her, but when I do, I feel like the air deflates from my lungs. All I want to do is take her into my arms and tell her everything is okay, that I don't mean a word that I've said but I can't. Not until she's safe, not until our baby is safe.

"What about *her*? We can leave her here. By the time someone finds her, we'll be long gone." Conflict flickers in Laura's eyes, and I know I've almost got her.

Take the bait, bitch.

"I don't know." Laura looks between Lily and me, once, twice, and then her gaze holds mine. "We should kill her. If you don't have a witness, then there isn't be a crime."

Lily starts to scream behind her duct tape, the sound is muffled, but I know without even looking at her that she's losing it. She doesn't know this is all an act, she doesn't know the things I'll do, the lengths I'll go to, to save her.

My heart aches, and a sour taste pricks my tongue at the words I speak next.

"You're right, but you shouldn't be the one to do it. Give me the knife, and I'll do it. I'm the one that caused all the problems." I keep my voice even, not giving away any deception. Holding out my hand, I wait for Laura to make the next move. The air grows tense, and I worry that maybe she's changing her mind. *Fuck.* No. "I need to do this, Laura. I need the closure. If I can't do it myself, I won't be able to completely give myself to you, not the way I want to, not the way I know you want me to." The words sicken me, and it takes everything not to double over and vomit all over the floor.

Laura smiles triumphantly and takes another step forward. She raises her hand as if she's about to give the knife to me. Only a few more inches and I'll have it. Only a few inches between Lily's safety, and...Laura freezes midstep. Every cell in my body tells me to grab the knife, to reach out and pluck the thing out of her hands. She's right there, right in front of me. Her eyebrows draw together, confusion appearing seconds before anger as we both hear the police sirens echoing off in the distance. For a moment, no one moves, but when it's clear that the sirens are coming closer, everything changes.

Laura's trust in me shatters, "You fucking prick, using my feelings, my fucking words against me. Now you can watch her die!"

Everything seems to happen in slow motion. She turns and runs in Lily's direction. A muffled scream pierces the air, and that's all I need to hear to get my body moving with superhuman speed.

Laura only makes it two steps before my chest bumps into her back. I wrap my arms around her body and pull her to my chest. The knife goes flying through the air with the collision, landing on the ground with a clang a few feet away from where Lily is sitting. Laura struggles in my grasp, kicking her feet, and tossing her head backward in an attempt to headbutt me.

"You've ruined everything. We could've been happy together. We could've taken the money and ran."

"No, Laura, you ruined everything for yourself." I grit out, squeezing her tighter while avoiding her head. I've never been more thankful for all the early morning workout sessions than I am now.

Laura stops struggling and instead turns on the waterworks, "I'm sorry, Sebastian, just, please let me go. Let me go, and I'll never bother you again. You know I have a family and a job. How will I care for them? My children will lose their mother. Sebastian, please, please...I can't go to jail!" She's doing her damnedest to break me down, but there isn't a bone in my body that cares about her or her family. If anything, this is what her family needs. It's obvious she's suffering from some mental issues.

"That's exactly where you belong. In jail, in a padded cell." She starts to struggle again, but she's no match for me. I'll hold her all day if I have to.

The sirens grow closer and closer. It sounds like they're circling us and finally, they seem so close, I wonder if they've driven into the building. Lily whimpers on the floor, and as badly as I want to look at her, to make sure she's okay, I can't. I can't do anything but concentrate on this batshit crazy woman.

The police seem to take forever getting inside, but I never loosen my hold on Laura, in fact, it's like the opposite happens. Like a boa constrictor, I tighten my grip every time she lets out a breath.

"You're hurting me." She cries, and I shut down completely. Heavy footfalls bounce off the walls of the hall, and I know then that everything is going to be okay. As soon as the police enter the room, I release her and watch as she stumbles away from me, sagging breathlessly against the wall.

"Officers, thank God you're here. He tried to kill me," Laura starts, the lies spinning from her fucked-up web.

The officers look between the two of us, and then Lily, who is still bound on the floor. In seconds I'm pushed against the wall, my hands pulled behind my back.

What the fuck?

"What the hell?" I growl as they drag me out of the room. Someone must have removed the tape from Lily's mouth because her voice is the only one, I seem to hear.

"No, it's not him. It's her! She drugged me, kidnapped me, and then she tried to kill me. That crazy bitch tried to kill me," Lily screams, and before I can comprehend what is happening, a small body crashes into mine.

My Lily. Mine. I wish I could wrap my arms around her. Instead, she does that for both of us. Another officer makes an attempt to pry Lily off of me, but she starts to cry, big fat tears slip down her face.

"I love you, baby, everything is okay. Don't worry, all that matters now is that you and the baby are safe."

"You, Sebastian Miller?" Someone that looks to be a detective rather than a police officer asks as he walks up to me.

"Yes. Yes, I am. I'm the one that called."

The guy gestures to the police officer, "Uncuff him. He's the one that called it in. Looks like we'll be taking this one in." He says, grabbing Laura's arms and slapping cuffs on her wrists.

Lily sighs with relief, and as soon as I'm uncuffed, I take her into my arms, kissing her forehead, cheeks, lips, anywhere that I can.

"Do you need an ambulance?" An officer asks Lily, who pulls away and shakes her head. I want to push the matter, but don't because honestly, I'm just so grateful to have her in my arms, to know that she's okay.

A few seconds later, they bring Laura out, she's handcuffed and fighting like a wildcat, "I didn't do anything! It was him! All him!" She screams, her tone is frantic and well, crazy. She continues to thrash as they all but carry her down the hall, only showing the cops more how insane she really is.

Once she's out of sight, I take Lily's face into my hands, and I stare into those big blues of hers. *Mine. All fucking mine.*

"You're pregnant?" I ask, needing to confirm what Laura already told me.

Tears fill Lily's eyes, "I am. I didn't want you to find out this way, it's the worst way ever to reveal a pregnancy, but yes, we're having a baby." She pauses, her eyes darting away from mine, and I can see the insecurity pouring into the open spaces in her mind. "Do you... Do you still want me? After the baby... and everything..."

Jesus fucking Christ, if this woman doesn't shut her mouth.

"Listen to me and listen to me well. You're it for me, Lily, you're it. Whatever I said back in that room, it was to protect you. Laura means nothing to me. It's all you, all you. That baby inside you. It's a part of both of us, and you're mine, no matter what you think or feel you're mine and I am yours. Do you understand me? I love you. I love you with every beat of my heart, and every breath that fills my lungs. I. Love. You." I press a kiss to her eyelids, cheeks, and forehead before kissing her pink lips.

Tears slide down her cheeks, and her chest rises and falls as if she's struggling to breathe, "I just feel horrible like I did this. Like it was my fault."

"No, none of this is your fault. Laura is batshit crazy, and you're the love of my life. Losing Amy hurt me, it felt like I lost a piece of who I was but losing you. I'd never survive that. You're inside of me, a part of me. There is no you or me, there is only us."

"I love you," Lily cries, and I pull her into my chest, wrapping my arms around her. My chin rests on her head, and I vow then right in the hallway of that abandoned building to forever love her, to forever cherish and protect her. Once upon a time, I vowed never to love, never to find joy in life because I thought I didn't deserve it.

As it turns out, I was still waiting for *my* person to come along.

22

LILY

"*H*ow did your grandparents handle hearing about the baby news?" Sebastian asks as he walks into the bedroom from the bathroom. He's shirtless, wearing nothing but a pair of boxers and the image before me does crazy things to my head. I want to lick those washboard abs of his and climb him like a tree.

Clearing my throat, I say, "It was good. Better than I expected them to take it. Surprisingly, the fact that I was pregnant was still not as bad as me dropping out of college. They're very old fashioned, I guess, so of course, my grandma asked when we're getting married. I told her we've got at least twenty weeks before we have to worry about that. I'm not going to roll down the aisle. I want to walk..."

Sebastian grins, "Is that what you want? To walk down the aisle and become Mrs. Sebastian Miller?"

Yes! "I mean it wouldn't be such a bad thing, now would it?" I can't believe I just talked so leisurely about getting married but talking to Sebastian is like talking to part of me, we have no secrets.

"No, not at all. I've dreamt of the day you'd become my wife," he confesses while crawling into bed. He moves up to where I'm sitting and pulls the blanket back to reveal the tiny bump hidden beneath my nightie. He cradles it as he does every night, whispering sweet nothings to our little peanut.

"Do you think Mommy and I should get married?" he asks, and all I can do is roll my eyes. I'm not worried about being married before we have the baby, it doesn't bother me, but I do want it to happen someday.

"Baby doesn't care," I mumble, but as soon as the words escape my mouth, I want to take them back because right there resting on my bump is a princess cut engagement ring with three diamonds in it. The air in my lungs evaporates, and I'm afraid to move, worried that I'll knock the ring off and it'll disappear.

"I told you I would make you mine forever. Our love hasn't been conventional, and the odds have been stacked against us from the very beginning, but we've always found a way to make things work, and that makes our love stronger than anything."

"Sebastian," I gasp, unable to form another coherent thought at that moment.

Plucking the ring from my lap he moves off the bed and drops down to one knee beside it, "Will you, Lily Kline, be my forever, my happily ever after?"

Tears well in my eyes and I lift a hand to my lips before squeaking out a *yes*.

Sebastian, of course, grins and places the ring on my finger. As soon as the ring is in place, I tug him off the ground and pull him into my arms. Our lips find each other's like they're two magnets being drawn together. Fire consumes my body as my need for him intensifies with each stroke of his tongue. Surrendering to him has always been easy, the desire for him instantly pooling in my core.

"I need you," I pant between kisses. I'm hungry, drowning in a sea of need. Sebastian doesn't make me wait long, thankfully. He's got my nightie removed, tossing it somewhere on the floor in a flash. With my stomach growing outward and my boobs growing heavier, I've become a little more self-conscious of my figure. No longer am I as skinny, and somedays I feel like a cow, but he doesn't care. He makes me feel beautiful and reminds me often.

"Beautiful, so fucking beautiful..." He murmurs, sucking one of my hardened nipples into his mouth. He licks and sucks, and nibbles on the hard nub until I'm half pushing him away while pulling him back at the same time.

"Please," I plead, when he finally releases me, his fingers trailing down over my belly. Gentle. Kind. Sweet. His touch would have me on my knees right now if it wasn't for this bed.

"Mine." The possessiveness in his voice makes me shiver. A gasp passes my lips as he enters me with two fingers, his movements are slow, leisurely, precise, and with each stroke, he brings me to life. A flush works its way through my body. It feels like I'm being burned by the sun. Scorched.

"Come, baby, come all over my fingers, and then I'll give you my cock." Such a filthy mouth. Mewling into the air like a cat in heat, I claw at the bedsheets. The entire time Sebastian keeps his eyes locked on mine, and with the heat of his gaze, and the stroke of his fingers, I come alive, shattering into a million pieces. My channel tightens around his fingers, and his hiss of pleasure meets my ears.

I'm hovering somewhere between heaven and earth when he enters me, filling me in one deep thrust, and though I'm wet, my body takes a minute to adjust to his size. In that time, Sebastian peppers kisses across my chest, making his way to my lips. Somehow, he always knows what I need, and when I need it. Once he's sure I'm ready he starts to move, his hips move slowly at first, but gain speed with every dip inside.

His fingers dig into the flesh at my hips as he owns me, branding our souls together. His thrusts become deeper, harder, and fire lights up my body, igniting only a part of me that he can reach, touch.

"Sebastian," I whimper feeling that common euphoric feeling building at the base of my neck. "I'm close…"

"Come, milk my cock, claim me." Sweat beads on his brow as he grinds his pelvis against my center. All over again, I go off like a firework filling the summer sky with an array of sparkling colors. Unable to keep my eyes open, I let the pleasure carry me away. One stroke, two strokes, three strokes.

Sebastian finds his own release, roaring like a lion as he fills me with his sticky seed. All I can do is cling to him, hoping and praying that this is how it will be forever.

"I love you," he says hoarsely, lips ghosting against my clammy forehead, "and I vow to love you forever, even after we're both nothing but dirt."

"I love you too," I respond as he takes us and situates us under the covers, wrapping his strong arms around me. As exhaustion threatens to take over, I'm hit with this gut feeling. It makes my heart pound and my insides warm.

Somewhere out there, I know Amy is happy and smiling down on Sebastian and me. Maybe we weren't meant to be from the beginning, but in the end, we found a way, because love always finds a way.

EPILOGUE

Sebastian

I watch my daughter's blonde little curls bounce on her head as she stumbles through the backyard. Maggie got her mother's hair; the light blonde locks fall down her back like spun gold in the afternoon sun. She hasn't been walking but a few weeks and her steps are still uneasy. She still frequently falls, and every time, I feel like I'm having a heart attack.

Kayla, Rem's little girl, is only a few months older but already quick on her feet, stomping through the yard easily and steadily. She sits down right in front of Rem and me picking up a dandelion from the grass.

Her small hand wraps around the stem of the flower, her big blues stare at it like it's the most fascinating thing she's ever seen. Then she puckers her lips as if she is trying to blow off the seed, but instead of air, spit flies out of her small mouth. The seeds don't take off flying but rather fall away to the ground.

"This is the cutest fucking thing I've ever seen," Rem says.

"You say that twice a week," I chuckle. "Everything your daughter does is the cutest fucking thing you've ever seen."

"Because it is!" Rem says defensively. "And don't act like you don't think the same about Maggie. Our kids are changing every day, and I find every single aspect of it cool."

I can't argue with that. I never thought I could be entertained and in awe about something so mundane as my girl holding a spoon for the first time, yet I was beside myself when she did. Being a dad is the strangest, most terrifying, most epic thing in the world. Right beside being a husband.

Lily and I got married two weeks after Maggie was born. I couldn't wait a minute longer to make her officially mine. Her grandparents finally came around and started to support her art exhibits, which I knew meant a lot to her. They were also happy about us having a baby and getting married, even though they would have preferred it to have happened the other way around. My dad and my brothers were overjoyed from the beginning, as I expected. They all loved Lily before I even knew I did.

Rem and Jules ended up getting married a short while after they found out they were having Kayla. Marriage suits my brother well, now we just have to get Lex on board with the idea of something more than a one-night stand.

Speaking of Lex. "Hey, assholes," he greets as he crosses the yard.

"Don't talk about the kids like that," Rem says sternly before a smile splits his face.

Lex rolls his eyes, "Not the kids, you guys are the *assholes*. I could never call my nieces such foul names."

It's my turn to roll my eyes, "How is life? Anything new happening?" Lex still doesn't like to talk about his love life, or anything for that matter really. Since the girls were born, he's kind of shut down, keeping to himself most of the time."

"Nope, same ole' same ole."

"Good, good, so no wedding planning anytime soon?" Rem busts his balls on the daily about how we're both married and have kids while our oldest brother doesn't.

Maggie staggers over to where Lex is sitting, a big smile on her face. Her eyes twinkle with excitement as she hands him a dandelion which he takes with a smile.

"Thank you, sweetheart." Maggie falls into his lap, a contagious giggle filling the air.

"Don't you wish you had kids?" Rem asks, "Now that I have Kayla, I don't think I could picture my life without having a kid."

Lex shrugs his shoulders, "It doesn't bother me. I'm not ready for kids, or marriage, or anything of the like. I'm still, too...unstable, unhinged. I need to get my shit together before I think about anything like that."

I know what Lex thinks; that no one will love him and all of his flaws, but he's wrong. There will be a woman that can handle him someday, that will build him up rather than cut him down. Before Rem or I can respond Lily and Jules come walking out of the house, one carrying a tray of sandwiches and the other a pitcher of tea.

"You boys hungry?" Lily asks, and I can't help myself. As soon as she places the pitcher on the table, I grab her by the hips and pull her into my body.

"I'm hungry all right but it ain't for any sandwiches," I growl, my cock already hard and standing at attention.

"Jesus, get a room," Lex gags.

"Oh, stop it," Lily gives me a gentle push backward, and I release her even though it's the last thing I want to do.

Maggie crawls out of Lex's lap and walks over to me, her tiny hands grip onto my pants, and I stare down at her, a tiny version of her mother. Never did I think I would have it all. The house, the wife, the kid, the dream job, but I do. When I lost Amy, I thought my life was over, but Lily showed me there was so much more to life. It wasn't easy, but together we achieved greatness.

"I love you," I say to Maggie and then look up at Lily who is watching me with wonder in her eyes.

"What?" I ask, pouring myself a cup of tea.

"Nothing, it's just I hope you can handle two."

"Two?" My brow furrows with confusion. She can't mean what I think she means...

"Two babies." She grins, "Maggie is going to be a big sister."

And just like that, I'm blessed all over again.

"Congratulations, brother, Rem and Lex both say, and I set my glass down and stand taking both Maggie and Lily into my arms.

"Thank you, baby, thank you so much for being my all, for giving me the best things in life." I seal my words with a kiss, wondering if life can get any better.

~

Thank you for reading The Vow! Lex's story is up next in The Promise. Keep reading for a sneak peek.

THE PROMISE

PREVIEW

JUDE

*M*y feet hit the grass-covered ground below my window, and I start on a dead run. I don't think anyone heard me sneak out, but I'm not taking any chances. I can't, *won't* get caught, this might be my only chance to do this. My only chance to escape my father's clutches. I have one single night of freedom, a few stolen hours away from a jail sentence I'll have to endure my entire life. Tonight is for me. It's my one saving grace.

Without turning to look back, I run nonstop until I make it to the bus station. My lungs burn, and my legs ache from the sprint, but I know it's all going to be worth it. When I get to the station, a bus is just about to leave. Getting in, I don't even bother looking where it will be going. I just need it to take me away.

Digging through my pocket, I get out the small stash of cash I've saved up. I pay the fare and find a seat toward the back of the bus. A woman about my age is sitting on the other side of the aisle, and curiosity gets the better of me.

"Excuse me," I say, getting her attention. "Where is this bus going?"

She looks up from her phone just long enough to answer. "North Woods."

"Thanks," I murmur and settle down in my seat. *North Woods, here I come.*

TWO HOURS LATER, the bus pulls into the North Woods bus station. I step out in awe. It's dark now, but there are still people out and about.

Looking around, I try to orient myself, but I have no idea where I'm going. So I decide to follow the others that got off the bus. Most of them are walking in the same direction, so I assume they must be going somewhere.

It only takes me a few minutes to realize where everyone is headed. After a short walk, a large building comes into view. No, not just one building, a whole campus.

I stop in front of the large sign decorating the pristine lawn. *North Woods University.*

Standing there for a few minutes, I think about how good it is that fate brought me here. I've always dreamed about going to college, but my father wouldn't allow it. *"Women don't need an education, they need to marry, cook, clean, and bear children."*

That might be the life my family wants for me, but I will not have it. If I run away, they will never stop looking for me, but if I do something else... something drastic enough... they will shun me. They will kick me out and disown me as a daughter. Which is exactly what I want.

"Let's go bar hopping!" A guy screams behind me, dragging me from my thoughts. His friends yell in agreement as the whole group walks across the street.

Keeping my distance, I follow them to wherever these bars are. That's exactly what I need. The guys ahead of me walk so fast that I end up losing them, so I just keep walking in the same direction until I come up to a bar.

Loud music and laughter filters through the closed door and tinted windows. A sliver of doubt runs through me as I reach out for the door handle, but then I remember my father's words, and the decision is clear again.

I open the door. The noises go up from a one to a ten. The music is so loud I can feel the pressure in my eardrum. The air is thick with the smell of alcohol, sweat, and cigarette smoke. I force my feet to carry me inside, regardless.

My heart is beating furiously against my rib cage as fear weasels its way up my spine. Taking in the people inside the place. I quickly realize that most of them are men... older men. In their late twenties and thirties. Definitely not the college crowd I was hoping for.

This was a bad idea. Maybe I should go to a restaurant instead. Spinning around, I head back to the door I just came through. Before I can take a single step, a large man cuts off the way, wedging himself between me and the exit.

"Hey gorgeous, why're you leaving so soon?" he slurs, his eyes glassy and unfocused. He looks down at my body, and I suddenly feel exposed and vulnerable.

"Sorry, I just want to go," I say, doing my best not to sound too desperate. I try to step past him, but he grabs my arm and pulls me closer to him, ignoring my obvious disinterest.

"Come on, I'll buy you a drink."

I'm already shaking my head, but he is still not getting it. He keeps pulling me in his direction, his fingers digging into the tender skin on my arm. I look around, hoping someone will come to my aid, but the other patrons are too busy with themselves. No one is even paying attention. Panic gets a hold of me, like claws ripping into my flesh.

Just when I'm about to scream on top of my lungs, the hand disappears, and the man is shoved away from me. Out of nowhere, a second man appears next to me.

"I don't think she wants to go with you, asshole," my savior growls. The creep stumbles backward but recovers quickly. I'm positive a fight is going to break out, but to my surprise, my attacker takes one look at the man beside me and shakes his head. With his tail tucked between his legs, he walks away, not taking another glance at me.

I turn to the man who saved me. As I take him in more closely, I realize why the other man backed off so easily. This man is nearly twice my size and probably twice my age as well. He is tall, over six feet for sure. His body is toned and muscular. His chest puffed out, and his arms thicker than my thighs.

"What's your name, sweetheart?" His voice is gentle and kind, the complete opposite of what he looks like. I decide then that he's an enigma.

Almost as if in a trance, I keep looking at him, studying his green eyes like they hold all the answers.

"Jude," I tell him. "My name is Jude."

LEX

JUDE. Her name rolls off my tongue with a smoothness I didn't expect. Her blue eyes are so big and wide, similar to that of a frightened kitten. Her hair is long and blonde but with a touch of white mixed in. It appears soft, and I'm tempted to reach out and touch it, but God knows that would be fucking weird. I drink in her tiny frame. She's young, probably too young to be in a bar. She is also a whole head shorter than me, and lean, frail.

She looks nothing like the women I've seen before, and that instantly has me intrigued by her. She's wearing a very long denim skirt that goes down to her ankles with a white turtleneck looking shirt. I can hardly make out the curve of her hips through the material and especially not in the shit lighting. Her face, though, I can see perfectly clear. She is angelic with high cheekbones, and a heart-shaped face. Her lips are a soft pink, and full, so full.

"Tha-thank you," she murmurs as she peers up at me through her thick lashes. She's watching me like she thinks I might do something to her. Innocent, naive, and fragile like a hundred-year-old glass. Those are the words that come to mind when I look at her.

I'm a better man than that, my dad raised me never to lay a hand on a woman, and my time in the Marines taught me that if you ever see someone in distress, you offer them a helping hand. And this girl was definitely in distress. That fucker wasn't taking no for an answer, and I wasn't going to stand there while a drunken creep manhandled her, and God knows, what else he had planned for her.

"My name is Alexander, but everyone calls me Lex," I say like we're two kindergarten students sharing first names.

"Lex." Her eyes light up, and her gaze roams over my frame as if she's assessing me.

Looking at her, I wonder if she's homeless or running. She is without a blemish or smudge of dirt, I presume that doesn't mean anything though. She can't possibly be a student? My head starts to hurt as I think about it. I decide the best thing to do is ask her some questions and see what she says.

"Do you want a ride home?" I ask, hoping maybe that'll answer at least one of my questions.

She shakes her head. "No, can you take me to your home?"

My home? I almost choke on my own spit. Maybe I didn't hear her right. Why does she want to come home with me? I'm certainly not any less scary than the guy who was just after her. I'm huge, muscled, and flawed. Much older than her. Though I'm a lot less leering and creepy than the other guy. This strange need to protect her overtakes me. I could see the panic rising up in her when that asshole refused to let go of her. It's why I stepped in, also because, like I said, I wasn't going to stand by and watch the fucker hurt her.

"Uh, sure," I tell her, assuming she has no home if she would much rather come back to my place with me. Maybe she needs a warm meal and a place to crash? I've been there before, and I've got the means to offer her help. It's a strange situation, but I'm not going to send her out on her ass.

Wrapping her slender arms around her middle, all I can see is how fragile she is, her eyes darting around the room. She waits for me to make my move while I stand there, staring at her. *Fuck.* I've got to get out of my head.

Turning around, I pull out my wallet and toss a twenty on the bar top to cover my beers. When I turn back around, the girl is nowhere in sight, and for some reason, that makes my heart clench in my chest. Storming out of the bar, I'm met with the cool night air. I also find Jude standing there, right beneath a streetlamp.

"Ready to go?" I ask.

She nods her head, her teeth nibbling on her bottom lip. I know she's not trying to be seductive. Something tells me she wouldn't know the first thing about being sexy.

Starting down the sidewalk, I turn the corner, heading for the parking lot in the back. Jude's soft footsteps bounce off the concrete behind me. I don't like her being at my back, so I stop and wait until she is in line with my steps. I walk slower to keep us together, and when we get closer to my truck, I hit the unlock button on the key fob.

Like a spooked horse, Jude jumps in the air at the sound, bringing her hands to her chest. Her eyes dart around, looking for an attacker, I assume.

"It's just the lock on my truck," I assure her.

"I'm sorry," she replies gently, the worry seeping from her gaze slowly.

Each step she takes seems to be measured with uneasiness, and yet she says nothing and continues into my truck. It's the strangest thing I've ever seen. Do I ask her if she is okay? If something is going on? I shake those questions away, deciding to ask a much more pressing question,

"How old are you, Jude?"

"Twenty-One," she answers without blinking an eye. Still, I have a hard time believing her. She doesn't look underage, but she doesn't look like she is old enough to drink either.

When we're locked and loaded in my truck, I turn to her and ask, "Are you sure you don't want me to take you home? It's no problem."

"No. I want to go with you." A smile tugs at her lips, and I nod, deciding she's made her choice.

When we arrive at my bungalow, I help her out of the truck, and we walk up the front steps. The place isn't much, a simple one bedroom. When you live alone, it's all you need.

Unlocking the door, I watch her out of the corner of my eye. She's looking around, almost as if she's taking everything in for the first time.

It's painfully obvious that she's sheltered, but I'm not going to pepper her with questions about her life. God knows, I fucking hate when people do that to me.

"You hungry?" I ask as soon as we step inside. It's not awfully late, so I can still whip something up for her to eat, plus she looks like she could use a good home-cooked meal.

As always, I was at the bar, drinking a beer, trying to figure out what the hell to do with my life, so it's not like the girl interrupted anything important.

"Sure," she says, and walks a little deeper into the house. Her eyes fill with wonderment as they move over the walls.

I decide to leave her be for a bit and walk into the kitchen to determine what I'm going to make. Upon inspection, I realize two things. One, I need to go grocery shopping, and two, frozen pizza is the meal of choice. Hardly, the home-cooked meal I envisioned making her, I would not make a good husband or boyfriend right now. *What the hell? Why am I thinking about that?*

Popping a pizza into the oven, I walk back out into the living room to find her standing near the fireplace, her fingers pressed against a photo. She's staring so intently, almost as if she's living the moment in that photo. It's one of my brothers and me. I can't remember the exact location, but the joy on our faces tells me it was a time before life got a hold of us.

I allow myself to look her over once more since the lighting in the bar was so shitty. She's pretty, gorgeous, even in the absurd clothing she wears. Her hips flare beneath the gaudy skirt, and though it's hard to make out, I can see the perkiness of her breasts beneath her shirt. My cock hardens in my jeans, simply thinking about stripping her bare and tracing her soft skin.

Whoa, dude, chill the hell out.

As if she can sense I'm standing there watching her, she whirls around, dropping her hand as if she's been caught doing something she shouldn't. Her creamy white cheeks flush pink with embarrassment.

"I'm sorry. I shouldn't have touched your things." Her words are so soft, almost as if she doesn't say them for me to hear.

"Don't be sorry, you did nothing wrong," I reassure her, running a hand through my hair. "I wanted to make you something, but as it turns out, I need to go shopping, so I popped a pizza in. I hope that's okay?"

She nods but says nothing else. I'm not sure why I feel so drawn to her, but I decide to push my questioning thoughts away. Silence blankets us as she moves throughout the room, examining each item on my wall, the knick-knacks, and books on my shelves.

The timer dings in the kitchen, letting me know that the pizza is done, and I go to check on it. Finding that it's bubbly and brown, I pull it out, turn off the oven, and get two waters from the fridge. Jude hesitantly steps into the kitchen as I'm slicing the pizza up.

She looks excitedly at the meal, and I almost laugh.

We eat in silence, a thousand and one questions swirling in my head. As I finish my food, I clean up the kitchen, giving my hands something to do. Jude takes small bites of her food, eating only one piece. I want to tell her to eat more, but consider how rude that might be.

She watches me, and when I get up and head into the living room, I find her hot on my heels, her movements tiny and hesitant.

Back in the living room, I whirl around, and she almost collides with me. A small gasp passing her lips. My hands reach out to steady her and an electrical current zings through me at the touch. I'm not sure where the hell my next sentence comes from, but I realize as soon as I say the words that I mean them. "I was thinking, if you don't have a place to stay, you can stay here for a while. No charge at all. I just want to help you."

She looks at me like I'm a flickering flame that might burn her if she gets too close. Tilting my head to the side, I stare down at her curiously. Wonderment, fear, and something else blooms in her big blue eyes. I drop my hands down to my sides, afraid that I might be the reason for her fear, but of course, she shocks me by pushing up onto her tiptoes.

Easing a little closer, there isn't even an inch of space between our bodies, and yet I welcome the warmth of her body against mine. Her chest brushes mine, and when her small hands lift and come to rest on my shoulders, a strange heat creeps through me, making my heart beat a little faster in my chest.

Then like an unexpected gift, she shocks the hell out of me, she leans forward and presses her plump pink lips against mine, and the entire world falls away around me.

~

JUDE

I'M KISSING HIM. I'm actually doing it. My heart thunders against my ribs, and I feel like I'm about to pass out. My lips move against his, and I wonder if he can tell how inexperienced I am? *Am I even doing this right?* Is he going to push me away any second? I try and think of how I can do this. I've never kissed a man before or even touched one.

Pulling away, I feel a heat forming between my thighs. My father always said that spot was sacred, meant for my future husband and no one else. The mere reminder of him has me pushing the fear of what I'm about to do away.

They'll disown you if you're not a virgin.

Chest heaving, I drop my gaze to the button on his jeans and reach for it with trembling hands. You can do this. It can't be that hard. I've merely flicked the button on his jeans open when his hands come out of nowhere, circling my wrists. They're rough, warm, and strong, so strong. It hits me then that he's halting my motions. *Oh no.* This is where he tells me no. Where he pushes me away.

Maybe he's realized I lied about my age. Maybe I'm too young for him? I'm only eighteen.

I have one chance at this, one singular chance, and it's about to slip away.

"That's not part of the deal. You don't have to..." I look up at him, noting the sharp angles of his face, his clenched jaw, how dark his eyes seem to have gotten in a matter of seconds. He looks angry. Did I anger him? Make a mistake in believing that maybe he wants me?

"Don't you want me?" I whisper, trying my best not to sound as rejected and hurt as I feel. I'm so far out of my element, I might as well be on another planet. Maybe I've done something wrong.

"I mean... yeah, of course, I want you. You're a beautiful woman, but you... I don't want you to think that you have to do this for a place to sleep or food. I'm not like that." His green eyes soften, and the honesty in them tells me everything I need to know.

He's a good person, kind, and the perfect man for this job.

"I know. I want you though." I force the words past my lips, realizing how true they are. I really do want him. Want him to be my first.

"Are you sure? I promise you don't have to do this. You can stay here, regardless. I'm asking for nothing in return."

"I really want you," I admit shamelessly. My parents would lose it if they could see me right now. If they knew how much I do want this, how sinful my mind is.

I've always known I was different from the rest of my family. The black sheep, even at a young age. Always testing boundaries, always rebelling, never following rules, and now I'm breaking one of the holiest customs. I'm giving away my virginity to a man I'm not married to, one I've known only a matter of minutes.

"If you're sure this is what you want?" Lex's voice grows deeper, reaching a spot inside of me that makes me shiver.

Wanting to show him rather than use words, I shove my skirt down my legs and tug my shirt off over my head. I do my best not to feel embarrassed over my plain cotton panties and bra and instead reach for his jeans, tugging the zipper down. My hands are shaking, and I swallow thickly when he reaches up and brushes the hair at my neck away. Leaning forward, he peppers kisses along my skin, and it's like my entire body is being lit on fire.

His lips feel so good on my skin, his fingers dig into the flesh at my hips as he tugs me forward, and I feel the hard ridge of his manhood resting against my belly. I'm consumed with a need to get this done, and so I push his jeans down his hips. At the same time, he pushes the straps of my bra down over my shoulders before tugging the cups down, exposing my breasts to the cool air.

My nipples are hardened, sensitive, and I gasp when his wet mouth moves down my shoulder, closing around one of the tight peaks.

Pleasure ignites deep in my core, and I move my hands to his head, holding him in place, wanting him to continue. His tongue laps at my nipple before he switches to the other, eliciting a gasp out of me. My face feels as if it's on fire, a wetness forming against my panties.

I want more, need more. I need to seal the deal before he changes his mind. Tracing a hand down his body, I'm mesmerized by the dips and hard plains. He's fit and firm, and strangely, I feel safe with him.

When my fingers graze over his length, he pulls back, his emerald gaze colliding with mine. A groan pushes past his lips, and he pulls away just enough to tug his shirt off and pull his pants down. Then he's on me. Wrapping his hands around the back of my thighs, he lifts me and hauls me against his chest like I weigh nothing.

I grip onto his shoulder and watch with amazement as he moves us into another room with a nice comfy looking bed.

"You should be fucked in a bed, not on the couch, or against the wall," he whispers against my ear. A lump forms in my throat at the words, and a sliver of fear settles deep in my gut. This is going to hurt, I know it is. I've heard the stories from the other women in our family.

Dropping me onto the mattress, he climbs onto the bed beside me. Drinking me in, I feel his eyes on every inch of my skin. Exposed and vulnerable, I contemplate lifting my arms to cover myself, but know I would be giving him the wrong idea if I did.

Pushing the fear away, I circle my arms around his neck and tug him closer. His hardness brushes against my panties, and I'm eager to get this done. Spreading my legs wide so he can fit between them, I kiss him hard. He gives back to me with the same intensity, and after we kiss for a bit, I move my hands down to his boxers.

Pulling away, he shakes his head. "I'm going to finger you first."

My brow furrows, I've never heard of such a thing, but I don't want him to stop or rethink, so I nod my head and rest back against the mattress, letting him do as he pleases. Grabbing my panties, he slowly pulls them down my hips. I bite the inside of my cheek until I taste the coppery tang of blood.

Don't show how nervous you are.

His fingers slowly trail down my body, his hand disappearing between my legs. I'm self-conscious, wondering what he plans to do. Is he going to inspect me, or just touch me? As soon as his fingers rub against the small bundle of nerves hidden between my lips, I whimper. He grins down at me, and I decide that smile is something I'll remember for the rest of my life.

"You're soaked, so wet for me. *Fuck.* I want to taste you. Lick you, finger you, and then fuck you with my cock."

"Yes," I gasp as he moves his fingers faster and faster. I'm so caught up in the pleasure he's giving me that I don't notice what he's doing next until he's easing a finger inside me. There's a sting of pain and uncomfortableness that follows, but after that, I feel nothing but pleasure.

He moves inside me with a tenderness that is frightening, almost as if he knows that I'm inexperienced and cautious.

"You're so beautiful, so pure and perfect. Come for me, come on my hand," he whispers the crude words into my ear, his teeth nipping the lobe, and I couldn't stop myself from being overtaken by the heat in my belly.

It spreads outward, overtaking my limbs and mind. My eyes fall closed, and all I can hear is the rush of blood in my ears. I'm aware that Lex is moving above me, and when I'm one with my body again, I open my eyes to find he's ditched his boxers.

I allow myself to look down at his length and almost gasp. He's thick and huge, and this is not going to work, not at all. I don't know why I thought this was a good idea.

Taking his length into his hand, he strokes himself a few times before lining himself up with my entrance. I clamp up, wondering if I can move forward.

"Jude, baby, you still with me, you still want this?"

I nod without thought. Even as afraid as I am, this has to happen. I have to give myself to this man because it's him, or a life of hell under my father's rule.

Hitching my leg up and over his hip, he prods my entrance once more. His body is shaking, coiled with tension as he hovers above me. Our gazes collide, and then in one swift movement, he pushes inside of me. The air rips from my lungs, and the pain between my legs explodes outward.

I squeeze my eyes shut to stop the tears from coming.

He's just saved me, and he doesn't even realize it.

≈

LEX

I COULD TELL she was inexperienced, but now that I'm inside of her, I'm starting to believe she's much more than that.

Did she just give me her virginity? Fuck, I hope not. Her eyes open once more, and I can see they're glassy, almost as if she was near tears. *Damn it.* I can't feel anything or see beyond the pleasure pulsing through my body.

She feels so perfect, small, soft, her pussy strangling my dick almost painfully. I want to ask her, but I'm so overcome by pleasure, the words are lodged deep in my throat.

A sheen of sweat covers my forehead, and my muscles tighten from the amount of effort it takes not to move right away. I want to let her adjust to my size first even though all I want to do is pull out just so I can slam right back inside of her.

Lifting her hips, I sink a little deeper inside of her as her legs wrap around me, and her heels dig into my lower back. "Please," she whimpers near the shell of my ear. "Please, move. It feels so good."

I didn't think it was possible, but my cock gets even harder. Her softly spoken words drawing the last bit of blood from my brain and redirecting it straight to my groin.

"You're so tight," I groan, making a fist against the mattress.

Pulling out a fraction, I ease back in, moving slowly, and giving her time to adjust while sinking a little deeper into the tightness of her channel. I've had sex many times, made love, and fucked, but nothing has ever felt like this.

"Please," Jude whimpers as if she's in pain—as if me moving slowly is causing her more harm than good.

"You want me to fuck you?" I grit out through my teeth. I feel myself slipping, my control being tugged right out from under me. Rocking my hips against her, I test the ground a little more, moving faster and faster.

Her delicate throat bobs, apprehension riddling her angelic features before she nods. "Yes, take me."

Giving in to my most basic needs, I pull out to the tip before pushing back inside her warm channel. That one fluid thrust causes everything to slip away. I move with agility and carnal need, rutting into her over and over again, trying to find something inside her, something I'm not even sure what.

Head tipped back into the pillows, her nails sink into my flesh with each hard stroke I give her. She's so fucking tiny and fragile. I don't want to hurt her, but my need to take from her until there is nothing left is all-consuming.

"Lex," she whimpers as I drive into her, the bed squeaking as I do. My chest is heaving, and sweat drips down my body.

"Yeah, baby…" I grunt.

"I need…" She gasps as I hit deep inside of her. "More…" I can tell she isn't sure what she's asking for just that she needs that little bit that's going to push her over the edge, so I balance on one arm and continue fucking her hard and fast while bringing a hand between our joined bodies. My fingers slide between her folds easily, and I rub fast circles against her clit, focusing my attention on her face, watching it morph into something more in a quick second.

"That's what you need?" I grit out, thrusting faster.

Unable to form words, she nods, her teeth sinking into her bottom lip, leaving an indentation. Pleasure builds at the bottom of my spine, my balls are begging for release, and my muscles ache. But I continue working her over until her pussy flutters around my cock, tightening all around me, letting me know she's gotten her release.

Then I bury my face into the crook of her neck and fuck her hard and fast until the pressure in my balls becomes too much to bear. Thrusting one more time, I go off like an atomic bomb, releasing ropes of my sticky release inside of her.

A heavy fog covers my brain, and I roll off of her a second before I collapse against her. Falling onto the mattress on the other side of her, I suck air into my heaving lungs. It's been a long time since I felt something that intense before.

Once I've caught my breath, I roll over to find Jude on her side, staring at me. She looks satiated and sleepy.

"Are you okay?" I ask, my voice husky.

"Yes, I'm great." Her eyes pinch at the sides as she moves, and I know she has to be in pain. I want to apologize, but what good would that do? Do I tell her that I've never felt the need to fuck someone like I did her? Surely, that will send her running to the door. Still, I want to apologize for hurting her if I did.

"I'm sorry if I... went too hard or fast."

"You didn't. It was perfect." She smiles, and the air in my chest evaporates. She's so damn pure looking right now that I just want to wrap my arms around her and protect her from the rest of the world.

"Are you... are you okay aside from that? Do you have somewhere to go?" I can't believe I'm asking her if she's homeless after fucking her.

She reaches down and grabs the blanket tugging it up to her chest. "My family isn't... They aren't very nice. They have strict rules and stuff."

The vagueness of her answer has giant red flags waving in front of my eyes. "Are they hurting you?"

She shakes her head, but there is an uncertainty in her eyes that tells me she's lying. Reaching for her, I tug her into my body and brush a few strands of hair off her face. Her cheeks are red, and her lips are swollen. She smells like sex, and me, and it's making my need to protect her a hundred times stronger.

"I promise that if you need somewhere to go, someone to protect you, I'll be that person. I've spent four years serving my country, protecting people is kind of my job. I'll protect you if that's what you need, I'll keep you safe."

Jude's blue eyes become misty, and she gives me a sad smile. "Promises were meant to be broken."

"Not mine. I keep my promises. Always." I get the feeling she's been let down a time or two in her life, and I want her to know that if she needs some type of safety, I'm here for her. I'll catch her if she falls.

Pulling her even closer, I hold her to me, showing her with my body that I've got her, that I'll keep her safe. She takes my invitation, cuddling into me, burying her face into my chest. She sucks in a harsh breath and then melts into me.

I try my best to fight against the exhaustion that's overcoming me, wanting this moment to go on forever, but I'm only so strong with her in my arms. Letting my eyes fall closed, I fall asleep with her warm breath fanning against my skin and the soft, steady beat of her heart on my chest.

JUDE

MY EYES BLINK OPEN, and for one single second, the unfamiliar room has me in a panic, but as soon as I take in my surroundings, those feelings vanish into thin air.

Warmth surrounds me, warmth and safety. Lex's heavy arm is

draped over me, holding me tightly to his chest like I belong to him. *Oh, how I wish that were true.*

I wish I could stay here in his arms forever, but I know that's just a dream. My family won't stop looking for me if I don't return. I need them to disown me first. I need to go back there so I can ultimately be free of them. I know they won't let me go without retaliation.

A crazy thought enters my mind then. Perhaps I could come back here? Maybe I could see Lex again. Just as quick as the thought enters my mind, I banish it away.

Don't be a fool, Jude.

This was a one-time thing. Just sex and nothing more. His words from last night were just that... *words.* I can't expect him to feel what I'm feeling. Plus, I'm pretty sure the only reason I'm feeling so drawn to him is the fact that he is the first man in my life who's shown me kindness. The first man who treated me with respect, who saw me as an equal human being and not as less because I'm a woman.

I'll be forever grateful to him; for what he's done for me without even knowing it. Quiet as a mouse, I slide out of bed and find my clothes on the floor. I wince, an ache throbbing between my legs as I dress.

When I'm dressed, I take one last look at Lex. It's almost completely dark, the only thing illuminating the room is the night sky that's filtering in through the window.

Even in the barely-there light, he looks magnificent, his bare chest on full display, rising and falling in an even rhythm, the sheet barely covering his nether region. It takes a lot of willpower to turn around and leave the room when all I want to do is crawl back into the bed to pretend the world around us doesn't exist.

On the way out, I spot a notepad on the coffee table and decide to leave him a little message. Last night might not have been special to him, but I can't leave without letting him know how much it meant to me.

Grabbing the pen, I take a deep breath before writing down what I feel in my heart.

Lex,

Last night meant more to me than you will ever know.
You gave me a gift.
You gave me a choice.
You gave me freedom.
And for that, I will forever be grateful.

Love, Jude

I DROP the pen and wipe the escaping tear from my eye before I head out. Closing the door behind me softly, I hope that one day I can find my way back here because I know...

Part of me will always be his.

Find The Promise on Amazon and FREE with Kindle Unlimited!

ALSO BY THE AUTHORS

The Blackthorn Elite
Hating You
Breaking You
Hurting You
Regretting You

The Obsession Duet
Cruel Obsession
Deadly Obsession

The Rossi Crime Family
Protect Me
Keep Me
Guard Me
Tame Me
Remember Me

The Moretti Crime Family
Savage Beginnings
Violent Beginnings

The King Crime Family
Indebted
Inevitable

STANDALONES

Their Captive

Runaway Bride

His Gift

Convict Me

Two Strangers

ABOUT THE AUTHORS

J.L. Beck and C. Hallman are an international bestselling author duo who write contemporary and dark romance.

Also check out our website for a list of all of our books.
www.bleedingheartromance.com

Beck *and* **Hallman**

BLEEDING HEART ROMANCE

f CASSANDRAHALLMAN
AUTHORJLBECK

Instagram CASSANDRA_HALLMAN
AUTHORJLBECK

BB CASSANDRAHALLMAN
JLBECK